"I'm going to h[...]

"What did you say?"

She lay there, gazing up at him, the oddest expression on her face. "I'm going to have a baby."

"You...are." He couldn't, for the moment, think of anything more intelligent to say.

Still wearing that odd expression, Susan nodded.

"Who is he? The baby's father."

"I don't know yet."

Whirling, he faced her. There'd been more than one man? "Well, when are you going to find out?"

"I'm not sure." She paused. "You're angry, aren't you?"

"Okay, yeah, I'm angry. I'm angry as hell at the irresponsibility of whatever man did this to you."

She frowned. "Did what to me?"

Michael swore, out of all patience. "Got you pregnant, of course."

Susan laughed. Shocking him. "In the first place, Michael, a man can't get me pregnant all by himself. And in the second, I'm *not* pregnant—yet. And in the third place, I haven't slept with anyone but you in my entire life."

Dear Reader,

I'm delighted to bring you this BY THE YEAR 2000 story. Though I'm still in my thirties and have a thirteen-year-old daughter, I relate so much to Susan and her dilemma. A woman's independence is a precious thing—something not easily won or sustained, yet essential to her becoming the person she was meant to be. The trick, of course, is to find the independence and then learn how to be *inter*dependent without losing anything. Because just as never finding independence is only half living, living *only* with independence is not experiencing life to the fullest, either. Like many women, I teeter on this line often as I struggle to be a mother, a wife, a friend, a writer.

But Susan showed me how it's done. I believe in her. And, like Susan, I believe we can have it all if we're determined enough, work hard enough—and remember not to take ourselves so seriously all the time.

I wish every one of you a new century of happy lives and happy relationships.

Tara Taylor Quinn

P.S. I love to hear from readers. You can reach me at P.O. Box 15065, Scottsdale, Arizona 85267-5065 or on-line at http://www.inficad.com/~ttquinn.

Books by Tara Taylor Quinn

MY BABIES AND ME
Tara Taylor Quinn

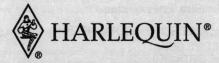

HARLEQUIN®

TORONTO • NEW YORK • LONDON
AMSTERDAM • PARIS • SYDNEY • HAMBURG
STOCKHOLM • ATHENS • TOKYO • MILAN • MADRID
PRAGUE • WARSAW • BUDAPEST • AUCKLAND

ISBN 0-373-70864-5

MY BABIES AND ME

Copyright © 1999 by Tara Lee Reames.

This edition published by arrangement with Harlequin Books S.A.

® and TM are trademarks of the publisher. Trademarks indicated with ® are registered in the United States Patent and Trademark Office, the Canadian Trade Marks Office and in other countries.

Visit us at www.romance.net

Printed in U.S.A.

For Deanna Reames and David Reames.
A woman couldn't ask for better in-laws.

CHAPTER ONE

WILL YOU have my baby?

No. Susan Kennedy shook her head, her layered shoulder-length hair tickling her neck and cheeks. That wasn't quite the line she wanted.

Can I have your baby?

Nope. She dusted the buttons on the telephone with one long slim finger. Misleading. Her *ability* to have a baby wasn't in question.

So how about *May I have your baby?*

She toyed with that one, actually dialed Chicago's area code before disconnecting this time. Her goal wasn't to ask his permission but to request his participation in the most monumental event of her life. At the same time she had to make it clear—abundantly, in-your-face clear—that she was asking nothing from him.

Other than the initial ten-minute participation. Grinning, Susan amended that last thought. There was no way any physical shenanigans between her and Michael would take less than an hour. They did sex very well.

Which probably meant she was asking for more like *two* hours of his time. Michael always claimed Susan had a way of making everything seem easier than it really was. Shorter than it was. Less expensive than it was. When she'd budgeted one thousand dollars for their trip to the Poconos, he'd counted on two.

Damn thing was, she'd somehow managed to run through every dime of the two-thousand dollars, just as he'd predicted. And Michael, being Michael, had never said a word.

Stupid, smug man.

Stupid enough to father her child? In spite of the fact that they'd been divorced almost as long as they'd been married?

He had to. Period. No other option was acceptable.

So how did she convince him of that?

How about *Would you lend me a sperm?* That didn't sound like too much to ask. And "lend" seemed so harmless, so…not-permanent.

But she wasn't planning on giving it back.

All the more reason to call him today. Because "lend" wasn't what she wanted at all. She wanted him to *give* it to her, willingly and for keeps, and as Michael always gave her wonderful gifts for her birthday…

January 21. Her birthday. She glanced at the office around her, the plaques on her walls, the windows overlooking the icy Ohio River, Cincinnati, Ohio and Louisville, Kentucky all at once. Sinking into the soft leather of the high-backed maroon chair, she sighed and hung up the phone. Gloomy suddenly, she reached down to pet the red setter snoring on the floor at her feet. She couldn't believe she was actually thirty-nine years old. For a person who'd always loved birthdays, she was doing a damn good imitation of hating this one.

Someone dropped a coffee cup in the hall. Hearing

it break, Susan hoped it had been empty. Annie, the setter who made her way to Susan's office every morning, didn't even budge at the noise. The dog was getting old, too, nearly thirteen. Susan's soul mate.

She didn't kid herself, though. In spite of the fact that Susan had known Annie since puppyhood, the dog didn't come to her every morning out of some incredible bonding experience they'd shared. No, Annie just preferred Susan's soft carpet to the cold but beautiful ceramic tile that covered the other floors of Halliday's. It was one of the largest, privately owned sporting goods supply companies in the world.

Susan jumped as the phone rang, echoing in her bright, luxurious, tomblike office.

"Hello?" She grabbed it after the first ring, eager for distraction, praying it wasn't Michael calling to wish her a happy birthday. She wasn't ready to speak with her ex-husband. Not yet.

"Hey, old woman, how about lunch?"

"Seth?" Holding the phone away from her ear, Susan grinned. "You in town?"

"Haven't missed a birthday yet, have I?"

"Well…" Susan used her best corporate attorney's voice to disguise how thrilled she was that he'd made it back. "I seem to recall there were those first two…"

Seth snorted. "Before I was born doesn't count."

Annie rose slowly and lumbered out to the hall, and as loneliness invaded the room, Susan's spirits plummeted again. "Lunch would be good. Can you go now?" she asked.

"At 9:30 in the morning?" Seth laughed, then stopped abruptly. "Something wrong?"

"Nope. Just don't feel like working today." Which *was* something wrong.

"I've got one call to make, and I'll be there," Seth promised immediately.

"Thanks." Tears in her eyes, Susan hung up the phone. As much of a pain as it had been growing up the only girl with five brothers, Susan was glad she had Seth. He was two years younger, the brother who came directly after her. She'd picked on him all the years they'd lived at home. She'd known she could get away with tormenting him. After all, Susan was the girl, the princess. And while she wasn't allowed to do any of the fun things they did—like go to the batting cages or play catch or go golfing—the boys were all under strict orders not to bully her. So she'd bullied Seth relentlessly. Even when he'd topped her by a foot and forty pounds.

She wasn't sure just when she'd started leaning on him instead.

"THANKS FOR meeting with me, Michael." James Coppel, of Coppel Industries, offered Michael Kennedy his hand.

"I'm happy to be here, sir," Michael shook his hand before taking a seat in Coppel's penthouse office suite. He'd just flown in from Chicago.

Although he was careful to do it covertly, Michael took in the opulence around him, his heart rate quickening. *Susan should see this,* was his first thought. Only his ex-wife could understand the importance of his being there, in that affluent Georgia office suite.

Only she would know what it meant to him. He caught a glimpse of himself in an ornate, gold-framed mirror that took up most of the opposite wall and was surprised by his reflection. Well-groomed, dark-haired, he looked...at ease. As if he belonged there.

"Would you like some coffee?" Coppel asked, relaxing in his chair as he surveyed Michael. The man's hair might have grayed, his skin wrinkled, but he'd lost not an inch of his imposing six-foot height in the seven years Michael had known him.

"Certainly," Michael replied. He wasn't a coffee drinker, didn't like what the stuff did to his stomach, but he'd been in business long enough to know that he had to appear as relaxed as his boss.

Though close to seventy, Coppel was a legend. A genius. The man had never missed a beat in the forty years since he'd purchased his first exterminating franchise. He'd built an empire that had interests in just about every industry in the country. Other than film. Coppel had even been smart enough to stay out of Hollywood.

If Michael had ever allowed himself an idol, Coppel would have been it.

The coffee was delivered and with one polished wing tip resting on a suited knee, Michael sat back to calmly sip the dreadful stuff.

"How old are you, boy?"

"Thirty-nine." Legally, Coppel had no right to ask that kind of question, and they both knew it.

"And you've been with Smythe and Westbourne for how long?"

Michael would bet every dime of the half million he'd saved over the past seven years that Coppel knew exactly how long Michael had been with the Coppel Industries' investment firm. To the day.

"Seven years."

"And in that time you've gone from director of finance of one branch to financial director of the entire operation, showing a three hundred percent increase over the past two years."

"Yes, sir." Michael was damn proud of those figures. They'd cost him. A lot.

"Mind telling me your secret?"

Michael knew he'd finally been asked a legitimate question. A question he could answer with deceptive simplicity. "Integrity toward the customer."

Coppel snorted. "I run an honest ship, young man. Always have. How do you think Coppel became the name it is? Honest business in a dishonest world. That's how."

And that was something Michael had known. Even before he'd earned his MBA, Michael had chosen the company for which he wanted to work. And set about being the candidate they'd choose when the time came.

"I take that one step further, sir," he said now, no longer aware of the opulence of the room or the other man's stature.

He had Coppel's complete attention.

"Each customer is different, with individual needs. My teams have been taught to treat the customer as a person, to sell him not what *we* have to sell—not what, in the short run, makes us the most profit—but what *he* truly needs. It hurts the small picture, sometimes, when we don't make a killing right off the bat. But in the big picture—"

"They go away happy," Coppel interrupted him, eyeing Michael with interest. "They come back. They bring their neighbors with them."

"Over and over again," Michael said with the conviction of seven years' worth of figures to prove his theory.

"Lose money to make money," Coppel said.

"Sometimes."

"Building a whole new level of trust, a new approach to doing business—which, I suppose is really an old-time traditional approach."

"At least at Smythe and Westbourne."

The other man nodded. "So you think you can determine what the customer wants."

"I do."

"How?" Coppel might be testing him, but he was intrigued as well.

"By becoming the buyer instead of the seller."

Coppel nodded, his brow clearing. "You put yourself in the shoes of the consumer."

"And realize that just as all people aren't the same, all consumers and their needs aren't the same, either."

Looking down at some papers spread in front of him, Coppel said, "You appear to have a real talent in this area."

Michael didn't know about that. He thought his real talent lay in profit-and-loss margins and personal infrastructures.

"What about your family?" Coppel asked. "How much of your time do they require?"

And for the first time since he'd been summoned to this interview more than a month ago, Michael allowed himself to hope. He wanted a move up to one of the bigger, more diverse companies in the Coppel holdings. He needed a new challenge.

"None, sir," he said with the confidence of knowing he had the right answer. "I'm divorced."

"No children?" It was a well-known fact that Coppel didn't believe a man should desert his children. Which was why he'd never had any of his own.

"None."

Nodding, Coppel broke into a small, satisfied smile.

"You have anybody else who might want a say on your time?"

You got a lover? Michael read into the question.

"No."

He saw women occasionally, but he'd been sleeping with Susan again, on and off, over the past three years, although they'd been divorced for seven. He couldn't seem to find a passion for anyone else.

"Any dependents at all?"

What is this? Michael shifted in his seat, suddenly uncomfortable. He sent a sizable amount of money to his parents and brother and sisters back in Carlisle, but that was nobody's business except his.

"Why?"

Eyes narrowed, Coppel sat forward. "I'm thinking about offering you a new position, a move from a subsidiary company to Coppel Industries itself."

Michael didn't move a muscle. Didn't breathe.

"But the position I have in mind would require constant travel, and I won't even consider offering it if that meant you'd be shirking personal commitments. I don't break up families."

Coppel had come from a broken family, had his

father run out on him, been forced to quit school and provide for his ailing mother. He'd entered high school at nineteen after his mother passed away. He'd put himself through college exterminating bugs, and the rest was history. Not only history, but public knowledge now that Coppel was one of the top businessmen in the country.

"I have no one," Michael said.

HE MADE HIMSELF WAIT until he was pacing the gate at the airport before calling Susan. Just to keep things in perspective.

Only to find that she wasn't in her office. A hotshot corporate attorney, Susan was out slaying dragons as often as she was in.

Picturing his ex-wife in her dragon-slaying mode, he grinned as he hung up the phone.

"I WANT to have a baby."

Seth spit the whiskey he'd been sipping, spraying it across the table. *"What?"*

Laughing, Susan wiped a couple of drops of Crown Royal from her neck. At least her silk blouse and suit jacket had been spared. "It's not like you to waste good whiskey," she admonished. Actually, she was a little concerned on that score. It was still only eleven. A bit early for her brother to be hitting the hard stuff. He'd ordered a drink the last time they'd met for lunch, as well.

Leaning across the table, Seth whispered, "Are you out of your mind?"

"Not as far as I know."

"Susan." He sat upright, every inch the imposing

engineer who flew all over the country inspecting multimillion-dollar construction sights. "Be *serious*."

"I don't think I've ever been more serious in my life." She was still grinning, but mostly because if she didn't, she might let him intimidate her.

"Why?"

"I'm thirty-nine." Neither of them touched the sandwiches they'd ordered.

"Yeah. So?"

Susan shrugged. "If I don't do it now, I'll have lost the chance."

"That's no reason to have a kid. You're supposed to want it."

"I do." Oddly enough.

Picking up a fry, Seth still looked completely overwrought. "Since when?"

"Since I graduated from law school."

He stared at her, fry suspended in midair. "No kidding?" She'd obviously surprised him.

"I have it all written down." She spoke quickly, eager to elaborate, to convince him that her decision was a good one. The right one. To win his approval. How could she possibly hope to convince Michael if she couldn't even get the brother who championed everything she did on her side?

"Before I married Michael, I spent a weekend at a lodge in Kentucky, assessing my life, my goals, my dreams. Life was suddenly looming before me and I was scared." She warmed beneath Seth's empathetic gaze. "Frightened that I'd lose myself along the way somehow." Her brother nodded, looking down at the plate between his elbows.

"By the end of the weekend, I'd mapped out all

my goals, both short- and long-term, in chronological order.'' Seth was staring at her again, his expression no longer empathetic. Unlike the sophisticated lawyer she was, she rushed on. ''It was the only way I could be sure I wouldn't let myself down, wouldn't end up sixty years old and regretting what I'd done with my life—when it was too late to do anything about it.'' Like their mother, she wanted to add but couldn't. The boys didn't know about those last hours she'd spent with their mother before she died. No one knew. Except Michael.

Seth continued to stare silently. ''I wrote down career goals first,'' she said, then took a sip of her brother's whiskey. ''Where I wanted to be by what time. Financial goals. Work goals. Personnal goals. For instance, I wanted to be able to play the violin by the time I was thirty-five.''

''That's why you took those lessons?''

''Because I wanted to learn how to play? Yes.''

''But did you still want to play the violin when you got to that stage in your life?'' Seth asked, pinning her with a big-brother stare he had no right to bestow on her. ''Or did you just take the lessons because you'd written down that you had to?''

''I wanted to learn to play.'' She'd just been unusually busy that year, which was the only reason she hadn't enjoyed the experience as much as she'd thought she would.

''When was the last time you picked up your violin?''

That was beside the point. She'd been too busy these past four years.

''I wanted to travel to Europe by the time I was

thirty-six.'' She steered Seth back to the original conversation. ''And,'' she added before he could grill her, ''I loved every second of the month I spent there.''

Of course, she'd been with Michael, and as a general rule, she loved every second she'd spent with Michael, period. They'd even made getting divorced fun. They'd rushed straight home afterward, tripped over his packing boxes on the way to their bedroom and made love furiously until dawn.

Seth chomped on a couple of fries. Brooding. His classically golden good looks were broken by the frown he was wearing.

''I've always known I'd have a baby by the year 2000,'' Susan said softly, seriously, begging her brother to understand.

''Listen to you! Learn to play an instrument, go to Europe, have a baby by the year 2000. It's ludicrous, Susan.'' When his intensity didn't sway her, he slowed down. ''What happens after you have this baby?'' he finally asked.

''Then I raise him or her.''

''You can't just bring a child into the world because some stupid plan tells you to, Susan.''

''Who says I can't?'' Not exactly an answer to be proud of, but he was making her defensive.

''You aren't mother material, for God's sake! Can't you see that?''

She opened her mouth but couldn't speak. Not one word came out. She just sat there, mouth gaping, staring at him.

Until her eyes filled with tears. ''How can you say that?''

"I'm sorry, sis." He glanced away, took a sip of whiskey. "I love you, you know that."

She'd thought she did.

"Look at your life, Susan, all mapped out, running right on schedule. The last thing children do is follow *your* schedule. They shouldn't have to. They should be free to follow their own way, their own hearts. And they need parents who can give them the time, the freedom of choice to do so."

"Like you'd know?" she asked, still hurt by his sudden abandonment.

He acknowledged his own lack of family with a nod. "I *do* know," he said, surprising her with his fierceness. "Which is exactly why I'm so goddamn alone." He finished off his whiskey with one swallow.

"Seth?"

There was a lot more going on here than she knew. A lot more that she needed to know.

"Not now," was all he said, flagging down the waitress for another whiskey.

Susan pushed her plate away, untouched. She'd had breakfast at nine. It was way too early to be thinking about eating again.

"There's another factor that's missing here. Unless something else has happened since I left town."

Susan shook her head. Life had been predictable, the same, for months now.

"A baby needs a father." Seth's voice was strong again. He made a show of glancing around them. "I don't see one hanging around."

Susan took a deep breath. "I'm going to ask Michael."

Eyes suddenly alight, Seth grinned and grabbed her hand. "You two are getting back together?"

She couldn't hold his gaze, couldn't watch it dim. Sliding her hand from his, Susan shook her head. "Of course not. Nothing's changed there."

"Careers still come first, you mean?" he asked.

Susan nodded, awash in the sadness she felt emanating from her younger brother.

"My point exactly." He finished off the second whiskey. "A kid deserves to come first."

CHAPTER TWO

"SO THIS BABY THING is the reason you didn't feel like working today?" Seth asked as he walked her to her car fifteen minutes later. He seemed huge and intimidating in his expensive overcoat.

And he was making her mad again with his refusal to take her seriously about the baby. If she couldn't convince Seth, how in hell was she ever going to convince Michael? But because she didn't want to face the fact that she might *not* be able to convince either one of them, Susan let his comment go.

To a point.

"No," she finally answered him, studying the shadowy trail her breath left on the air.

They'd reached her Infiniti, and Seth opened the door she'd unlocked with her antitheft device as they'd approached. "I've actually got a small problem at work that was making me wish I was somewhere else this morning."

"A small problem?" Seth leaned into the car, one arm on the hood, one on the open door. "That means there's something major coming down. What is it?" He paused, frowning again. "Your job isn't in jeopardy, is it?"

Susan laughed then, but without much humor. "Hardly." They both knew she could write her own ticket as far as Halliday Headgear for Sports was concerned. She'd saved them enough money over the years to buy them out twice.

"Then what is it?"

"Just a case I'm working on. No big deal." Susan started the car, turning the heat up full blast.

"Is Halliday in trouble?"

"Nope."

"You going to tell me, or you want me to just keep asking questions until my ass freezes?"

"It's nothing, really." Susan grinned up at him. "Just a little suit I could have won even *before* I attended law school."

"And?"

It was annoying how well Seth knew her. She'd have to remember to stay away from him when she was having birthday blues in the future. "I just feel for this boy, okay? His face mask snapped, a production problem with one of the hinges. The kid suffered a subdural hematoma which is pushing against his brain, causing paralysis on one side of his body. His father's out of work and the family doesn't have insurance. They don't have money for surgery, let alone the months of physical therapy he's going to need."

"If his face mask malfunctioned, isn't Halliday responsible?"

"We would be if he'd been wearing it to play softball—the mask's intended use."

"Why was he wearing it?"

Susan looked up at her brother. "He was playing soccer."

"Halliday's getting off on a technicality?"

"A big one."

"And the kid?"

Susan shrugged. "I don't know. Even if the surgery's performed, he's not going to be able to walk again without rehabilitation." She took a deep breath. "I could win this one for him if I were on his side. I know of a loophole that would override ours."

"Damn!" Seth whistled. "You sure as hell don't need to be wasting energy worrying about babies, Susan. Sounds like you've got some soul-searching to do a lot closer to home."

"Yeah." She'd be doing some soul-searching, all right, but having a baby was about as close to home as she could get.

A MESSAGE FROM Michael was waiting for her back at the office. Susan was inordinately disappointed to have missed his call. Especially in light of the dissatisfying hour and a half she'd just spent with her punk of a brother. Who the hell did he think he was telling her she wasn't mother material? How would he know?

Of course she was mother material. She just hadn't had the occasion to use those maternal skills or instincts or whatever they were…yet. But she would as soon as she could.

Her fingers didn't falter this time as she punched out Michael's number. She had a goal. A purpose. And no one was going to stop her.

"I'm sorry, Ms. Kennedy, Mr. Kennedy is out of town today.…"

And that about summed up the day for her, Susan thought as she dropped the phone back in its cradle. He'd left town on her birthday. He'd left town without telling her. What in hell was the world coming to?

She listened indifferently to the remainder of her messages. Her father had called to wish her happy birthday. No round of golf for her. Only her brothers got *that* invitation for their birthdays. Julie, her brother Scott's wife, not only called to wish her happy birthday, but to invite her to little Joey's second birthday party the following week. Scott was her oldest brother. And her least favorite. He was so much like their dad he made her crazy. But he was a good man and when she was in a normal mood, she had to love him.

Spencer, the doctor in the family and the youngest brother, had called for him and Barbara, his wife, who was also a doctor. What was this? It seemed as if everyone was ganging up on her. Like there was a conspiracy to make her feel better or something. Did they know how miserable she felt? How much she wished the day would just go away?

The thought gave her chills. She didn't want any of them to guess that she wasn't just hunky dory and happy-go-lucky with her perfect little life. She'd been defending it to them forever, and she'd bloat up and burst if she suddenly had to eat all those words.

Besides, Stephen and Sean hadn't called yet. Which meant no conspiracy was afoot. Sean, the brother between Seth and Spencer, was the organizer of mutinies in the family. He'd have been the first to call and gloat if he thought he had a way to get to her. And Stephen? Well, she wouldn't be surprised to get a birthday call from him sometime in March. If it weren't for the fact that he was a renowned nuclear scientist, she'd worry about his IQ. The man was about as clueless as they came. He was also closest to Susan in age, being only one year her senior. He was going to hit forty this year.

Snatching the phone back up, Susan buzzed her assistant. "I'll be out for the rest of the day," she said the second Jill answered. She didn't want to enter into any discussions about research and cases on the docket. It was her birthday and she was damn well going to enjoy it. Somehow. She loved birthdays.

"The McArthur boy lost his lawyer," Jill reported anyway. "I figured you'd want to know."

That was true. Susan did want to know. Later.

"Any change in his condition?" she asked in spite of herself.

"Still paralyzed."

"Thanks." Susan made a mental note to seek out Tricia Halliday the following week. Surely they could find a compromise on this particular case.

She just wondered how much groveling or bribing she'd have to do to get the hard-hearted woman to budge. Tricia cared about being right. Not about being human.

"I'm taking tomorrow off, as well," she decided out loud. The next day was Friday. She was giving herself a birthday present.

"Heading for Chicago?" Jill asked. Susan could hear the impertinent grin in her assistant's voice.

"Not that you know about."

"Don't worry, Susan, there'll be no calls from me unless the old lady croaks."

"Even that can wait until Monday," Susan muttered as she hung up the phone.

Michael's secretary had said he'd be back that night. She was going to be there to welcome him home personally. She needed a fix.

And maybe, just maybe, she'd get up the guts to ask for the present she wanted most in the world.

A tiny little life to nurture and love and fill her up again.

She had a feeling she'd have to put forth the most convincing argument of her life if she hoped to win this one. Of course, that was what she'd thought when she'd been set on talking Michael out of their divorce. And look where that had gotten her.

MICHAEL TRIED to reach Susan again when he touched down in Chicago. Not only was he dying to share his news, even if everything was only in the possibility stages, he'd also remembered on the flight home that today was Susan's birthday. To celebrate, he stopped at the American Airlines counter and bought them both tickets to Hawaii for Easter weekend. It had been too long since either of them had taken a vacation.

The tickets were open-ended, as always. He could change them if Easter wasn't good for her.

She was out of the office until Monday. Still no answer at the condo. Knowing how much Susan loved birthdays, knowing more than anyone how she did everything to excess, he was sure she'd found some crazy way to celebrate this last birthday in her thirties. Things like that mattered to Susan. Celebrating. And momentous birthdays. Michael usually had to stop and think to even remember how old he was. Age wasn't anything that had ever mattered to him. He supposed it might be different for women.

Catching sight of a departure board as he walked by, Michael found himself searching for any flights leaving for Cincinnati that evening. He wanted to be with Susan. To share his news. To share her celebration. To make love to her...

He wanted to go home.

And because his wanting threatened to override good sense, Michael went to pick up his forest-green Pathfinder from the airport's parking garage instead. His home was here for now, in the condo he'd purchased when he'd moved to Chicago seven years ago. He and Susan had made their choices then. Forced to decide between staying together and climbing to the top, neither one had been willing to give up on career success. As great as their marriage had been, their careers had meant more—to both of them.

He had the day's industrial summaries to go over. Reports to study. He'd catch Susan later when she was all celebrated out.

And maybe he'd be able to talk her into a quick trip to Chicago in the not-too-distant future.

TWO DRINKS AT LUNCH. Another one instead of dinner. And peace was as elusive as ever. Seth Carmichael stayed at his desk until his eyes stung from lack of sleep, and he knew he had to pack it in. Go home. He'd been up for more than twenty-four hours. He'd taken the red-eye after last night's meetings in Alaska to make it back here in time for Susan's birthday. He'd like to think that meant he'd fall into bed the second he hit his apartment, that he'd sleep the sleep of the just. Or the dead.

But he knew he wouldn't.

And that was why he was still at work two hours after everyone else had gone home for the night. Of course, they all had families to go home to. Seth had an apartment filled with stale air. There weren't even any plants sharing the place with him. He was gone so much any plants he brought home just shriveled up and died.

He locked up carefully and walked out of the building that housed the offices held by Hier Engineering. In the parking lot, Seth climbed into his Bronco, pleased with the power beneath his hands as the engine turned over instantly.

Bitch of it was, he liked his life. Or he had. He loved his job. Enough to know that when he was seeing double like this, he had to leave the figures alone. He couldn't risk a mathematical error that could result in a tragic accident—a building not as sturdy as it needed to be, a bridge that cracked. These were his real nightmares.

Almost of its own accord, Seth's Bronco headed in the opposite direction from home, toward a part of town he no longer had any reason to visit.

So why were his nights filled with a couple of sullen little faces and a more determined beautiful one? It had been four months since Laura's ultimatum. Four months.

He felt as raw as if she'd hurled those hateful words only yesterday. They were as clear in his mind as if she had.

Hell, it wasn't like she'd been a permanent fixture

in his life. Or her kids, either. He'd only met them the previous summer when he'd shown up to coach soccer to a bunch of underprivileged kids and met a little boy with a whole lot of defensiveness but a lot of talent, too. He'd been drawn to Jeremy from that very first day, thinking of him at odd times through the weeks that followed—trying to figure out a way to help him.

And the boy's mother... He could still remember the first time he'd stopped by Jeremy's house to speak to his parents about the boy's talent. He'd thought Laura was the boy's sister when she answered the door. Her silky blond hair had been hanging loose over a frayed tank top. And her cutoff shorts had had more holes in them than her tennis shoes.

He'd been poleaxed right from the start. And that was before she'd even opened her mouth, before he'd discovered her indomitable strength. Before he'd found out the good news—she was single. Divorced.

The Bronco sped down the exit ramp. Seth didn't reduce his speed as he continued on.

And Susan. What in hell had gotten into his sister? Didn't she know she was his hero? That he measured everything he did by her standards? How could she do something as stupid, as *heartless,* as to even consider bringing a child into the world simply because she'd written it down in her damn planner? Who was going to raise that child, nurture him, love him, while Susan spent fourteen hours a day at work?

The soccer field came into view before he slowed down enough to be cautious. Jeremy might not even be there. He'd probably quit practicing the second Seth walked out the door of his mother's house. Or maybe it had been the next week, when he'd gone to soccer practice and discovered that Seth was no longer his coach.

At least he knew the kid was still on the team. He supposed that was something.

And what would Seth say to the boy if Jeremy was at the field by himself? "Hey, kid, good to see ya. Sorry you weren't important enough to me."

Right. Just what a nine-year-old needed to hear. *Face it.* That was exactly what Jeremy was thinking, anyway. The kid's father had run out on him. He'd *expected* Seth to do the same. And Seth had obliged.

The field was empty, just as he'd realized it would be. Of course, it *was* January. Freezing. Who kicked around soccer balls at eight-thirty on a January night?

Jeremy would have. If Seth had still been around to encourage him. The boy had ability. And he loved to play. Soccer was the one thing that could help Seth get through to Jeremy. That could make Jeremy feel good about himself.

Driving by Laura's house was a given.

Maybe he should stop in to say hello. Just to make sure they were all right. There were lights on in the front room, and a glow from the television that appeared to be Jeremy's only solace these days, his only escape.

The front yard was still nothing but a tiny square of hard dirt; the sidewalk was cracked, pieces missing; half the porch sagged. He'd repeatedly offered to set her up in a better place, a better part of town. She'd refused every time. And when he couldn't stand having her there any longer, when he'd found her a place on his own, made all the arrangements for her to move, when he'd insisted she accept his offer, she'd given him the ultimatum that had ended everything.

Light flickered on the homemade curtains, probably a reflection from the television screen. He wondered if Jeremy was still looking out for his little sister.

Seth had driven by Jenny's school last month, and the little girl had been off by herself, leaning against a corner of the building while her classmates played. She'd seen too much in her young life to be capable of make-believe. To find any joy in childish antics.

Seth had hoped to change that, too. Just as he'd once thought he'd be able to bring an easy sparkle back to Laura's eyes. But the bastard who'd helped create that family had done some real work on all of them. The bruises he'd left behind, both physical and mental, were more than Seth had been able to eradicate.

He'd wanted to be their friend. They'd needed more than that. A single-parent family usually did.

Slamming his gloved hand down hard on the steering wheel, Seth sped away from the run-down neighborhood where Laura lived; he didn't slow down until he'd reached the bar right around the corner from his apartment complex. He could walk home from there if he got lucky enough to be too wasted to drive.

He just couldn't believe Susan was actually *planning* a single-parent family. What if she had a boy? Boys needed fathers. Jeremy was proof of that.

He'd given his sister credit for having more sense.

SHE'D COME PREPARED. Slipping into the public rest room in the lobby of the condo sales office in Michael's complex, Susan quickly took off her suit, bra and panty hose, donning nylons, a garter and a lavender French-cut negligee. She might be pushing forty but her body still looked good—curved in the right places, tight where it should be. Touching up her makeup didn't take but a second, just long enough to coat her lips with wet luscious red. Her nipples puckered with cold, and probably a bit of anticipation, too, as she slid her overcoat and shoes back on, picked up her weekend bag and sedately reentered the lobby.

She'd brought protection, too, just in case Michael hadn't replaced the box they'd finished off the last time she was in town. There was no place in her plan for an unexpected pregnancy, no place for manipulation or dishonesty. If she was going to have Michael's baby, it was going to be with his permission.

An evening sales associate tossed her a welcoming smile as Susan sailed regally past her and into the night, shaking back her hair. Gold with streaks of light chocolate—that was how Michael had always described her hair. Gold and chocolate. Of course, he'd also said it almost exactly matched the oak of her desk, but that was when he'd had her lying on top of it.

Her desk would have been a little cumbersome to bring, so she'd settled for his favorite whiskey—a rich golden Scotch—and a box of his favorite chocolates—all lights. While he'd understand the significance of her offering, he might think her a little odd for bringing him presents on *her* birthday, but she wasn't leaving anything to chance. She wanted his senses overflowing. She wanted distraction.

She wanted to ask a favor and she was scared to death he'd think she was crazy. Of course, his immediate answer would probably be no. She'd wait until he was stone-cold sober before she'd accept that decision.

MICHAEL WAS ELATED and instantly hard when he opened the door of his condo to see Susan standing there, coat gaping, his own personal paramour. But he wasn't really surprised. He'd been thinking of her all day. Needing her. And she was here.

That was just the way it was with them.

"Lady, you read my mind." He gathered her close, his hands sliding inside the open overcoat, as he kicked the door closed.

"Hello, Michael," she laughed when he let her up for air.

He kissed her again, tasting her, turned on as much by the familiarity of her as the luscious breasts he felt against him. "Happy birthday, sweetheart." He nuzzled her neck, her collarbone.

"Thank you." Her voice wasn't quite steady. She was on fire, too. Even after all these years, it was still instantaneous combustion. For both of them.

"Mind if I put these things down?"

Michael took her bag and the gifts she held without removing his lips from her body. He set her things on the high-backed wicker chair in the foyer and then, turning, forced her backward toward the stairs that led to his bedroom.

He was damn glad she was here.

"WHERE WERE YOU TODAY?" Susan's words were soft, sleepy, her finger toying with his nipple as he lay facing her, still *inside* her.

"Atlanta."

Her eyes were closed, but her face was taut, her body tense as she continued to play with him. "On business?"

"Later." At the moment, Michael couldn't even remember why he'd thought the day's meeting so important.

"Mmm-hmm." Susan's tongue darted out to his lips and then was gone. "Later."

"MICHAEL?"

"Mmm-hmm?" He'd just been thinking he should rouse himself enough to tell her his good news. As soon as he was strong enough for another celebration.

"We can always talk to each other about everything, can't we?"

Although he didn't shift from his position propped on the pillows with Susan cradled against his chest, Michael was instantly alert. Lethargy evaporated to be replaced with caution. And maybe something else. Maybe fear.

"I've always thought so."

"Yeah, me, too."

Her breathing became more regular as she lay there silently, more relaxed, as though she were going to sleep. Was that it, then? Just a reaffirmation of what they were to each other?

Granted, their relationship was far from traditional, an open-ended friendship with no strings attached. But it worked for him. And for her, too, he thought. Had she just needed reassurance? He was loath to move, to disturb her. Loath to find out there was more.

"So, if…something…changed for me, I could tell you?"

What had changed? "Of course you could."

Had she found someone else? Someone in Cincinnati? God forbid, someone she wanted to marry?

Michael's throat was dry, but he tried to be calm, reasonable. She wouldn't have shown up here tonight, wouldn't be lying naked in his arms, satiated with a couple of hours of healthy love if there was someone else, right?

Unless…

He thought back to the day—and night—of their divorce. Sex was exactly how she'd said goodbye.

He couldn't stand the idea of her with someone else.

"So *has* something changed?" He finally had to ask. Had to know.

"Maybe."

Maybe? Could you *maybe* be in love with someone else?

He continued to hold her, to run one hand lightly up and down her naked back.

"You're not sure?"

The entire conversation was ludicrous. Susan in love with someone else? *Making love* with someone else? He might have worried about something like that in the beginning, seven years ago, right after their divorce. But now?

"I'm sure."

His hand stilled. "You are."

Her hair was rough against his chest as, slowly, she nodded.

Then why in hell are you lying here, naked, in my bed, in my arms? He wanted to shout at her. Almost did.

Until it occurred to him that Susan had every right to fall in love with someone else. And that he had no rights at all. Not anymore.

Once, he had.

But he'd given them up.

CHAPTER THREE

"I'M GOING to have a baby, Michael."

Michael flew out of bed, hardly aware of her head flopping onto the pillows behind him as he stood on the thick carpet covering his bedroom floor.

And then, feeling incredibly foolish, he realized he must have misunderstood, heard her wrong. He'd thought, for a second there, that she'd told him she was pregnant.

"What did you say?" He stalled, looking for a way to explain his bizarre behavior without actually telling her what he *thought* she'd said.

She lay there, gazing up at him, the oddest expression on her face. Half fearful, half belligerent. Her chocolately golden hair was scattered about her face and tangled on the pillows beneath her, her lips bare and swollen, her eyes wide. She'd pulled the covers up to her chin. She looked about sixteen.

"I'm going to have a baby."

The breath knocked out of him, Michael felt as though he'd been sucker punched. If he hadn't been butt naked he'd have sunk to the floor.

"You...are." He couldn't, for the moment, think of anything more intelligent to say.

Still wearing that odd expression, Susan nodded. He hated the way she was looking at him. Hated seeing her so unsure. Hated everything about this damn evening. This day. This life.

"You're going to have a baby." He just couldn't make sense of it.

She nodded again.

Susan was pregnant. His Susan. The woman whose career meant more to her than anything, including him, was going to be encumbered with someone else's child.

He'd kill the bastard who'd done this to her.

"Who is he?" Michael reached for his slacks and, not taking time for underwear, pulled them on. He would hunt the guy down and kill him with his bare hands for not loving Susan more responsibly. Hell, for loving her at all.

"I don't know yet."

So intent was he on finding some shoes, a shirt, he barely heard the words when she first uttered them. But as he buttoned his shirt, cussing at every little buttonhole, her voice slowly sank in.

Whirling, he faced her. "You don't know *yet?*" He had to be asleep, having the craziest nightmare of his life. There was no other way to explain the things he was hearing.

Unusually winded, Susan shook her head.

There'd been more than one man? "Well, when are you going to find out?" Didn't they have to wait until after the baby was born to determine paternity?

"I'm not sure."

"I'm going downstairs."

Michael took the stairs three at a time—half sliding, half running in his hurry to get away from her. To get away from the whole sordid mess. With a

Scotch in hand, and one small light on above the bar, he paced his living room, doing some quick desperate math. He'd seen Susan at Christmas, but he'd only been able to spare the one day and her whole family had been around. He'd been busy as hell all through the fall with year-end approaching, and dammit, this baby couldn't be his.

His gut hard, he figured out that it had been a good four months since he'd made love to Susan. And there was no way she was four months along. Her belly was as flat as always. He knew. He'd just spent the past two hours intimately acquainted with it.

Not that he'd *wanted* the baby to be his. He finished off the shot of whiskey he'd poured. Not at all. Certainly no more than Susan wanted to be pregnant. He couldn't think of anything she'd want less. Except maybe death. Or anything *he'd* want less, for that matter.

He also couldn't get past the sick feeling of knowing that another man had done this to her. Dammit! Why hadn't she been more careful?

"You're angry, aren't you?"

She'd appeared behind him, wearing a rumpled men's shirt. She'd found the shirt he'd worn to work earlier and wrapped herself in it. The shirt reminded him of his meeting with Coppel.

"No."

"Don't lie to me, Michael."

He turned toward her. She was right. Lying to each other was one thing he and Susan had never done.

"Okay, yeah, I'm angry." So angry he could feel his nostrils flaring.

"Why? It has nothing to do with you."

So why, if that was supposed to make it okay, didn't he *feel* okay?

"For one thing, I'm angry as hell at the irresponsibility of whatever man did this to you."

She frowned, dropping down to his leather couch, folding her feet beneath her. "Did what to me?"

Michael swore, out of all patience. "Got you pregnant, of course." Did pregnancy make a woman stupid, too? He'd thought it only caused pickle cravings and crying attacks.

Susan laughed. Shocking him. "In the first place, Michael, a man can't get me pregnant all by himself."

She had him there.

"Secondly, I'm not pregnant—yet."

The whiskey was clouding his brain.

"And in the third place, I haven't slept with anyone but you in my entire life."

Well, that was okay then.

Michael fell down to the couch beside her, feeling a little drunk, though he'd only had the one shot. "Thank God."

Only him. In her entire life. He started to grin.

She grazed his face with one slim hand. "Would it really have mattered so much if there was someone in Cincinnati?" Her words were soft, easy, but the light in her eyes was soul-deep.

"It would." In seven years' time, they'd never discussed fidelity. Or infidelity, either.

"I'm glad."

Pulling her into his arms, Michael held her, wondering if they'd just made some kind of crazy commitment in this relationship that wasn't. And hoping, irrationally, that they had.

Slowly, though, as he sat listening to her breathing in the quiet of the night, Michael's mind started to clear. He still had his good news to share. But first...

"Why did you say you were going to have a baby if you aren't?" he asked, frowning in the near darkness.

"Who says I'm not?" She turned to look at him.

"You just did."

"No, I didn't."

"Susan..." His tension was building again. "You just said—"

"That I'm not pregnant," she finished for him. "But I'm going to be."

"When?"

"Soon, I hope."

Aghast, he stared at her. "Why?"

"Because I *want* to be."

"But..." He was adrift. Lost. He stared at a scrap of paper he'd been doodling on earlier and left on the coffee table. "...then you'd have a child."

"I know." It was the quiet conviction in Susan's words that got to him. And scared the hell out of him. *Who was this woman?* Susan didn't want children.

Did she?

"Will you give me a baby, Michael?"

Michael jumped up again. "No!" He hadn't meant the word to be so loud—so harsh. "You're kidding, right?" It was late; she'd been working long hours. That must be it.

As soon as she started to shake her head, Michael looked away.

"Please try to understand, Michael."

Looking back at her, he nodded. He wanted to understand.

"Having a baby is something I've always planned to do."

"Since when?"

"Since before you and I were married."

"And you don't think I should have known about this?"

"Probably, but we were young. We had so many goals." She shrugged. "Neither one of us wanted a child then."

"But you planned to have one later." He was trying to understand. He really was.

"By the time I was forty."

"You never mentioned it because you weren't planning to stay married to me?" He supposed the question was a bit ludicrous considering that they *weren't* married, but had she gone into the marriage knowing it wouldn't last?

"I just figured that once we'd both done what we had to do, reached our career goals, we'd be ready to talk about having a family."

He nodded. At least she hadn't been planning their divorce before she'd even married him. And they'd never actually *said* they were never going to have children. He'd just assumed, since she was as career-driven as he was—since she put job above all else and completely accepted the fact that he did, too—he'd just assumed she didn't want a family as much as he didn't want one.

Maybe he knew her better than she knew herself.

Sitting down beside her, Michael once again took

her in his arms. Having her there with him was the only thing that felt right, natural…normal.

"Susan, honey, you're at a particularly vulnerable time in your life. A time when people make rash decisions. And then spend the next twenty years regretting them."

"Don't patronize me, Michael." She pulled away from him, one-hundred percent intimidating attorney, even while wearing nothing more than his shirt. "I am not going through a midlife crisis."

"It's perfectly natural."

"And I'm not going through one."

"Most people don't realize that they are."

"And do they start them in their twenties?"

"You can't honestly consider some half-baked thought you once had about having a child as proof that you really wanted it. If you did, why'd you wait so long?"

"Because I knew I could afford to wait. That I needed to wait." Her eyes pleaded with him to take her seriously. "The thought, even back then, wasn't half-baked."

"How can you be so sure about a decision like this?"

"Remember when I went to Kentucky that weekend before we got married?"

"Of course." He'd been scared to death she was going to change her mind.

"I went because I was having second thoughts. I was afraid that by marrying you, I was going to lose me."

"You never told me that." Michael pulled at a

string coming loose from the button at the bottom of his shirt.

"I know." She smiled sadly. "You'd just have told me you wouldn't let that happen, that you wouldn't take away who I was or needed to be."

"Because it's true."

"But sometimes these things happen to people without their even noticing it." She took his hand, held it in her lap. "You wouldn't knowingly or purposely have distracted me from my goals, Michael. Just my loving you, wanting to make you happy might have done that." She paused, then began again, her voice low. "Once you start…subjugating yourself, you don't even know anymore whose interests you're really protecting. And then you're fifty or sixty years old and resenting everyone because you haven't done what you needed to do in life and it's too late. Look what happened to my mother. Because of our family."

And suddenly Michael began to understand. He'd been the one to pick up the pieces of Susan's tortured heart after Rose Carmichael died. They hadn't been married yet, but he'd helped her come to grips with that last, painful conversation. Helped her work through the regrets, the recriminations.

"I wrote out a life plan that weekend in Kentucky, Michael. My goals, my dreams. And target dates by which I either had to decide they no longer mattered—or I had to fulfill them."

Michael started to feel a little sick. "Having a baby was on that list."

Susan nodded.

"And it still matters."

"Yes."

The last thing in the world he wanted was a baby. He had his own reasons. And, like Susan's, they came from examples set by his parents. To Michael, having a child meant his life was over.

He'd felt that even before the meeting with Coppel. "Have you talked to anyone else about this?"

"Just Seth."

"And?"

She was silent. Her eyes fell for a moment and then returned to his. "Seth's hardly one to understand."

Based on her brother's bachelor life-style, he supposed not. But Seth had always championed his big sister, had walked in her footsteps as long as Michael had known him. Michael had even begun to wonder if maybe Seth was still alone, married to his career, because he was following Susan's example.

"He thinks you're crazy?"

Susan shrugged, shocking Michael when her eyes filled with tears. "He doesn't think I'm mother material."

Seth's lack of confidence had shaken her. "He's nuts." Michael heard the words before he'd even realized he'd had the thought.

"Really?" Her beautiful eyes glowed with uncertainty in the dusky room.

"Just look at Seth if you need evidence," Michael said. "You practically raised him." Which was one of the reasons Michael had thought she'd never want children. With three younger brothers, she'd had more than her share of babysitting and housework and driving her brothers to practices and games. Her mother had needed her at home, so her high-school years had been rife with missed opportunities.

Somehow she was back in his arms and Michael soaked up her warmth, her soft feminine scent. The evening washed over him—the good and the bad. Was her need to have this child so great that she'd be willing to give up her job? Move to Chicago?

The thought wasn't as displeasing as it might have been. He'd lost track of the number of times he'd wished he'd never had to divorce her in the first place. The number of sleepless nights he'd spent lying beside her, trying to convince himself that a long-distance relationship could work. Instead, he'd been tortured with visions of needing his wife at some important function and her not being there, or vice versa. He'd imagined them wearing themselves out trying to be together every weekend out of obligation to each other. And he'd thought of what marriage meant, of the expectations it brought, of two people being one unit—and just couldn't picture the link between him and Susan stretched across two states. Visions haunted him of the damage they'd eventually do to each other by trying to hang on when they kept disappointing each other, when expectations couldn't possibly be met. He'd tried to imagine himself being a good husband to Susan from Chicago and knew that he'd had no choice but to let her go. He'd finally had to face the fact that they couldn't possibly be true to themselves, to their own needs and desires, and to each other, as well. There wasn't room in either of their lives for anyone else's expectations.

But that was before he'd known she wanted to have a baby.

"You want us to get married again," he summed up.

She didn't say anything right away. "Nothing's changed for us, has it Michael?" she finally asked, frowning.

"How do you mean?"

"Our reason for divorcing. Your career needing you one place, mine needing me another."

So, she *wasn't* planning to move to Chicago? "Not for me, it hasn't."

"Then why would we get married again?"

"So you can have your baby."

"This is almost the new millennium, Michael." Her voice was a little arrogant as she settled back against him. Hard. "You don't have to be married to have a baby."

He was apparently too damn tired to think straight. "Do you mind telling me then, what exactly you do want from me?"

"Your sperm." Susan grinned up at him. And he saw in her eyes, in the cocky tilt to her mouth, the woman he'd fallen in love with so many years before. The one who always made everything sound so easy.

ALMOST FOUR DAYS LATER, Susan couldn't believe how relieved she was to have asked the question. She knew there was a good chance Michael was going to say no. But she couldn't ignore the fact that he hadn't already done so. And couldn't help but hope that he wouldn't.

She'd spent the rest of the weekend in Chicago, and it had been just like old times. He'd taken both days off in deference to her birthday and they'd played to their hearts' content. In bed and out of it.

They'd done the city, gone to the zoo, walked along the skydeck of the Sears Tower, taken a walking tour through downtown Chicago to view the skyscrapers. They'd been sidetracked before they'd actually seen many skyscrapers, however. The cold and their hunger had driven them inside. After an hour and a half spent stuffing themselves at Michael's favorite restaurant down by the lake, Michael had driven her through the Lake Shore Drive Apartments—glass houses he called them—and out to the Widow Clarke House, the oldest surviving building in Chicago.

And not once, throughout the entire weekend, did they mention Susan's baby—or anything else remotely serious.

But she knew Michael. He was thinking about the baby. And he'd let her know when he'd made a decision. She just hoped it was sometime before her fortieth birthday.

In any case, she was feeling better Monday morning than she had in a long while. She'd asked him. She could afford to wait. At least for a week or two.

In the meantime, she had another little problem to attend to. A problem named Tricia Halliday. Tricia's office—it was still hard for Susan to think of it that way—occupied the whole floor above Susan's. Formerly belonging to Tricia's husband, Ed, the room was a sportsman's dream. It had a half basketball court at one end, basketball being Ed's favorite sport, a putting green running along one wall, and a ceramic tile floor underneath the furniture to accommodate

Ed's best friend, Annie. And it was all wrong for Ed's widow, Tricia.

Susan had gone to work for Ed right out of college. Having grown up with five brothers, she fit right in with the sports talk, understood the needs of athletes. She could even hold her own on the basketball court if she had to. And she'd adored Ed. She'd been devastated when he'd died of a heart attack last year, playing tennis at his club one Sunday afternoon.

He'd reminded her of her dad with his patience, his ability to see what was done well rather than focusing on what hadn't been done, his insistence on looking at the bright side, the right side. The major difference between the two men, as evidenced by Susan's position in the company, was Ed's lack of chauvinism. He hadn't thought, as Susan's father did, that men and women had to be pigeonholed into particular roles.

Unfortunately, Ed's character hadn't rubbed off on his widow. Tricia was honest and hardworking, but her only interest was in the bottom line. Her pocketbook. And as Halliday Headgear was a privately held company, there wasn't a lot anybody could do once the CEO made up her mind about something. Except live with it. Or quit.

Dressed in her red power suit, Susan faced Tricia across Ed's desk, determined not to leave without some sort of compromise in the McArthur case.

"Are you telling me you can't win this suit?" the older woman asked, her brows almost touching with the force of her frown.

"No. I'm not telling you that."

"It was my understanding that my ten-year-old nephew could win this one for us."

"Probably."

"So why are we wasting my valuable time, and yours, discussing it?"

"Because the McArthur boy didn't do anything wrong, Tricia. True, he was playing soccer instead of softball, but the mask would have broken, probably with more serious repercussions, if he'd been hit with a softball rather than a soccer ball."

"He wasn't."

"No, he wasn't." Susan paused, eyed her boss, and started again. "But that boy is still paralyzed because of the malfunction of our equipment."

"What do you want from me, Susan?"

Susan stood, leaned over the front of Tricia's imposing desk. "I want us to settle out of court, to fund the boy's operation—and his physical therapy afterward."

Tricia stood up, too. "That's got to be thousands of dollars."

"The lawsuit could cost you a lot more than that."

"But we're not going to lose the suit."

"I had Jill spend a day with Grady Moses down in production." Looking around at the motivational posters on the walls, the peaks being scaled by climbers, the shots being made, the rides and runs and jumps, Susan took heart from Ed's memory. "She found out that there was a malfunction several months ago on one of the machines. Six cases of masks were damaged before the error was noticed. Their hinges didn't have double sealings."

"I'm aware of the problem." Tricia nodded. "The machine was fixed, the cases were pulled."

"Five of the six cases were pulled," Susan corrected. "While Grady was at lunch someone used the sixth case to fill an order. The masks had been on back order for weeks and someone in shipping was a little too eager."

Carefully, slowly, Tricia sat back down. Her eyes never left Susan's face. "You're telling me we're going to have more lawsuits, and somewhere along the way, one of them's going to be the result of a softball injury."

And the McArthur incident would come to light giving Halliday Headgear some very bad press.

"No." Susan almost wished she didn't have to be honest. "Grady was able to track down the orders and make exchanges."

Relief softening her face, Tricia spread her arms wide. "Then we don't have a problem."

"The men's club in Valdez had ordered five of the recalled masks. They sent back four damaged ones, but the fifth one they returned was a first-quality mask. By mistake, they kept the fifth damaged one for the boys at their church to use."

"I see." Tricia folded her hands on top of the desk.

Breathing her first easy breath, Susan hoped Tricia finally did see, and waited patiently for instructions to prepare the out-of-court settlement.

"We're certain this is the only mask that escaped notice?"

"Positive." Susan nodded, perching on the edge of the desk. "Grady checked and rechecked the serial numbers."

"Then we'll proceed as originally directed."

"But..." Susan stood, staring down at her boss. "We know the mask was faulty," she said, trying very hard not to raise her voice. "We *know* the boy would've been hurt no matter what ball hit him. It's only a technicality that he happened to be playing soccer instead of softball."

"And court cases are won on technicalities all the time."

"You realize that if this information is made known, your chances of winning will drop considerably."

Tricia's eyes narrowed. "Are you threatening me?"

"Of course not!" Susan backed away from the desk. "I've been with Halliday Headgear since college, Tricia. I've always, *always* seen to the best interests of the company."

Head bowed, Tricia said, "I'm sorry, Susan. Of course I'm fully aware of how much you've done for us, how lucky we are to have you." She looked up and Susan saw the sincerity in the other woman's eyes.

"Thank you."

"Now, was that all you needed to see me about?"

Just like that, Tricia expected this to go away. "I can't rest the case yet, Tricia. An eight-year-old boy may never walk again."

Shrugging, Tricia pulled a pile of papers toward her. "I pay you to be thorough, Susan. Keep searching if you feel you must to protect the company, but unless you've got something new to tell me, I don't need to hear about this case again.''

Too furious to do anything else, Susan turned and left the office.

CHAPTER FOUR

IF HE DIDN'T make her pregnant, someone else would.

No matter how many different ways Michael looked at the situation, he always ended up back in the very same place. Susan wanted him to impregnate her, but if he said no, she wasn't going to give up on this crazy idea. He'd be sending her directly into the bedroom of another man.

By Thursday afternoon he had one hell of a headache. And still no answers. In desperation he turned to the only other person he could possibly call. His ex-brother-in-law, Seth—and, next to Susan, his closest friend.

"What's up?" Seth asked as soon they'd assured each other they were fine and that both of them had absolutely nothing to do next Sunday but watch the Super Bowl.

"I'm sure you can guess." Michael was finding it a little difficult to say the words. He was that opposed to the whole idea. Picking up a pencil, he started to sketch a couple of cartoon characters, a man and a woman, jumping out of an airplane without parachutes.

"Susan told me she asked you about the baby."

"And she told me you think she's insane." He dropped his pencil.

"I never said that!"

"No." Michael remembered the tears in Susan's eyes. "You told her you didn't think she'd make a good mother."

Sounding unusually defensive, Seth said, "And you think she would?"

Swiveling his chair away from his desk, Michael looked out the window behind him. He gained no inspiration at all from the barren tree limbs outside.

"She did all right by you and Sean and Spencer."

"She didn't have a career then."

"She has a career now and she still looks out for you."

Seth swore softly. "Come on, Michael, you know it isn't the same thing. A kid deserves better than absences, vague promises, excuses."

"So, it isn't her mothering abilities you doubt." He rested his feet on the windowsill. "It's her time management."

"Or her priorities," Seth said. "You know her, Michael, she's been biting off more than she can chew her entire life, all the while insisting she'll manage. She always thinks that whatever she's tackling is a piece of cake."

He agreed with Seth. But... "She does manage in the end."

"Up until now she's only had one priority."

That was true, too. But who was to say she wouldn't handle two priorities as successfully as she handled one? If she wanted both of them badly enough...

Michael brushed a piece of lint off his navy slacks. "Answer me something..."

"If I can."

"Do you think she really knows what she wants?"

"If you mean do I think she really wants this baby, then yes, I do."

Michael was afraid he'd say that. "Yeah, me, too."

"So…you going to give it to her?"

This had to be one of the oddest conversations in the history of man—or at least of brothers-in-law. But Michael was getting nowhere on his own. And the decision was too important to be clouded by confusion or wishful thinking.

"I don't know," he finally said.

Seth hesitated. "You know she'll, uh, find someone else if you don't."

"I had considered that." At least a million times in the past six days. "But she might not."

"I don't think anything but an act of God is going to keep Susan from having her baby."

Neither did Michael. Dammit. And damn Seth for saying so. "There's always artificial insemination."

"I really doubt she'd consider it."

So did Michael.

"She'd want to know the man who's going to be, biologically speaking, the other half of her child," Michael said before he had to hear it from Seth.

"She'd insist on having the inside scoop on the littlest things, like how soon he'd learned to tie his shoes, how close his family was, whether or not he liked to go to the movies." Seth twisted the knife a little deeper.

"She'd ask for a complete genealogical workup going as far back as possible." Michael rubbed more salt into his wound.

After all, Susan was a lawyer. A damn good one. She wanted all the answers.

"Of course, all that extra effort, getting to know someone that well, tracking down someone's heritage—it might be a little off-putting, might make her reconsider...." Seth was obviously trying his best to help.

"Not Susan." Michael voiced what both men knew. Turning, he picked up the pencil and added some finishing touches to the cartoon. "Because she'd underestimate the work involved, the difficulties. Just like she always does." Just like she had that night she'd tried to talk him out of the divorce. She'd made it all sound so simple. Him living in one state, her in another. But he'd known a marriage could never survive under those circumstances. Marriage meant commitment, expectations. Sharing one life. Not two.

"So, you going to do it?" Seth asked painfully, as though he were suffering right along with Michael. And, in a sense, he probably was. Seth obviously felt pretty strongly that Susan was making a big mistake.

Michael tossed the pencil. "The last thing in the world I want is to be a father."

"I don't think Susan's looking for a father," Seth said. "I had the impression she just wants the...you know. The genes." He could tell Seth didn't approve of that, either.

"Yeah," Michael said. "That's the way I took it." She wanted his sperm. Not him.

And that rankled, too.

THE OFFER FROM Coppel Industries came through on Friday morning. Coppel stockholders wanted to make

Michael a vice president of finance. If he accepted, he'd be on the road, traveling around the country, analyzing current holdings, but mostly seeking out new ones. Diversification was the key to success. And Coppel felt that Michael could pick winners.

He'd have an office, too, a posh one, at Coppel headquarters in Atlanta.

The offer exceeded his expectations; it was a culmination of everything he'd worked for his entire life. More than a dream come true, it was a mountain successfully scaled, a goal reached, years of endless toil rewarded. Of course, it also came with Coppel's words of warning still ringing in Michael's ear. *No entanglements. No dependents.*

Michael took the job.

"OKAY." •

"Okay?" Susan sat down. She'd been waiting for his call all week.

"I can't pretend I'm happy about this."

Sitting on the floor of her bedroom, wearing nothing but the slip and panty hose she'd been in the process of taking off, Susan couldn't stop grinning. "I know." She couldn't believe it! He was really going to do it.

"You don't have a child on a whim, Susan."

"I don't do anything on a whim, Michael."

"Single-parenting is tough."

Susan glanced at her watch. Seven o'clock on Friday night. She wondered if he was still at the office.

"I can handle it."

"And you think it's fair to the kid, bringing him into the world without a father?"

"I have five brothers, Michael, all of whom live within twenty miles of my home. I don't think he— or she—will be lacking male attention."

"This is nuts."

"I don't think so." It felt right. To be having a baby. To be having Michael's baby. Of course she'd prefer to be doing it the traditional way. To be sharing more than just the conception with Michael. But she'd be happy.

A baby!

"What about your job?"

"What about it?"

"You're still planning to work?"

Susan frowned. "Of course." And then, "Who do you think's going to support this child?"

"And you honestly think you can work fourteen hours a day and still be a good parent?"

Her arms about her empty stomach, Susan leaned her head back against the wall and closed her eyes. "The only reason I still work fourteen-hour days is because I have nothing to come home for." It was the first time she'd admitted the truth, even to herself. "I'm not climbing up anymore, Michael. I'm at the top."

"There are always higher mountains to climb."

"I like the one I'm on." She used to, anyway. And she would again. In spite of Tricia Halliday.

"I can't be a father, Susan."

"I'm not asking you to be."

Ice clinked in a glass and she heard him swallow.

"Hell," he swore softly. "I don't even live in the same state."

"Which has nothing to do with anything." She wished he'd just relax about it. "Michael, we're divorced. All I want from you is biology."

He swallowed again. "You make it sound so simple."

"Because it doesn't have to be complicated." Opening her eyes, Susan stood, finished undressing. "I'm a single woman who's made the decision to have a baby," she told him. "It's happening more and more. Single women are even adopting babies. But I really want the full experience, carrying the child, giving birth. All I'm asking from you is the missing ingredient I need to get started."

Susan stopped, pulled on a pair of sweatpants. The line was silent. "I could ask a total stranger to provide the sperm," she said, exasperated. "Would you rather I do that?"

"Hell, no!"

"You're my friend, Michael." Throwing herself down on the bed she'd once shared with him, Susan gazed, still topless, at the picture of Michael laughing up at her from the bedside table. "My best friend." She had to stop for a second. Catch her breath. Swallow the tears that had suddenly appeared. "Who else would I go to when I need a favor?" she finished.

"No one." He sighed. "You were right to come to me."

She couldn't believe how good it felt to hear him say so.

"So when do you want to do it?" His voice dropped, low and gravelly, sexy.

Covering her naked breasts with her arms, Susan wanted to tell him that this weekend was perfect timing, as far as her cycle was concerned. "Whenever it's…convenient…for you," she said instead. It felt odd to be *discussing* it. She and Michael just kind of fell into sex—mostly because they couldn't help themselves.

They'd certainly never planned it before. It was slightly embarrassing. And she was freezing. Scrambling into her sweatshirt, she barely caught his words.

"…this weekend…off for the Super Bowl."

"Good!" She pulled the phone back to her face. "This weekend's good." She'd already decided to take both days off. While that would mean two full weekends in a row, she needed a little extra distance right now. Needed time to think objectively about the McArthur case. "Probably too late to fly in tonight, huh?"

Michael laughed and her toes curled. There just wasn't another man like him. She knew. She'd searched frantically during those first few years after the divorce.

"I'd like to think it's my body you're so eager for."

It was. "That old thing? Had it last weekend."

"Keep it up, woman."

"So you'll come in the morning?"

"First flight out." His voice sounded muffled, as though he were already on to the next item on his evening's agenda.

"Michael?"

"Yeah?"

"Thanks."

SEX. He wasn't going to think about anything but the sex. And sex with Susan was always incredible. He had to admit, as far as favors went, this one was relatively painless.

As long as all he thought about was the sex.

He occupied himself with business during the short flight from Chicago to Cincinnati, mentally reviewing possible candidates for his replacement at Smythe and Westbourne, making a list of the projects and problems his replacement would need to know about.

He still hadn't told Susan about the promotion. He had some irrational feeling that if he was going to get through this episode intact, he had to keep his private life, his own personal self, out of it. Susan's request had erected a wall between them that he was afraid to scale. Somehow, he knew that for his own self-preservation he had to keep his distance. Sharing this, the greatest success of his life, with her, the realization of all his goals, made him too vulnerable at a time when he couldn't afford to be vulnerable at all.

Besides, there was a small part of him that was afraid she'd be hurt because he'd accepted a job that required no familial obligations, even though he'd agreed to father her child. And the fear wasn't just born from an aversion to hurting Susan. If she was hurt, that would mean she'd been harboring some desire for him to share more than just the conception of her child.

And he couldn't do this for her if he thought, for one second, that she'd be asking for more than he had to give.

Staring out the window at the expanse of anonymous farmland passing beneath him, Michael forced his mind back to the loyal staff he'd built over the years. He'd pretty much decided on the person he was going to promote, and he looked forward to breaking the news. That thought gave him the balance he'd been seeking.

Business was the only thing he felt sure about. The only way he knew how to cope. To shut off the fears and concerns that were nagging at him, the uneasiness he couldn't seem to dissipate with logic.

A man could only think so much about sex without embarrassing himself.

SETH'S DARK-BLUE Bronco was parked in front of the condo when Michael pulled up in his rental. Fond as he was of Susan's brother, Seth sure as hell could have picked a better time to come visiting.

"I heard you were going to be in town," the big blond man greeted him as Michael let himself in. "Thought I'd stop by and see if you two wanted to take in a movie or something."

Susan, curled up on the couch, raised her brows and grimaced behind her brother's back.

Michael shrugged out of his overcoat and hung it on the brass tree by the front door. "Don't think so, buddy," he said. There was no way in hell he'd be able to sit through a movie right now.

"The new Star Trek movie's playing downtown," Seth coaxed.

Exchanging glances with Susan, Michael shook his head. Trekkies though they were, a movie was still a two-hour wait in the dark. "It was just released," he told Seth, pulling his keys out his jeans pocket to drop them on the hall table. "And it's Saturday. The theater'll be full of kids."

Dressed in beige khaki slacks and a black long-sleeved fleece shirt that hugged her waist, Susan looked great. And eager. Her eyes were glowing as she shared an intimate glance with him.

"How about a game of basketball, then? I can call for a court." Seth picked up the phone and dialed.

"I didn't bring gym clothes," Michael said, disconnecting the call. He met and held his friend's gaze. "Seth, go home."

"There's a new restaurant on the other side of the river I've been meaning to try," Seth said, still clutching the phone. "We could have lunch...."

Turning his ex-brother-in-law toward the door, Michael grabbed Seth's coat off the rack and handed it to him. "Go home."

Seth took his coat, put it on, and turned back, looking from Susan to Michael. "I think we should talk about this."

"I think—" Susan began.

"Go home," Michael interrupted her, giving Seth a little shove.

"You're sure?" Seth asked quietly.

Hell no, he wasn't sure. But Susan was. And he'd never be able to live with himself if he forced her to ask another man to do this.

"Go home," he said one last time.

Swearing, Seth let himself out, slamming the door. Michael locked it behind him.

SUSAN STARED at Michael's back. He was still staring at the door he'd just locked, almost as though he were thinking about heading out himself.

"You want something to eat?"

He turned, walking slowly back into the living room, not meeting her eyes. "Nah, I had breakfast at the airport."

He slipped his hands into his pockets, stretching the denim of his jeans taut across his fly. Susan couldn't help noticing how attractive he was. She'd never been able to look at Michael without thinking about sex. But today there was more. Today she saw the man who was going to give her his baby.

The thought scared her just a little. What if this changed things? Not her life; of course *that* was going to change. But what if things between her and Michael weren't the same afterward?

"We don't have to do this if you don't want to," she blurted suddenly.

His gaze swung to hers, intent, hopeful. "You've changed your mind."

"No." Susan shook her head. She needed to be a mother. "But it doesn't have to be now, today," she said even as she realized that putting it off wasn't going to make any real difference. "It doesn't have to be you."

But she wanted it to be. She couldn't imagine carrying anybody's baby but Michael's.

"Are you having doubts?"

Looking down, Susan studied the pattern in the tweed fabric of her overstuffed couch. "Not about the baby."

"You're having doubts about me?"

She'd hurt him. Damn, it was getting messy already and they hadn't even *done* anything yet.

"Could you sit down or something?" she asked as he continued to hover over her, the hands in his pockets distracting her. "Please?"

Michael sat. On the very edge of the couch, knees spread, his elbows on his knees.

Susan couldn't look at him. She hadn't felt this tongue-tied with Michael since before the first time they'd made love. She'd been crazy with wanting him. And a little frightened because of her virginity. Her inexperience. A little frightened that she wouldn't be able to satisfy him. After all, he'd had the prettiest girls in college chasing after him.

She'd been a boring little tomboy bookworm.

Not knowing what else to do, she'd been honest about her feelings then. And been honest with Michael every day since.

"I can't imagine anybody but you as the father of my child." The words, though softly uttered, were filled with the emotions tumbling through her.

She wasn't looking at him, but she felt him flinch.

"I'm not asking you to *be* a father, Michael. I'd never do that to you. Any more than you'd ask me never to be a mother."

Chancing a peek at him, she quickly looked back down at her hands. He was staring straight ahead, the muscles in his jaw working fiercely.

"I'm fully prepared to raise this child myself. In fact, I'm intent on doing so," she assured him. Just as she'd been assuring herself for months.

"I just want it to be your baby growing inside me."

She wasn't doing this very well. "I want my son or daughter to be a part of you."

The more she talked to her silent ex-husband, the more her needs became clear to her. She didn't just want a baby by the year 2000. She didn't just want a baby, period. She wanted *Michael*'s baby. Even though she knew that having Michael's baby meant raising the child herself.

"What I—" she said, stopping and then trying again. "What I don't—" She reached across to lace her fingers with his, willing him to meet her eyes, waiting until he did. "What I *don't* want…is to lose you in the process."

He seemed about to say something but didn't.

"You're my best friend, Michael. I don't want that to change."

Slowly, tenderly, he brought his lips to hers. Kissing her softly. "In seven years I haven't learned to stop caring about you," he said, his lips still brushing hers. "I don't think I ever will."

Susan tried to block her mind as she gave herself up to his kiss, but for the first time, she wasn't in a hurry to make love with Michael.

And that frightened her most of all. Things were changing already.

SETH TOOK the corner so hard he felt his outside tires leave the road. How could they be so *stupid?* The sister who'd never made a mistake in her life, as far as Seth was concerned. And his friend, who was exactly like Seth himself. It was as if he didn't know either one of them anymore.

By what right could they bring a new life into the

world without the means to nurture it? Children needed parents. Two of them. Full-time.

Rounding another curve, he heard a grinding in his steering column and lightened up on the vehicle. His Bronco didn't deserve this abuse. It was faithful to him. Loyal. There when he needed it. And it never asked more from him than he could give.

Some gas. A wash every month. An occasional new tire. Tune-ups. All stuff that could wait until he happened to be in town.

Seth drove until he calmed down enough to stay within the speed limit, then slowed even more. He wanted a drink. And he'd have one. Maybe, considering that it was Saturday, and the day before the Super Bowl to boot, he'd have two. Or three.

Keeping the Bronco out of sight of the field, he slid in behind the big weeping willow across the street and to the west, and put the truck in park. But he didn't turn it off. He wasn't staying. Couldn't. He couldn't risk being seen.

He also couldn't seem to stay away.

Every week that he was in town he tried. And every week he ended up right in this same place. He'd thought that maybe today, in his efforts to prevent his sister from making the biggest mistake of her life, he'd be spared this little sojourn.

But even that peace had been denied him.

So here he sat, champing at the bit as he watched Mitch's dad massacre what had promised to be a damn good soccer team. The city league was sponsored by the Y and played all year, no matter what the season, in an effort to keep kids off the streets and in organized activities.

Last year, Seth had been their coach.

"Use your head!" he yelled. And then, ducking his own head, looked around furtively to see if anyone had heard.

Someday he'd learn to keep his big mouth shut. He'd have been a lot better off if he'd done that *before* he volunteered to coach soccer for underprivileged kids. Before he'd met Jeremy Sinclair. Or his mother.

"Finesse, Jeremy," he muttered fiercely. "Keep your eye on the ball and your feet in motion."

The boy watched the ball, but he was practically tripping over his feet in his hurry to get down the field.

"Dance, son."

Seth itched to get out of the car. To stand at the side of that field and holler. He noticed Peter Adams sitting on the bench, his lower lip jutting out like he was going to cry. None of the boys were smiling. Wishing he could motivate their butts, Seth swallowed instead.

And saw Jeremy glance over. There was no way the kid could see him. He was too far away, camouflaged by a tree. But it was time to go. He couldn't risk practice ending early. Couldn't risk Jeremy finding him there.

Anyway, he wanted that drink.

CHAPTER FIVE

THE MAN WAS enough to drive her to drink. Two o'clock Saturday afternoon and they'd spent barely a moment at home. So, of course, Michael still hadn't made love to her. He'd touched her. Hell, he could hardly keep his hands off her. Yet the second things started to progress, he'd find something to talk about.

Without really talking about anything at all.

And Susan thought *she* was nervous about taking that final, irrevocable step.

This morning, after he'd thrown Seth out, he'd decided he was hungry, after all. So they went to the new restaurant Seth had recommended for lunch, and a couple of hours disappeared. Then he'd asked to see her office on the way back to the condo, giving as his reason the fact that he hadn't been there since she'd moved her desk in front of the window.

Eventually, they'd ended up back at the condo. It was either that or go see the Star Trek movie.

"Let's make a gingerbread house," Susan said as they pulled in the drive.

"What?" He looked over at her as though she'd lost her mind. Putting her Infiniti in park, he shut off the engine and handed her the keys.

"Come on." She grinned at him. "It'll be fun." And it would give them something unthreatening to do—at home, where there was at least a possibility of babies being made.

"You need special candies and stuff to do that," Michael told her as he followed her into the house.

"Got them." She'd meant to make a gingerbread house with Spencer and Barbara's five-year-old daughter, Melissa, at Christmastime. Thank goodness she'd never mentioned her intentions to Melissa, because she hadn't had a Saturday off in the entire month of December.

Hanging his coat on the rack, Michael reached for hers. "Gingerbread houses are for Christmas."

"If you promise not to tell Santa, I won't."

"Susan." Michael took her in his arms, pulled her against him. Kissed her once—and let her go. "A gingerbread house isn't something you finish in an afternoon. They take hours of planning."

Hurt by Michael's unwillingness to make love to her, Susan headed for the kitchen. "Then we'll design a simple one."

Michael had always had artistic flair. His doodles were proof of that. But he'd hardly ever stopped working long enough to do more than doodle. She'd like to see him turned loose on a gingerbread house.

"Just waiting for the gingerbread to bake and cool takes all day," Michael said, walking into the kitchen.

"We've got all day." Susan was taking ingredients from cupboards, piling them on the kitchen counter. "Besides, it won't take that long. We can always pop the pieces in the freezer when they come out of the oven." She had to stand on tiptoe to get the molasses from the cupboard above the stove and Michael was suddenly there, reaching over her, bringing it down.

He brushed his body against hers, then let her go. And told Susan something she desperately needed to know. He wanted her. He was hard as a rock.

But before she could so much as turn in his arms, he'd stepped away from her to study the recipe she'd put on the counter.

"It says you have to chill the dough overnight before you cut it."

"So we'll pop it in the freezer *before* we bake it, too."

"Susan, I'm telling you, if you start this now, you'll still be at it tomorrow afternoon."

"Not with you helping me I won't." She grinned at him to hide her hurt. "You want to mix or dump in the ingredients?"

"Dump." Michael didn't sound any more excited about that than he had about the baby. She hoped he was a little quicker at the dumping or they *wouldn't* get the house made.

HE'D BEEN RIGHT, of course. There was no way they were going to finish her damn gingerbread house that day. They'd been working on it for a couple of hours already and he was still at the designing stage.

But he had to admit the idea had been a good one. He couldn't remember the last time he and Susan had laughed together like this.

"You have flour on your nose," he told her, reaching up to brush the dab of white away. His fingers lingered. He'd always loved the softness of her skin, the contrast between it and his rough stubble.

"Remember that time we were fooling around in the trees outside my dorm, and Connie Fisher dumped that bag of flour all over us?'' she asked now, leaning over his shoulder as she surveyed his drawing. He'd been sitting at the table with paper and pencil for the better part of an hour.

"She was lucky she was up three flights," he grumbled, remembering all right. Susan had just let him under her shirt for the first time and right before he'd had his first real handful of the breasts that had been driving him to distraction all semester, they'd been ambushed.

And she'd been dormed the rest of the week for missing curfew. He'd had to wait another five days to finally touch her.

She'd been so worth the wait....

"I think this is it." He reined in his thoughts, not trusting himself to travel along the road they'd taken. Which was ironic, considering the fact that sex with Susan was his whole reason for being there.

"I love the turret," she said, smiling at the intricate drawing.

He handed her a stack of pages. "Your pattern pieces, madam."

Taking them, she headed over to the dough she'd rolled out on the counter and said, "This is great, Michael. I can't wait to see the finished product."

And because she sounded so happy with herself, neither could he.

THE PIECES were all cut out, baked and cooling in layers in the freezer. Susan was washing the last of the dishes. It was still only seven o'clock.

Too early to go bed. Or at least, Michael amended that last thought, to go to sleep.

"I'll dry," he said, grabbing a towel out of the drawer and moving to the sink beside Susan. She had a perfectly good dishwasher, but Susan preferred to wash the dishes by hand. He'd long since concluded that she just liked playing in the suds.

He couldn't count the number of times he'd seen her standing at that very same sink, her arms elbow-deep in warm sudsy water. Or the number of times he'd stood beside her, drying the dishes as she washed, wanting her.

He *could* count the number of times it had happened since their divorce. Not once.

"Why is it that we always seem to eat out when I come to town?"

Shrugging, Susan focused on the task at hand. "Guess it's just easier."

Maybe. Or had she been keeping a distance between them? A distance he hadn't even noticed until now.

Her arm accidentally touched his side. "Sorry."

"No problem." He continued to dry. And to watch the curve of her neck. She always shivered when he kissed her there. And tightened inside. He'd made that particular discovery years ago.

Rinsing a dish, she glanced over at him. "I've got this case I'm working on..." she began, then stopped. "What?"

"Nothing," he said, but he continued to hold her gaze with his own. He couldn't stand it anymore. He had to love her.

The consequences be damned.

She was going to do this with or without him. And though he had a feeling he might hate himself for the rest of his life, he couldn't let her do it without him. He also couldn't spend another minute standing beside her, sharing her space, sharing their memories, without making love to her.

So he would. He'd leave his sperm inside her as she wanted. He just wouldn't think about what changes that might bring. Except, perhaps, to pray that there wouldn't be any changes at all.

Susan, with her heart in her eyes, fell into his arms as he reached for her, clinging to him. And opened her mouth for his kiss.

He didn't want this to happen. But, God help him, he was only a man.

FINALLY. Susan's quivering body cried out the word. Picking her up without even taking the time to dry her arms, Michael carried her down the hall to her bedroom—their bedroom—and put her on the bed. He followed her down, still fully dressed, kissing her again before either of them could speak.

Not that she had anything to say. He was coming at her so fast she couldn't even think. But she could feel. Oh, could she feel. His hands glided over her possessively, knowingly, hungrily. It was almost as if he were trying to possess all of her at once, to claim her, and she couldn't succumb fast enough. For either of them.

She wanted to touch him, too, to reassure herself that he still felt familiar, that he was still hers. But he was consuming her senses with his urgency and it was all she could do to keep from splintering into a million pieces. She held on—to him, to the covers beneath her, to whatever she could clutch in her fists.

There wasn't room for gentleness. Not that he hurt her. He didn't. He never would. He was careful with his passion, but not controlled. Not at all controlled.

His shirt came off one arm at a time but his searching caresses didn't stop for a second. Susan helped him with the waistband of her slacks, pulling her shirt up to her neck. She helped him with the waistband of his pants, too, needing him desperately, needing to finish what they'd started. Before she could think about it. Question. Worry.

She knew in her heart that this was right, that something far stronger than either of them was driving her to her eventual goal. And that was all she knew. Michael left her no time for any further thought.

Because of the day's frantic and—until now—unrelieved tension, she climaxed before Michael had even straddled her. Her gaze traveled his body as he suspended himself above her, loving the firm lean lines she knew so well, the dark hair tapering down his belly, the sweat on his brow.

Entering her with one quick thrust, he lowered his body to hers. Then, chest to chest and belly to belly, there was nothing left but feeling. He was so strong, so confident in his strokes, his caresses, she came a second time, experiencing wave after wave of sensation, until she was only aware of how much she loved the man in her arms.

And as the waves passed, as the sweetest peace followed, Susan felt him empty himself into her unprotected body. He groaned as he held himself deep within her and she knew he was doing that for her. Only for her. He was giving her the most precious gift, the gift she'd wanted, and Susan did the only thing she could.

She wept.

Silently, softly, the tears dripped off the sides of her face onto the mattress beneath her. Her arms still wrapped tightly around Michael, she prayed that he wouldn't know, that he wouldn't ask her to explain her tears. Or worse, be angry with her...

Michael began to move again, to settle himself inside her, to caress her body as thoroughly as he had before. Whether he knew about her tears or not, she wasn't sure, but they dried, forgotten on her lashes, when he loved her again.

And later, as she was sleeping in his arms on top of the covers, he woke her and made love to her a third time.

There was still, in spite of their satiation, something frantic in Michael's loving. Something that called out to Susan even though she didn't want to hear its voice. Something she answered even as she denied its existence.

Almost as though he were telling her goodbye. And she was accepting that he had to go. That he wouldn't be back. Not as she knew him that night. Not as she'd ever known him before.

It shouldn't have mattered. They were, after all, divorced. Living separate lives in separate states. It shouldn't have mattered.

But it did.

She was deathly afraid she'd just made the biggest mistake of her life.

AS MISTAKES WENT, the gingerbread house ranked right up there. All day Sunday, Michael and Seth were in her living room, roaring along with the players on the field at the Super Bowl. While Susan was stuck in the kitchen building, frosting and decorating the dream house she'd never, ever own in real life.

That house, scaled up to size, would take a big family to fill. A single mom and one kid didn't qualify. A divorced woman living alone even less so.

She didn't even have a use for this mammoth gingerbread house now that it was finished. The original plan had been to send it home with Melissa.

"Seth's gone, and I'm about ready to head out." Michael stood in the kitchen doorway, his hands in those damn jeans pockets again.

Not trusting herself to speak, Susan nodded. She'd been weepy all day and she couldn't blame that on Michael. He'd done exactly what she'd asked him to do—and only because she'd pushed so hard. Regrets were hers alone.

"You okay?" Sliding his arms around her from behind, Michael kissed the side of her face.

Resting the back of her head against his chest, Susan nodded. "Just tired."

"Hey—" he let her go "—the house looks great!"

She nodded again. She felt chilled, needed a sweater.

"What are you going to do with it?"

Susan busied herself with the last of the dishes. "Give it to Annie." Actually, she'd decided to call Seth's friend Brady. The disadvantaged kids in his care wouldn't mind that the house was a month late.

"Who's Annie?"

"Ed Halliday's dog," she reminded him. "Tricia still brings her to work every day."

"I thought you didn't like that dog. You always complained that she sheds."

Shrugging, she put away the frosting utensils. She'd complained about Annie a time or two when she'd first gone to work at Halliday Headgear. A dog at the office hadn't seemed quite professional.

"Annie grows on you," she finally said. "I've actually been thinking about getting one."

"An Annie?"

"A dog, or maybe a cat."

She turned in time to see Michael shaking his head, as though he didn't know her at all.

"I've thought about it myself," he shocked her by saying. "I'm just not home enough." Taking a seat at the kitchen table, Michael started munching on the gumdrops lining the side of the house. For someone who was heading out, he was doing it slowly.

"We had a dog when I was growing up," he continued.

Susan joined him at the table. "You never told me that."

"Haven't thought about it in years."

"What was his name?" They'd never been allowed pets when she was growing up. Too much commotion.

"Her." Michael grinned. "Samson."

"Samson was a girl?"

"What did I know? I was only six." He grabbed another gumdrop. "Besides, she was a mutt. She didn't care."

She'd known Michael for almost twenty years, and

she was seeing a part of him she'd never known. A part that mattered, somehow. "How long did you have her?"

"Until I left home."

"What happened to her?"

"She was old." He shrugged, pushed the house a little farther away.

"She got sick?"

"Not really. She just sort of...stopped wanting to live."

He wasn't making any sense. "She must have missed you an awful lot."

"Yeah." Michael glanced up at her and then away.

Suddenly she understood. The dog had died of a broken heart. And Michael still felt the sting of not being there for her.

"I'd best get going." He stood up and stretched. "I still have to turn in the rental."

Nodding, Susan followed him as he collected the satchel he'd brought. His things were already packed.

"Well—" he gave her a quick peck on the lips "—take care...."

Susan nodded, feeling a little bereft. "Michael?"

Michael stopped on his way out, one hand on the doorknob. She'd sounded almost...needy. Susan was never needy. On the contrary, she always thought she could handle anything, better than she probably could most of the time. Except that eventually she always seemed to manage.

"Do you want to know?"

No! He didn't want to know about it, think about it or talk about it. He turned, satchel in hand, not knowing what to say.

''Whether or not it worked, I mean,'' she clarified.

''Uh, sure.'' That seemed to be the answer she was hoping for. ''I guess I need to, don't I, in case we have to try again?''

Nodding, Susan grinned—the emptiest grin he'd ever seen. ''I hadn't thought of that.''

He'd thought of little else. And reached his limit. ''See ya,'' he said, dropping one last kiss on her cheek.

He'd never in his life felt such a strong need to escape.

THE FOLLOWING Saturday night, Seth was once again hell-bent on escape. He spent the evening wiping the barroom floor with one of his closest buddies, who'd dared to challenge him to a round of darts.

''Good God, Carmichael, you missed one yet tonight?'' Brady Smith muttered as he laid another five-dollar bill in Seth's outstretched palm.

''Nope.'' Seth grinned at the other man. He turned the five-dollar bill into a couple more beers at the bar and brought one back to Brady. ''You want another go?''

''I guess,'' Brady grumbled good-naturedly. ''Might as well enjoy the beer as long as I'm buying.''

Resetting the electronic dart board for another game of 501, Seth motioned for his buddy to go first.

Brady hit a bull's-eye, and then one twice. ''Fifty-two.'' He cursed eloquently as he finished reciting his score.

Seth hit a bull's-eye as well. And then two triple

twenties. He collected his darts silently, celebrating with a long swallow of beer.

"A hundred and seventy," Brady said, his voice filled with reluctant awe. "How do you do that, man?"

Seth just shrugged. Truth was, he had no idea. He'd never known how he came to be so good at sports. He just was. At every sport he'd ever tried.

"You still coaching that soccer team?" Brady asked later as the two men abandoned darts to give more serious attention to the beers they were consuming.

"Nah."

"I thought you liked it." Brady finished his last beer, wiping the foam off his mouth with the back of his hand.

"I did."

"You ever looking to volunteer some more, let me know," the other man said, pulling his keys from the pocket of his jeans. "I can put you to work in a second."

Brady ran a local detention home for troubled youths. "I'll think about it," Seth said. Maybe he would—if he was unlucky enough to remember this conversation in the morning. "You okay to drive?" he asked his friend.

"Yep. Only had two," Brady reported, patting Seth on the back as he headed out. "Marge was baking cookies when I left. They should be done just about now."

"Tell her I said hi." Seth ordered another beer. He'd had more than two. But he wasn't ready to stop yet.

"You could always come tell her yourself," Brady offered. "Those cookies'll be mighty good."

"Some other time," Seth said, shaking his head. He'd been shying away from family situations these past few months. They just seemed to make him cantankerous.

"Sure," Brady called over his shoulder as he made for the door. "I hear ya."

Brady sounded kind of offended. Seth was sorry about that. And he had a feeling he was going to remember every damn word of their conversation in the morning. He was sorry about that, too.

"JILL, GET ME Joe Burniker on the line."

Though she suspected her assistant was trying to escape, at least for lunch, Susan continued to push. Both of them. She'd been doing little else in the week since she'd seen Michael.

She jotted notes while she waited for her phone to buzz back, Jill's mission accomplished, and picked up on the first ring when it did.

"Joe? Susan Kennedy."

"Susan, how the hell are you?"

She said something noncommittal, then asked about his wife. She told him she was sorry when he explained that they'd split about six months ago. They commiserated only long enough for her to figure out that Joe, every bit the playboy he'd always been, was really quite relieved by his personal situation. And then she got down to business.

"I need a favor, Joe." She picked up the McArthur file. The boy was from Tennessee. And so, coincidentally, was Joe.

"I certainly owe you one after saving my butt in the Crone case last year."

She'd given him a little piece of research she'd unearthed in a similar case the year before. It had been no big deal. But she was calling in the favor, anyway.

"I have a case I need you to take, no guarantee you'll ever get paid."

"I'm sure there's a good reason you aren't doing it yourself."

"I am."

"And you need *my* help?"

"I'll be opposing you."

Joe laughed. "I don't know whether to be insulted or flattered."

"Why's that?" Susan sat back, starting to relax. Joe always made her feel better.

"Either you're asking because you want to ensure a win and think I'm a guaranteed loss, or because you're bored, want a good challenge, and I'm it."

Laughing, she tossed the McArthur file back on her desk. "Wrong on both counts. Actually—" sobering, Susan leaned forward. "I'm pretty sure I can win, just not sure I want to."

"Curiouser and curiouser."

"I need to know that if I *do* win, I should have, Joe. And in order to do that, I need the best attorney I can find to fight the other side."

Which all sounded great, except that Joe didn't have a hope in hell unless he unearthed the one vital piece of information that Susan ethically, as Halliday's attorney, couldn't give him. She was gambling on the fact that Joe was no less thorough than he'd been in college.

"What are we fighting for?" he asked, suddenly as serious as she.

"A boy's life."

"How is she?"

"You know you could always call her yourself and find out."

"Yeah."

It had been three weeks since Michael's weekend with Susan. Three weeks since he'd cashed in their tickets to Hawaii, exchanging them for a couple of trips to Denver and several to Atlanta. Three weeks since he'd spoken to Susan. And in spite of the fact that she seemed to be on his mind twenty-four hours a day, he still couldn't bring himself to call. Seth would have to do. For the fifth time in three weeks.

"She's fine," his ex-brother-in-law finally answered him. "Working her ass off as usual."

"Yeah." He'd expected that.

"How's the new job?" Seth asked.

"Great." A lot of work. A lot of hotel rooms. But he'd never been happier.

"You ever planning to tell Susan about it?"

Someday. Maybe. But when he told Susan he'd have to tell her all of it. That was how they did things. He couldn't give her only the basics, like he'd done with Seth. No, he'd spill it all. And when he did, she'd see right inside him, know how much the promotion meant to him, share his deepest feelings. He wouldn't be able to accept her congratulations casually, either. He'd feel her happiness for him clear to his bones. And he wasn't ready to get that close.

Without answering Seth, he asked, "She's looking good?" Picking up the complimentary pad of paper and pen next to the phone, he drew a stick figure sitting on a bench.

"Fine."

"The same?" If Michael hadn't known what a good friend he had in Seth, he'd be doubting that the other man cared anything for him at all. Seth was making him work too damn hard for every scrap of information.

"Last time I saw her."

"She's eating?"

"How the hell should I know? I'm out of town."

Right. He knew that. He'd called Seth's hotel room in Washington from his own hotel room in Burbank. "You're home weekends." Which was more than *he*'d been.

"I didn't eat with her last weekend."

"Seth…"

"Look, man, this is between you and her, okay? And I—" He stopped abruptly.

"…want no part of it," Michael finished the sentence for his friend. Michael could sympathize. He wanted no part of it, either.

CHAPTER SIX

SHE'D MISSED HER PERIOD.

"Susan, do you want me to fill out these forms for Ronnie McArthur or send them to his mother?"

This might be the start of the most momentous event of her life, and nobody knew. "Let me see them." She held out her hand for the forms.

Annie raised her head as Jill approached Susan's desk. Reaching down instinctively, Susan gave the dog a reassuring pat, perusing the forms at the same time.

"Why don't we fill in the argument section, then send them on for his mother to finish," she said, frowning. "They really should come from her."

Jill took the forms back, but didn't move from Susan's desk. "Aren't you the least bit worried that Ms. Halliday's going to hear about this?"

Susan was worried, all right. But not about her boss. In moments of excitement, of happiness, she wanted to scream from the top of Cincinnati's tallest high-rise, tell the whole world her secret. But in moments of despair, which were occurring with far more frequency, she wanted to run so far her body would never find her.

"All I'm doing is a little private charity work," she told her assistant. "There's nothing wrong in my arranging for funds through a children's charity I happen to be involved with. The child needs surgery and his parents can't afford it.''

Her brows disappearing beneath her fringe of dark bangs, Jill said, ''I suppose not.''

''Besides...'' Susan shot a glance outside her window, to the tepid March day. She could empathize with the weak ray of sun trying to burn its way through the haze. ''It's not enough, anyway. The surgery will solve part of his problem. But he won't have a life without physical therapy and there are no funds for that.''

''This is really getting to you, isn't it?'' Jill asked, still standing in front of Susan's desk.

''Yeah.'' Along with everything else. For once in her life, Susan wondered if she'd taken on more than she could handle.

So she rationalized. Her period was late because she was tense. She hadn't gone this long without talking to Michael since the first year after their divorce. And she'd been late then, too. Of course, that could have been because she'd gone off birth control pills and her cycle was messed up.

However, not having seen or heard from Michael in six weeks, she knew she couldn't stall any longer. She was well and truly on her own. Or rather, well and truly without Michael. It was time to find out if she was alone or not—a single woman or a mother-to-be.

She'd bought the home pregnancy test weeks ago. The time had come to use it.

If nothing else, she rationalized as she drove home from work, once she knew, she'd have an excuse to call Michael. Maybe even get him to make love to her once more...

She remained calm until she actually had to go and see the test result. Trembling, she started to cry even before she was in the bathroom door. Either way, the news was terrible.

Either way, she needed to find out.

She'd give *anything* to know she could have Michael back, return to the way things had been.

And she'd give just as much to know that she did indeed have a baby, one she and Michael had created together, growing right there inside her.

Like a child fighting the inevitable, she shut her eyes the second she stepped through the door. But not before she'd seen. Shaking, moving a little closer in her self-imposed darkness, she counted to three and quickly flashed her eyes open, then shut them again.

The result was the same. She didn't need to look a third time. Tears squeezed out of her tightly closed lids, slid down her cheeks and off her chin. Susan sank weakly to the floor, her legs no longer capable of supporting her.

And yet, as she sat there, propped against the bathroom door, a small burst of joy exploded within her, spreading until it touched her face, her lips. She was grinning like an idiot. And crying, too.

She was pregnant.

"HELLO?" Home for the first time in weeks, Michael had a premonition as soon as he heard the telephone ring.

"Michael?"

He knew he shouldn't have answered the damn

thing. "Hello, Susan." What else was there to say? *I've been waiting to hear from you?* He'd been avoiding her like the plague. *It's good to hear your voice?* It wasn't. He felt panicked.

"How are you?" He asked the innocuous question only when the silence had dragged on so long he couldn't stand that, either.

"Pregnant."

Oh. God. She wasn't supposed to just blurt it out like that!

"Well, goodbye..." she said—and hung up.

Stunned, Michael pulled the phone away from his ear, looked at it a moment before dropping it back in its cradle. She'd never given him a chance to think, let alone speak.

He'd been on his way out to buy some groceries, but took off his jacket and threw it on the couch instead. Pouring himself a drink, he downed it in one gulp. Then, for want of anything else to do, he poured another. And paced. His living room. His kitchen. His office. The bedroom. And when he ran out of rooms, he took a hike around the complex.

Everything looked exactly the same as it had when he'd arrived a couple of hours before. Hell, it all looked exactly as he'd left it two weeks ago, when he'd made a quick trip home to pay some bills.

Why, suddenly did it all feel so different? Nothing had changed. His life was no different from the way it had been an hour before, a year before, *five* years before. He was single. Married to his job. He lived alone. Was responsible for no one. Not even a pet.

Nothing had changed.

"There's absolutely no reason to go," he told himself as he rounded the corner of his building.

"What was that, Mr. Kennedy?" the elderly widow who lived next door to him called out.

She was pruning her rose bushes—and his, too.

"Nothing, Mrs. Leets."

"It's good to have you home," she offered with a friendly smile.

"It's good to be home." He stopped to watch her carefully pull off a couple of dead leaves. "How's your back?"

"Better." She smiled at him again. "I never did thank you properly for helping me move that couch." She'd been rearranging her living room the last time he was home. Said the sun was fading the fabric on her couch.

"No problem." He was glad he'd been there when she needed him. Chances weren't in favor of that. "You want anything else moved, you just let me know."

"I will."

He had things to do here. Laundry to send out and pick up. Mail to get through. He'd scheduled himself home for the entire week, intending to spend a good fifty hours or more at the Smythe and Westbourne office.

But he packed anyway. Just an overnight bag. And drove himself to the airport. Pulling out his credit card, he paid for a flight to Cincinnati, then sat down waiting for it to be called. He had no idea what he was doing. Or why.

OKAY. He knew why he was here. He had to see her.

She was his friend, for God's sake. He could spare

a few hours to make sure she was all right.

To congratulate her. Swerving into a small plaza on the corner by her condo, Michael jumped out and grabbed a bottle of champagne. Dom Perignon. Her favorite.

He was back in the rental before he realized she probably couldn't even drink the damn stuff.

Her condo looked the same as always. Same yard. Same trees. Same Infiniti parked in the drive. So why did everything *feel* different? As though he'd stepped into someone else's life.

Hurrying up the walk, he rang the bell, giving himself no time to reconsider—to run.

"Congratulations!" He forced the hearty greeting as soon as she opened her door, handing over the bottle. "Guess you'll have to wait until later to drink it."

"Michael?" She took the champagne. Of course, he'd given her little choice, shoving it into her arms that way.

She looked the same, too. Sort of. She didn't look like a mother or anything.

"Well, see ya," he said, turned and headed down the walk again, toward the car.

"Michael Kennedy, get back here!"

He stopped but didn't turn. He'd done what he came to do. Now he had to run.

"If you've ever cared for me a stitch in your life, you won't just leave it like this."

Damn her.

"Like what?" He played stupid. Except that he wasn't playing. Glancing at her, he shook his head.

He was moving through some surreal version of his world. He had no idea what was happening.

"You can't just walk out of my life and pretend I didn't even exist," she told him.

Sure he could. They were divorced. He was foot-loose and fancy-free. Wasn't that the point?

Hands in the pockets of his jeans, he turned again and followed her into the condo they'd purchased together all those years ago.

"So, what'd you want to talk about?" He stood in the living room, defensive as all hell.

"Us." She was also standing, looking way too good in those designer jeans. Her hands on her hips told him she meant business.

Fine. Business was what he did best. "What about 'us'?"

"That's what I want to know."

"We're divorced." He said the only thing he was sure of.

"That was years ago. I'm talking about *now*."

"I didn't know divorces expired."

"Why are you doing this, Michael?" She actually stomped her foot. "Are you trying to tell me we aren't even friends anymore? Is that it?"

Staring down at his feet, he said quietly, "I don't know."

"Don't know if we're friends?"

He couldn't look at her, was afraid he might see the tears he heard in her voice. "I don't know why I'm doing this. Any of it."

"Can we talk about it?" Her voice softened as she grabbed his hand, pulled him gently toward the couch.

"If I knew what to say, we'd have talked weeks ago."

She was so beautiful sitting there, her hair tumbling in stylish layers about her face. "Can't you at least tell me a little of what you're feeling?" she asked.

"Trapped."

"By what?" Her eyes were clouded with worry— and hurt. "Me?"

"No." He wished he could give her what she wanted, wished he knew what that was. "I don't know."

"Are you angry with me?"

"No!" He almost wished he was. Anger he knew what to do with.

"Do you hate me?"

Reaching out, Michael ran his hand along her face, loving the softness of her skin. "Of course not," he said.

"You've never gone six weeks without calling."

"I know."

She waited, obviously needing more. He could only give her what he had to give.

"I missed you." She continued to hold his gaze bravely.

"I missed you, too." He had, he realized. Desperately.

"Does it have to be this way now? Not keeping in touch?" Her voice broke and she looked away.

"I don't know, Sus." His answer was straight from the heart.

She nodded. Stood. Moved away from him.

"I have a new job." He hadn't meant to blurt out the words. He wasn't sure he'd meant to tell her at all. But being there with her, he couldn't keep the news to himself any longer.

She spun around. "You do?" Surprise replaced the pain in her eyes.

"A promotion, really."

"With Smythe and Westbourne?" She frowned. "I thought you were already as high as you could go with them."

"I was." He wished she'd sit back down. "But I had a meeting with Coppel in Atlanta a couple of months ago."

"A couple of *months* ago?" She sank down to the couch.

Michael nodded. In the old days, this would have been good news. "I've been promoted to vice president of finance for Coppel Industries."

"My gosh!" She smiled, her eyes round. "Congratulations!" She even leaned over and planted a quick kiss on his lips before she remembered herself.

"So..." She was frowning again. "You're moving to Atlanta?"

"No." Michael shrugged. He wasn't sure what he was going to do. One place was the same as another when he was mostly away in hotel rooms. "I'll probably keep my condo for now."

"But isn't Coppel's home office in Atlanta?"

"It is." Now he was the one who couldn't sit still. Rising, he stared out her living room window into the darkness that had fallen. "And I'll have an office there, but the majority of my work is on the road. I've been home twice in six weeks."

"Oh."

She didn't seem upset by the news. Maybe he'd

misjudged her. Maybe he'd been worrying for no reason. Maybe nothing had changed, after all.

"That was one of the things Coppel wanted to speak with me about, the traveling."

"One of the things?"

Michael turned around and faced her.

"Before he'd recommend me to the board, he wanted to be sure I had no personal responsibilities— no ties—that would suffer by my accepting the position."

"What did you tell him?"

"That I had none."

She nodded, her eyes steady as she held his gaze. "Was that before or after I flew to Chicago?"

Before or after I asked you to give me a baby? he translated.

"I'd just met with Coppel that day."

"That's where you were when I called and your secretary said you were out of town."

Michael nodded.

"So you already had the job?" She sounded confused.

Taking a deep breath, Michael shook his head. What did it matter? *Why* did it matter? He'd been asking himself the same questions for six weeks. And still had no answers. Except to know that…somehow…it did.

"The official offer came the following Friday."

"The day you called to tell me you'd give me your baby."

Michael nodded.

HOPES SHE HADN'T even known she had began to slip away, leaving such a sadness in their wake that Susan's entire body felt the impact. Feeling tired and heavy, she looked up at him.

"Why didn't you tell me?"

"Does it matter?" Defensiveness in every line of his body, Michael stood before her.

"Of course it does." She tried not to sound hurt, but wasn't sure she succeeded. "Didn't it ever occur to you that I'd care about such a…a momentous step in your life, just like I've always cared, because I care about you?"

"Well, I…yeah…"

"Come on, Michael," she said, standing up. She couldn't let him tower over her anymore. "This is big-time, a huge coup. The result of years and years of effort. And you didn't think I'd *care?*"

"Don't you get it, Susan?" He took a step closer. "What it means is that I've got no intentions, ever, of having any part in your baby's life. That I went into this knowing I'd already denied all responsibility for it. That I denied responsibility *knowing* I was going into this. For all intents and purposes, I'm not your baby's father."

"Yeah." She promised herself she wouldn't let the tears fall. Not in front of him. "I do realize that."

"And?" Arms crossed at his chest, he challenged her.

"That was always the plan, Michael," she reminded him. "You forget, I know you. The request was a strictly biological one. It was never for you to be my baby's father."

She wanted so desperately for him to know she understood.

"I guess it's just damn lucky we aren't still married, huh?" He tried to joke, but she saw how much he was hating himself.

And hated herself for doing this to him.

"That's what these past weeks have been about, isn't it?" she asked him, taking a step toward him. "You've been beating yourself up for not wanting to be a father, haven't you?" That was as straightforward as she could be.

Staring at her, his eyes full of emotion, Michael was silent.

"You can't help needing other things from life, Michael," she said softly. "You didn't ask to feel like you do. Nor have you ever made any secret of it."

"Maybe not."

"You're a good, honorable man." She slid her arms around him. "A hardworking man. And fair. You've always been completely honest with me."

Michael held himself stiffly, hands at his sides.

"What you did was wonderful, selfless, forgoing your own desires to give me what I needed."

Pouring her heart into every word, Susan was determined to get through to him. "You're the best friend I've ever had...." She broke off as the tears that had been waiting to fall finally did.

His arms came around her slowly, pulling her against him. And for those brief moments, she felt strong enough to make it alone.

CARLISLE LOOKED exactly the same, too. Other than the addition of a twenty-four-hour convenience store about five years back, nothing had changed there in decades. He'd been born and raised in the downtrodden little town, as had his parents before him. And their parents before them.

Pushing his rental to the limit, he made the two-hour trip from Cincinnati in a little over an hour, arriving at his parents' home just before the end of the ten o'clock news. Any later and they'd have been in bed.

"Michael! Sam, look, it's Michael!" His mother came running down the porch steps in her slippers and robe, wrapping him in her hug. "Sam! Michael's come."

"Yes, I see." Michael's father came out of the house, as well, a bit more slowly, but with a grin as wide as his mother's. "Good to see you, son!"

Shaking the hand Michael offered, he pulled his son in for a quick hug, too.

"Come on in," Mary Kennedy said, yanking Michael by the hand. "Have you eaten? I've got meat loaf left over from dinner. Or I can mix up a batch of biscuits if you'd like."

"It's okay, Mom, I'm not hungry." Michael allowed himself to be led into the house, dropping his satchel by the door before he followed both his parents into the kitchen.

It seemed that every important event in the Kennedy family had happened right there in that kitchen. He and Susan had announced their engagement, sitting at this very table, with cups of hot chocolate between them, just about this same time of night. Only that evening they'd driven like bats out of hell from Cleveland State University, instead of from Cincinnati.

They'd announced their divorce here, too. The Sunday after they'd signed the papers that made it official. He'd wondered a time or two why they'd put off telling his parents for so long. Had he maybe hoped it wouldn't happen? That Susan would find a way to convince him a divorce wasn't necessary?

"Here, have some pie." His mother dropped a plate completely covered with apple pie and vanilla ice cream in front of him. And another one in front of his father.

"Thanks, Mom, this looks great," he said, suddenly more hungry than he'd thought. He'd always loved his mother's cooking.

Smiling, she bustled about the kitchen, probably fixing some hot chocolate—and pulling more bacon out of the freezer for breakfast, too, now that she knew Michael would be there.

"Something wrong, son?" his father asked quietly, calmly savoring his apple pie.

Astute as always.

Michael could have gotten away with this visit if it had been only his mother at home. While she was the best cook, the best friend, the best mother a kid could want, she wasn't...well, she wasn't what you'd call clever. Or discerning. And not just because she hadn't finished high school. She was just a little slow on the uptake, saw the world through the innocent eyes of a child, took everything at face value.

His father was another story. The man was brilliant.

And wasted in this two-bit town.

Mary, finishing in the kitchen, hurried out with a comment about clean sheets for Michael's bed.

"I was just in Cincinnati," Michael finally answered his father. "Couldn't get a flight out until to-morrow."

"How's Susan?"

Yep, Dad was as bright as ever. "Good. Fine." Michael took another forkful of pie. His father waited. "Busy."

"Too busy to put you up for the night?"

Pushing his empty plate away, Michael glanced over at his dad. "Guess I just wanted a night at home."

"That's fine, then." Sam Kennedy pushed his plate away, too. Michael hadn't fooled him a bit.

CHAPTER SEVEN

"WHAT TIME'S your flight out?" Sam asked over an early breakfast Tuesday morning.

Michael tucked into the bacon and eggs and biscuits and gravy with relish. He'd slept well, was glad he'd come home. "No particular time," he said between bites. "I thought I might hang around for a couple of hours, catch something early this afternoon."

"Well, then, you'll have to come down to the station!" the older man said with a broad smile. "I'll show you around. We got a new air pump since you were here last."

"Yes, your father's the boss now, you know, since Mr. Hanson retired." Mary brought a bowl of fresh fruit to the table.

"Now, Mary, I'm doing the same work I've always done."

"Well, maybe so, but..."

"Old man Hanson retired?" This was news to Michael. And he was usually filled in on every little change during his weekly calls home. They had to fill him in on the little ones; there usually weren't any big ones.

"Not really," Sam said. "There just isn't enough

work for both of us anymore, so Hanson doesn't come in much.''

''Business has dropped that much?'' Michael's father worked at the local service station, had done so since he'd married Michael's mother during his senior year of high school.

''What with that new self-serve station out by the highway, and all.'' Sam shrugged.

''But you still have the mechanic's bay, and you're right here in town.''

''Oh, yeah.'' Sam gestured with his fork. ''We're still showing a profit. We're charging a buck per use for the new air pump,'' he continued enthusiastically. ''You should see the thing. It's computerized to check gauge and shut off automatically. You don't ever have to worry about filling your tires too much or too little.'' Sam sounded like they'd just invented a cure for the common cold.

Michael felt the old familiar anger take root. His father could have been a scientist. He damn sure was smart enough to find a cure for the common cold. And here he was, forced to settle for amazement at a stupid air pump that had seen the light of day at normal gas stations at least three years ago.

''Pop, why won't you let me buy Hanson out, bring the station up to date so you *can* compete with the place out by the highway?''

With a shake of his head, Sam added to his son's frustration. ''You do enough, boy, sending the money you do. I didn't raise you to live off you.''

''But—''

''No more.'' Sam spoke firmly, holding Michael's eyes with the gaze that had always been able to take

Michael down a notch or two. "I support your mother and myself just fine, and that's the end of it."

And the money Michael sent was banked for his mother's wish fund or treats for the grandchildren. Once, out of sheer necessity, it had bought a new hot water heater.

Sam slathered some homemade jam on a biscuit. "You see that new sign that went up on Rutherford?"

"Don't think so." Michael tried to remember. "It was dark when I came through."

"It's right pretty," Sam told him, grinning proudly, as though the rest of the conversation had never taken place. "The Dairy Bar put it up hoping to get some highway traffic this summer. They got a picture of Main Street during the Strawberry Festival last summer. Your mom thinks we're in it."

"We are in it," Mary said, coming to the table with a pot of coffee. "We was standing by the stoplight when they took it. I remember clearly because I thought the flash was the light changing and then we could cross the street, but it wasn't, it was the camera going off."

Sam gave his wife an affectionate smile. "Yes, well…" He sipped his coffee. "It's a pretty sign."

"How are the twins, Mom?" Michael asked as his mother finally landed in her seat long enough to take a bite of her breakfast.

"Fine." Mary smiled. "Those babies sure keep them busy, you know."

Yeah. Michael knew. His sisters, almost twenty years his junior, had both married right out of high school, and started families immediately.

"And Bob got a promotion down at the shoe factory," Sam interjected.

"He did?" In midchew, Michael stared at his father. His brother had advanced?

"He's crew manager now."

"No kidding! What's it pay?"

"Oh." Sam helped himself to more eggs from the platter in the middle of the table. "There wasn't a pay raise. Not yet anyway." He added more bacon to his plate. "They're waiting to see how he does first."

Nodding, Michael finished his own breakfast and sat back. Only a year younger than Michael, his brother took after their mother.

"Bobbie Jayne got a part in a musical at school," Mary said.

"Oh, yeah?" Bob's ten-year-old daughter, on the other hand, took after Sam's side of the family. She was smart as a whip and an outgoing delight. Michael figured she'd be great on stage. "Which musical?"

"I'm not sure," Mary said, frowning, "but we're all going to see her. She gets free tickets for the whole family."

"I'm sure she can get one for you—and for Susan, too—if you want. You just say the word," Sam offered.

"When is it?"

"Sometime before school's out."

Would Susan be showing by then? "Let me know when, and I'll check my schedule," he said. He really would like to see it. Sometimes Bobbie Jayne reminded him of himself at that age, always looking for bigger things than Carlisle had ever seen.

"Oh, jeez, it's twenty after seven," Sam said, jumping up. "I gotta run or I'll be late."

"The station doesn't open until eight, does it?" Michael asked.

"No, but Fred Hanson likes me there by seven-thirty in case we have early customers."

"He drives by the station every morning to make sure your father's there," Mary added.

"He does?"

Sam covered his embarrassment with a laugh. "Yeah, but it's no big deal. He's been doing it since I went to work for his dad forty years ago."

Acid burning in his stomach, Michael watched his father hurry out. Fred Hanson had been ahead of his father by two years in school. Yet that hadn't stopped Sam Kennedy from beating the older man out of a first-place win at the state-wide school science fair during Fred's senior year.

The win had cost Fred a scholarship. One that went to waste when Sam had to marry his pregnant girlfriend instead of attending college.

And Sam Kennedy had spent the rest of his life settling. Because once you had children, if you were a good person, a worthy parent, your own needs didn't matter anymore. Your primary purpose then became to meet the needs of the lives you'd created.

Sam and Mary spent every waking moment doing just that.

"SUSAN, Joe Burniker called...."

Jumping, scaring Annie, whose head she'd been resting her hand on, Susan smiled guiltily at her secretary. This was the third time in as many days that

Jill had caught her daydreaming. She'd known about the baby for a whole week, and the shock still hadn't worn off.

"I'm sorry, what was that?" she asked, sitting up at her desk. She grabbed a pen, trying to look like she belonged there.

"Are you okay?" Jill was frowning.

"Fine. Who'd you say called?"

"Joe Burniker, and it's okay if you don't want to tell me, but I'd like you to know that I'm here if you need to talk," her secretary said in a rush. They were the most personal words she'd ever said to Susan.

Susan put down the pen. Arm folded across her chest, she met her secretary's eye. "I'm pregnant."

"Oh." Jill's expression filled with consternation— and embarrassment. "I'm sorry," she said, looking anywhere but at Susan.

"I'm not." Susan grinned.

That got Jill's attention. "You're not?" She stared at Susan.

"Nope, I planned the whole thing."

"But you're not, I mean—" Jill broke off.

"Married?" Susan helped her out.

"Well." Jill glanced down. "Yeah."

Taking pity on her secretary, Susan pulled herself together. "I'll be a good mother, Jill," she said, sounding far more controlled than she felt.

Jill's gaze shot up, her eyes locking with Susan's. "I never thought any differently."

"It's perfectly acceptable for single women to adopt babies these days," Susan said, preparing to repeat herself several more times as her associates discovered her condition. "I just chose to have my own, instead."

"Then you're not planning to marry the father?" Jill asked.

"No." But she couldn't leave it at that, couldn't have them thinking she'd been foolish enough to get knocked up by someone who'd deserted her. "In fact," she added, "I chose him deliberately because I knew he *wouldn't* want to marry me. I don't want to share this child."

So what if the words were only half-true? No one but Susan was ever going to know that.

EVERY DECISION Laura Sinclair made—which included forcing Seth Carmichael out of her life—was with her kids in mind. She'd made a huge mistake staying with their father when it was obvious his abuse wasn't going to stop. But since she'd been freed from that tyranny, she'd never once broken her vow to put the kids first. Always.

She just wasn't sure of the best way to handle her current dilemma. Which was worse—the physical problem posed by the bees swarming their house or the potential emotional problem if she called the only person she could think of to ask for help?

Her long blond hair hanging loose, she stood outside her little house on the second Saturday in April, arms wrapped around her middle, staring at the dirt that made up an excuse for a yard. She'd just come home from dropping the kids at a birthday party— one neither had been eager to attend—to find her kitchen infested with bees. The buzzing had been like something from an Alfred Hitchcock movie.

And there was no money, anywhere, to pay for a pest control company to get rid of them.

But, perhaps, if she was lucky, she could still see to the kids' physical safety without jeopardizing their fragile emotions. She studied the holes in the toes of her tennis shoes for a second, glanced at the Pooh bear hanging limply across her stomach on a T-shirt worn and stretched from too many washings. But at least it was wrinkle-free, tucked into her jeans, and clean. And loose enough to hide the extra weight she'd lost. Either way, it would have to do.

Mind made up, she marched next door, explained about the army of bees keeping her from her phone and asked the crochety old couple if she could use theirs. And coughed up the quarter they charged her.

She needed a man's help and there was only one man in the world Laura trusted. The one who'd walked out of her house the previous fall and hadn't been back since.

"Seth, it's Laura." She hoped she didn't sound as breathless as she felt.

"Is everything okay?" Grinning at the fact that he hadn't even said hello after all these months, Laura tried not to cry, too. She'd missed him so much.

"Yes and no," she said now, aware of the older couple listening to her every word. "We're all fine. It's just that I've got bees in my kitchen and I don't know how to get rid of them."

"How many bees?"

"I don't know." She couldn't stop smiling, couldn't believe she was really talking to him. Couldn't cry in front of her neighbors. "Too many to count. Hundreds, maybe."

"I'm on my way." He hung up before she could assure him that a trip out wasn't necessary, all she really needed was some instruction. Tell her to buy some leather gloves, let her know what can of poison would do the trick. Give her the name of a beekeeper friend.

But if she was honest with herself, she'd have to admit that he could have stayed on that phone for an hour and she wouldn't have asked him not to come. She was a strong woman, just not that strong.

Hurrying next door to wait for him, she promised herself he'd be gone before the kids got home.

Armed with a motorcycle helmet, boots, rubber gloves that reached past his elbows and a can of Raid, Seth stepped out of his Bronco half an hour later and strode past her toward the back door that led to her kitchen.

"Are you sure you should go in there?" Laura asked, worried about him.

"Somebody has to." His voice was muffled by the face plate on the helmet. "I'll be fine."

She couldn't believe that after all these months they were carrying on as if they'd only seen each other the day before.

"Stay out here," he commanded when she would have followed him through the door. "They're going to be pretty damn mad when I start spraying."

Laura watched him go, trying not to remember all of the scary things she'd heard about bees. "Be careful," she called. There'd been that article in the paper last year—a kid had died due to a bunch of bee stings. He'd been allergic, if she recalled correctly.

Was Seth allergic to bees? God, she hoped they

didn't get inside that helmet. They'd be trapped. And angry. And—

He'd looked so good. So strong and sure. And he still filled out his jeans as well as she'd remembered. Everything else, too, for that matter. Seth's shoulders used to make people turn around for a second look.

Trying not worry, she paced the yard for another ten minutes, wondering why weeds could grow there and grass wouldn't. But then, that was about the extent of her life, wasn't it? Hard as she tried, she could never get the grass to grow.

And then she reminded herself of the decision she'd made less than a week before. She'd taken the kids to church for Easter and had been moved, herself, by the sermon about faith. About hope. About their power to change lives. And she'd promised herself she'd try to have a little more of both.

So, how long did it take to kill a swarm of bees? Laura approached the kitchen door, trying to hear what was going on inside. Should she go for help? Call 911?

"All done." Seth held open the door, helmet in hand. "Do you have a broom? It's a mess in here."

"You got them all?" she asked, amazed, eyeing him carefully for any sign of damage.

"Yep." He was grinning like a schoolboy.

Laura shivered when she walked past him into that little room and saw the carpet of dead bees on her floor. She'd underestimated the number of them.

"Where'd they all come from?"

Seth was pulling at the vent above her stove. "That's what I'm about to find out."

While Laura swept, trying to pretend the bees were

dust bunnies, Seth investigated her kitchen for possible entryways. It was almost as if that last horrible scene between them had never happened. Except that she knew it had.

"How's Susan?" she blurted when she started to worry that he'd be thinking about the last time he'd been in her kitchen, too.

"Pregnant," Seth grunted.

"Pregnant?" She stopped sweeping and stared. She'd never met Seth's older sister, but from all he'd said about her, she'd have found it easier to believe the other woman had flown to the moon.

He snapped the stove vent back in place. "Yep."

"Did she remarry?" After all, it had been almost eight months since she'd seen him.

"Nope." He was pulling things out from the cupboard under her sink.

Laura leaned on her broom, watching him. "So who's the father?"

"Michael."

"Her ex-husband?"

"Yep." His voice was muffled, coming from somewhere in the cupboard he'd just emptied, but not so muffled she couldn't catch the disapproval in his voice.

"Are they getting married again?"

"Nope."

"Wow." She didn't envy his sister, having a baby on her own. She didn't envy her raising the child on her own, either. Laura knew all about being a single mother. And she didn't recommend it to anyone.

"They went into this knowing Michael wasn't going to have any part in raising the child," Seth said. "It's all been very friendly."

"So he's still in touch with her?"

"Some. Not a lot." He moved farther into the cupboard. "He's on the road a lot. Checks in with her occasionally. Mostly he calls me."

"At least he cares."

"Far more than I think he knows," Seth said, poking around.

"So why don't you tell him that?"

Half sitting up beneath the cupboard, Seth looked out at her. "There's no point," he said, as though he were making perfect sense. "Wouldn't change a thing." He lay down, reaching for something Laura couldn't see.

"Nothing under here," he said, turning to back out of the cupboard.

Momentarily distracted by the tight buns moving straight at her, Laura forgot what they were talking about.

But only for a second.

"Her ex isn't the responsible sort, huh?" she said a little bitterly. She could really feel for the woman by whom Seth measured all other women. Even if she *had* spent the past eight months hating the woman's guts. With Susan as an example, there was no way in this life, or the next, that Laura was ever going to measure up.

"That's just it," Seth said, frowning. "He is. Very. So's she, for that matter."

"He just doesn't think being a father requires responsibility?"

Shrugging, Seth turned away. "He travels," he said, like that was some kind of crime.

"Yeah?" So did Seth. So what?

"He can't very well be a father if he's not around, now can he?" he muttered and left, letting the screen door slam shut behind him.

Laura felt like she'd been punched in the stomach. She couldn't breathe, couldn't think. Couldn't believe he'd just walked out on her. Again.

She also couldn't go after him. She needed him to leave. Her children would be home soon. So she started to sweep, slow, methodical strokes, collecting her dust bunny bees into a nice neat pile. Picking the pile up was a little bit more of a challenge than she wanted to face, but maybe she'd leave it for Jeremy. He'd think it was cool....

"Just as I thought." Seth came back inside, pulling off his gloves. "There's a hole in the netting covering the outside end of your stove vent. The grease must have attracted them."

Laura was so shocked that he was still there—so relieved—she teared up before she could stop herself.

"What?" Seth was there immediately, taking her shoulders in his hands. "Did you hurt yourself?" He glanced around. "Did I miss one?"

Not trusting herself to speak, she shook her head. And willed the tears away.

"What's wrong?" he asked again, searching her face.

"I thought you'd gone." More tears came.

Though she wasn't even sure he was aware of it, Seth's hands were softly rubbing her arms. "I just went outside to—"

"I know," she interrupted him, tried to laugh.

"Laura…"

"Shhh." She put a finger on his lips. "Nothing's changed," she whispered.

She couldn't be the woman he needed, a woman worthy to be his wife, and she couldn't let him any further into the lives of her children without that permanence.

If nothing else, the past eight months getting over him had proved it. His going had practically killed her children. She could only imagine how much worse it would've been if he'd stuck around for a year or two before he'd decided to split.

"Nothing's changed," she said again.

He didn't even try to argue with her. He lowered his lips to hers, instead, kissing her softly—and then not so softly. Telling her with his body how much he wanted to stay.

And then he was gone. Leaving her with her empty house and her broom and her pile of dead bees.

"SUSAN'S SICK."

Recognizing Seth's voice, slurred though it was, Michael sat up in bed, reaching for the lamp on the nightstand beside him. It was two o'clock in the morning. Monday morning.

"What's wrong?" he asked, throwing off the covers, mentally calculating how long it would take him to get from Denver to Cincinnati.

"Dunno," his friend said. "She says nothing's wrong."

Feeling stupid for overreacting, Michael lay back

on the bed and wondered how many drinks Seth had had. "Then how do you know she's sick?"

"We were all out to Scott and Julie's for Easter dinner a couple weeks ago. She could barely eat a thing."

"Maybe she just wasn't hungry," he said, remembering life with his ex. "She probably had a craving for a burger on the way over and stopped for one, thinking she could eat that and dinner, too."

"She threw up." It sounded as though Seth had been drinking for hours. Much as he didn't want to stick his nose where it didn't belong, Michael was going to have to have talk with his ex-brother-in-law. Soon.

"She could've had a touch of the flu."

"She missed work two days this past week."

"You're sure?" Michael sat up again, his stomach tight.

"'Course I'm sure. I may be drunk but I know when my sister isn't at work."

Even when she'd had that fever of 103, Susan had gone to work. She'd worked with a sprained ankle, with strep throat, and with a cold so bad she was blowing her nose every five seconds. "Something's wrong," Michael said, thinking out loud.

"S'what I've been trying to tell you."

"She won't talk to you about it?"

"Nope, jes tol' me I worry too much."

"I'll call her."

SUSAN HAD an appointment with her obstetrician at eight o'clock Monday morning. She'd had an amnio centesis, recommended because of her age, at her last visit and was eager to be reassured that everything was normal. That her violent bouts of nausea amounted to no more than morning sickness. She was twelve weeks along and miserable.

At least physically. Emotionally it depended on the day—or the minute. Tired all the time, she found it hard to be positive about single-handedly preparing for the birth of her child. Yet she was floating in a dimension of happiness she'd never known before.

And she missed Michael. Desperately.

"Ms. Kennedy?" A uniformed nurse stood at the waiting room door. "The doctor will see you now."

Half an hour later, Susan walked back through the waiting room, seeing no one. Stunned, she didn't even respond when the receptionist called out to her to set her next appointment. Just kept right on walking.

She found her car, climbed inside and sat—but had no idea what to do next.

Eventually she started to laugh. And then to cry a little. And to laugh some more. Passing by the car, a middle-aged woman stopped and peeked inside. Susan waved, and kept right on laughing. Smiling, the woman waved back before continuing on her way.

Pulling her lips between her teeth, Susan tried to sober up. But laughter erupted again before she could stop it.

At least now she knew why she'd been feeling so rotten.

Dialing her brother's number on her car phone, she tapped her foot impatiently. She knew he was in town. He had meetings at head office all week. "Seth?" she cried as soon as he answered. He wasn't the person she'd *really* wanted to call, but he'd have to do.

"Yeah?" She'd woken him. And couldn't feel the least bit sorry.

"It's twins!" She practically screamed her news.

"What? Twins? You're kidding." He was wide awake now.

"Nope. Twins." She figured *she* should be daunted by the news. But she wasn't. Twins sounded wonderful. Fun. Two for the price of one. Piece of cake. "Gotta go," she sang, tossing her cell phone into the seat beside her as she started her car.

She had an appointment in fifteen minutes with the attorney representing a bankrupt padding company Halliday Headgear had done business with. She couldn't be late.

CHAPTER EIGHT

THE PHONE RANG and rang and rang.

"Dammit, where is she?" Michael paced as far as the cord would allow in his hotel room Monday morning.

Glancing at his watch, he tried to pretend his tension was because he had a decision to make—and very little time in which to do it. He had a flight booked from Denver to Cincinnati in an hour, and another from Denver to Chicago at the same time. If he could just get hold of Susan, he'd know which of the two flights to take. He'd prefer to go to Chicago first, pick up some more clothes. And his Pathfinder.

"Answer." He swore again, telling himself there was nothing to worry about. As she'd so often told him, she had five brothers and a father in town. If she was really in trouble, she'd have called one of them.

And if she was in the hospital, Seth would have called Michael back.

He jabbed his finger on the disconnect button and dialed Cincinnati again, Susan's office this time. At least someone there would pick up the damn phone. And they'd probably be able to tell him where she was, too.

Five minutes later Michael hung up, grabbed his bag and hailed a cab for the airport. After speaking with Susan's secretary he'd decided to take the Chicago flight. With Susan in a meeting, things obviously hadn't reached critical stages.

But he was still going to drive over to Cincinnati. He had a business lead there he wanted to pursue. An insulation company that was on to something. The work in Denver could wait.

DAYDREAMING ABOUT look-alike outfits and double strollers, Susan waited for her microwave oven to finish heating a cup of chamomile tea. If she could only get her stomach to settle, she might find the energy to start cleaning out the spare bedroom. There was a lot of work to be done, some of it double, and her doctor had warned her to prepare early. She might not be able to count on herself for much during her last trimester.

Susan opened the microwave door and reached for her cup of hot tea before she realized that the buzzing she'd heard wasn't the oven, but the front doorbell. She wasn't expecting anyone.

Maybe Seth had come by. Maybe he'd help her take apart that bed in the spare bedroom.

It wasn't Seth.

"Michael." He looked so good to her, it was all she could do to keep from throwing her arms around him. She hadn't greeted him that way since they were married.

"I've got business in town." He was making her uncomfortable, studying her closely. "I tried to call, but you weren't home." Could he tell she'd gained a few pounds? See the slight bulge beneath her overalls?

"Well, come in." She stepped back, opening the door wider. "I'm just heating up some herbal tea. You want some?"

Shutting the front door, he hung his jacket on the rack. "You never used to drink that stuff."

"The doctor says it might help settle my stomach."

"Seth told me you've been ill." He followed her into the kitchen.

"Just morning sickness." She looked away as she said the words. She'd rather not mention the pregnancy in front of him.

"You're sure that's all it is?"

"Positive. I just saw my doctor today."

Susan dumped a couple of spoonfuls of sugar in her steaming cup in an attempt to camouflage the taste, took a sip and grimaced.

Leaning back against the counter, arms crossed, Michael watched her.

"How long are you in town?" she asked, trying desperately to think of what she'd be saying had she not been pregnant with his child. With his children, she amended.

"I'm not sure." He turned to help himself to a can of soda from the refrigerator. "I'm investigating a company here in Cincinnati. They've come up with a new form of spray-in foam insulation that's not just fire-resistant but eighty-nine percent fire-proof."

Putting ice in a glass, pouring his soda, Michael had his back to her.

"Fire-proof insulation—can you imagine how that'll take off?" she asked him. "A fire that started in one room of a home might burn the drywall, but the wall itself would still stand,'' she went on. ''And the room right next door might not even be touched.''

''Exactly.''

''How much is it likely to cost?'' She'd have to look into getting some. After all, she had to protect the babies who'd soon be sleeping innocently in their cribs, relying on their mother to keep them safe.

Michael shrugged, coming to sit with her at the table. ''That all depends on production and distribution costs.'' He wiped condensation from his glass with one lean finger. ''If everything checks out as the preliminaries seem to indicate, this will be a whole new niche in the market. One I'd like to see Coppel pursue.''

Blood stirring in spite of her admonitions to be careful, Susan sat back and listened. This was vintage Michael, the way he'd been in their college days, his mind churning with plans, his entire body buzzing with energy. She'd fallen in love with him during just such a conversation.

''Miller Insulation is the only company that's got the technology at the moment, but it won't be long before others are figuring out what they've done,'' he continued. ''Miller doesn't have the capital to hit the market big, but we do. So we buy Miller Insulation, put up plants in a few strategic places across the United States to keep distribution costs in line, and then, when everyone in the country's demanding the product, we own the niche.''

''I'm impressed.'' She smiled at him. Wanting him.

His eyes, so alight with intent, broke contact with hers. ''By the time I do a complete analysis, figure profit margins, meet with Miller Insulation officials—

well, I'll probably be tied up here for a couple of weeks. Or more."

She tried not to be excited about the prospect of having him in town for so long. Considering their current circumstances, it wouldn't be a good idea for her to expect anything.

"Will you have time to go out for dinner or anything?" Should she ask him to stay with her? Four months ago she wouldn't have had to ask.

No answer. Susan told herself not to be hurt. Her pregnancy was bothering Michael far more than she'd ever thought it would. How could she possibly have imagined she could carry the man's child and not have it affect their relationship? Such as it was.

He broke the silence. "I'm worried about Seth."

Susan looked back at Michael, taking way too much comfort from the concern in his eyes. "Me, too."

"You have any idea why he's drinking so much?"

"None." She grimaced and shrugged her shoulders. "I asked him about it and got my head bit off for my trouble."

"So you have noticed it," he said. "It's not just my imagination."

Shaking her head, Susan related the last few times she'd met Seth for lunch. Her brother seemed to drink more than he ate.

"Do you think it's affecting his work?"

"Not at all." Susan shook her head again. "From what I can tell, he's better when he's on the road. Hasn't missed any work at all. He only seems to drink when he's in town."

"Seth told me you missed a couple days of work."

What *was* Seth, anyway—his sister's keeper as well as a lush? "Just that morning sickness I told you about. It's no big deal."

"You've never missed a day of work before."

And, that quickly, he was a polite stranger again, awkward, finding it difficult to meet her eyes. Love, fear, despair. They all rolled into one mass of emotion that threatened to consume her.

"I've never been pregnant before."

His eyes, when they finally met hers, were troubled. "I'm sorry, Susan."

"I'm not," she said, then added, "At least, I'm not sorry I'm pregnant."

"What *are* you sorry for?"

"Sorry I put you in this position, sorry I didn't see what my asking you to play a part in this was going to do to you. To us." She reached for his hand across the table. "I wish it didn't have to change things."

Michael turned his hand over, threading his fingers between hers. "There doesn't seem to be any way around it," he finally admitted. "How can I see you and not see that child you're carrying?" He didn't give her a chance to respond. "And seeing that child, how can I not find myself grossly lacking?"

"I went into this with my eyes wide open, Michael," she reminded them both. "We had a very clear understanding that I would take, that I *wanted* to take, complete responsibility for this baby."

He pulled his hand away, sitting back, his expression stormy.

"You very generously did me a favor, Michael. Why can't we just leave it at that?" It had all sounded so simple to her when she'd first come up with the idea.

"Because you're sick, for one thing."

"It's normal. It'll pass." She hoped. With twins, chances weren't as good, but either way, she'd manage.

No matter what she said, though, she couldn't seem to wipe the lines from his forehead.

"I guess I'd better go." He stood up. "I've still got to check into a hotel."

Taking a deep breath, Susan told herself not to push, not to be a fool. "You could stay here," she said.

"Not this time." He retrieved his jacket from the rack by the front door. "I'll be in touch."

And, once again, he was gone.

THE NEXT NIGHT, with some half-formed thought that he'd be doing Susan a service, Michael made plans to meet Seth at the bar around the corner from Seth's apartment.

Two drinks into the evening, he wasn't sure who was helping whom.

"Is there something that says a man has to be a father to be a decent human being?" Michael asked, studying the amber liquid in his glass. He'd never found any answers there, but he kept looking just the same.

"Not that I've ever read."

"Then how about something that says a man can't be decent if he doesn't want children?"

Seth gazed at him across the scarred wooden table, his eyes tired. "Isn't that the same thing?"

"Hell, I don't know, man." Michael downed the last of his drink. "I can't figure what in hell's the matter with me that I've never wanted kids."

"You don't like them?" Seth asked. "There might be something wrong with a guy who can't like kids."

"It's not that," Michael was surprised to discover. "I like them well enough—at least I think I do. I love my niece a lot."

He waited while another drink was placed in front of him, thinking he was going to have to take Seth up on his earlier offer to bunk down at his place for the night.

Seth was having another drink, too, staring down into his glass just as Michael had done.

"You find anything in there?" Michael asked.

Raising his head, Seth appeared to ponder that for a moment. "Nope. Not a damn thing."

"You looking for something?"

Seth just shrugged. And then glanced across at Michael. "So how do you know you don't want to be a father if you think you like kids?"

Meeting the other man's eyes, Michael wished like hell he could explain. "Every time I even think about the possibility, I get claustrophobic, like I gotta run as far and as fast as I can," he said, wondering if he sounded as stupid as he felt. "You ever feel that way?"

"Maybe," Seth said. "I guess that's how a guy feels when he knows he should do something, and knows he shouldn't at the same time."

"Exactly." Michael couldn't have said it better himself.

''Like, a man's gotta work, and sometimes what he does just doesn't allow him to be other things.''

''Exactly.'' They drank to that.

''Sometimes his work is all he *can* do, all he's trained to do.''

Well...not exactly. Michael didn't have to take that job in Chicago seven years ago. He could've stayed with the firm in Cincinnati, could have grown old and died there.

''But what if it isn't?'' he asked, trying to focus on his ex-brother-in-law. This was too important to slur his way through. ''Is it wrong for a man to want to love what he does?''

''Hell, no.''

Thank God for that. But... ''Does it make him a self-centered bastard to pursue his goals?''

''It shouldn't.''

''But it might.''

''I guess it could, depending on how he goes about it.'' Seth nodded, as though pleased with his answer.

''I've always been completely honest with Susan.''

''I know you have.''

''I could've stayed here, you know,'' he confessed, although he knew Seth had figured that one out long ago. ''I didn't have to take the position with Smythe and Westbourne.''

''Sure,'' Seth said. ''You could've stayed and rotted away.''

Michael froze. ''What do you mean?''

''How happy would you have been, knowing what you'd passed up, knowing for the rest of your life that you had a chance to be everything you wanted and turned it down?''

"Does it matter, as long as Susan was happy?" he asked. "Isn't that what we're talking about, being selfish bastards?"

"I don't know about that," Seth said, frowning. "But I do know that Susan would never have been happy holding you back. Just like she wouldn't have been happy giving up everything she'd worked for at Halliday's to follow you to Chicago."

"Kids hold a man back."

"Not some men," Seth said bitterly. "Some men can be who they wanna be and still have kids."

"Not me," Michael admitted. "I travel too much."

"Tell me about it. I spent all those years going to school, and then making a name for myself. Engineering's all I know how to do."

Surprised at Seth's tone, Michael tried to concentrate a little harder. "You unhappy in your job?"

"Hell, no," Seth said so boisterously a couple of guys shooting pool looked over at them. "I love what I do."

"So where's the problem?"

"I do what I do, that's the problem."

The answer made no sense to him where Seth was concerned, but it summed up almost perfectly what was troubling Michael.

AFTER A BOUT of throwing up so hard her ribs hurt, Susan crawled back into the spare bedroom, determined to give some serious thought to making it into a nursery. Michael had been in town for three days and she hadn't heard another word from him. She had to quit thinking about him, quit hoping he'd call, and get on with having his babies.

As soon as she answered the door, she told herself when the bell rang.

Of course, it *would* be Michael, just when she was looking her absolute worst. He didn't even know she'd kept his old T-shirt from the intramural basketball team he'd played on in college. It was old and stained, and ripped on one shoulder. And to make matters worse, she was wearing the baggiest pair of sweats she owned and looked like a big grey elephant.

"What's the matter?" he asked once she'd managed to pull open the door.

"Nothing…" she started to assure him, but ruined the effect by bolting for the bathroom again.

"THIS IS WHAT it's like for you?" Michael was sitting on the floor by the bathroom, waiting, when Susan finally came out. He was shocked by how much she was suffering.

"Not always."

"You look terrible."

"Thanks." Susan slid down the wall to the floor across from him.

He swore when he saw the tears that sprang to her eyes. "I didn't mean it like that, Sus, you just look like you *feel* horrible."

"Well, I don't."

"Still insisting things are easier than they really are, huh?"

"I don't," she said, pouting so much he wanted to haul her into his arms. "I like to be positive. It accomplishes more."

He couldn't argue with that. "And what are you accomplishing tonight?"

"Decorating the nursery."

He couldn't believe even she was attempting a project that huge, feeling as awful as she obviously did. Getting to his feet, Michael went down the hall to take a peek.

"Funny, a nursery looks a lot like a spare bedroom."

Following him, Susan gave a weak grin. "I'm still in the thinking stages."

"Want some help?" He didn't know why he was offering, why he was even there. He just knew he couldn't be in town and not see her.

"I don't want your pity, Michael." Her voice was stronger. "Or your misplaced sense of responsibility. This is my life, a challenge of my own choosing. I can handle it."

"No one said you couldn't."

"I never intended you to be involved—"

"Susan," he interrupted, not sure what he intended to say. He *couldn't* let her finish that remark. "This isn't about the child. It's about you, a person I care about, a person who needs a little help. Can't you let me help while I'm in town?"

He was relieved to discover that she was smiling. "You could take the bed apart for me."

HE CALLED HER at work the next morning.

"Just wanted to make sure you're completely recovered," he explained when she answered the phone.

"I feel fine," she told him, not bothering to mention the bout she'd had that morning. It had been a comparatively mild one. And she'd eaten two stacks of pancakes for breakfast afterward.

"Good enough to have dinner tonight?" he asked. "I figured since this is Friday night, you might want to get out."

"I'd like that." Susan's eyes filled with tears, and she cursed the stupid emotionalism that was taking over her body.

Making plans to meet him at her place at six-thirty, she rang off, determined to concentrate on business. The McArthur case was coming up in a couple of weeks and as far as Susan knew, she was still a sure win. Joe Burniker seemed to have lost his touch.

MICHAEL TOOK HER to a little place just across the river where they had a window table for two in a quiet alcove by the water. She'd worn a short black dress, more because it was the loosest one she owned than because she was trying to be fashionable, but she was gratified by the appreciation she saw in Michael's eyes. He looked great, too, his short dark hair a little wind-tossed, his sweater matching the green of his eyes. She was just so darn happy to be out with him.

"I'm not sure, but I think Seth has woman problems," he told her while they waited for the pasta they'd ordered.

"No kidding?" Susan's spirits lifted even more. "I'd given up hope."

"I'm not sure there's any reason to hope," Michael said, frowning. "I think his job's been getting in the way."

"Oh." Susan could understand, but she hoped Seth

knew what he was doing. What he might be giving up. She hoped the job was worth it to him.

"I've been meaning to ask you something." Michael wasn't meeting her eyes and Susan's stomach tightened. It was the first bout of nausea she'd felt all evening.

She nodded.

"What are you going to tell your baby about his father?"

Her heart dropped. Oh. God. That he—they—didn't have one?

"I'm not really sure," she answered honestly. "I mean, what do the women say who have artificial insemination?"

"I wouldn't know."

"Would you hate it terribly if I said you were the father?"

"And how would you explain that I don't act like a father without making the kid feel neglected?"

This was so much more complicated than it was supposed to be. "We're divorced," she said. "Lot's of kids have divorced parents."

"You don't think he's going to figure out eventually that we were divorced seven years before he came along?"

Susan looked across at him, so close to her. She loved him so much. She'd never realized quite *how* much. "Can't I just tell the truth?"

"I don't know." He grabbed a pen from his pocket and started doodling on his napkin. "I suppose."

"Michael?" He glanced up. "That napkin's cloth."

Going back to his drawing, he said, "I'll pay them

for it.'' And then, ''Don't you think he's still going to wonder why I'm never around?''

Her heart stopping, Susan promised herself she wouldn't cry. ''You aren't planning to be around after the birth? Ever?''

It was what she'd been afraid of since the night she'd conceived. The night she'd known he was telling her goodbye.

''How can I possibly come and visit the mother while remaining nothing to the child?'' he asked. His eyes narrowed as he watched her. ''How can I see him and not be his father?''

Susan stared at him, frightened, without any answers at all.

CHAPTER NINE

ALMOST AS THOUGH they both realized their time was running out, Michael and Susan spent the rest of the evening sharing everything they could about the things going on in their lives. With one exception. Neither mentioned the pregnancy.

Susan knew she should tell him she was carrying twins. She'd promised Seth she would, but she just couldn't do it. Michael was hardly able to handle the thought of *one* child.

Michael talked a lot about his insulation project. The Miller family had shown interest and were meeting with their father in Florida that week.

And he talked about a project he was working on in Denver.

"We're buying into the landscaping business," he told her over fettucine alfredo. "Starting in the Denver area, we're buying out individual landscapers and combining the smaller businesses into one stronger business with many locations. There's a common cost structure, a common service agreement, one place to call for customer service." His warm green eyes glowing, Michael was in his element. "And once we've finished in the Denver area, we'll move on to other areas around the country, doing the same thing until, eventually, Coppel owns an entire market. But the best part is, the consumer benefits.''

"Sounds to me like you're creating a monopoly," Susan said, challenging him. She remembered many weekend mornings when they were both home, sitting at their kitchen table with the newspaper, having conversations just like this one. She'd never realized how much she'd missed them.

"Not really." He shook his head. "Say there are one hundred landscapers in the area. We buy out thirty of the best. Of the remaining seventy, some— hopefully the worst—go under, but the most reputable stay in business with loyal customers and referrals.''

He reached for the salt, brushing her hand, lingering, as he did so. "The major benefit here is that when the consumer calls a Coppel landscaper, he's not at the mercy of one particular person. There's a regulated price structure, a fair price structure and an accepted standard of business he can count on.''

Susan smiled at him. "Still set on making the world a better place, eh?" she teased him.

Shrugging, Michael grinned back at her.

As they ate apple cobbler, Susan filled him in on the latest with the McArthur case. If she couldn't find a way to stall, it was going to court in the next couple of weeks.

"So what are you going to do?"

"I don't know," Susan murmured. "Ethically, I'm bound to protect Halliday's, but my heart tells me it's wrong to see the ruin of a young boy's life.''

"Business life versus personal life." Michael nodded as though he knew exactly what she was saying.

"I don't think so," Susan said. "When I walk out

my door in the morning, I don't suddenly become less personal because I'm going to work, and I don't become more of a person when I get home. I'm a businessperson, Michael, wherever I am.''

Fork in mid-air, he stared at her. "And you take who you are to every decision you make." He sounded surprised, as though the thought had just occurred to him.

"Right." She knew he'd understand.

"Have you stopped to look for other possibilities in the McArthur case?"

"I've been over it so many times I can quote the defense in my sleep," she told him. "I just don't see any way for Joe to win without the evidence I can't give him."

"So, maybe winning or losing isn't the only solution."

"What else is there?"

"I don't know. Maybe nothing. I'm just suggesting that if you take off your lawyer's hat and look at the situation again, from another perspective, something might occur to you."

It was worth a try. One thing was for sure. It couldn't hurt.

"I CAN'T BELIEVE you finished that second desert." Michael was laughing at her as they drove through the dark Cincinnati streets half an hour later.

Laughing too, Susan said, "I seem to eat with the same intensity that I get sick."

"You do everything with intensity, Susan." All traces of laughter were gone. "It's one of the things I always loved about you."

The words took her breath away. "Thank you."

They drove the rest of the way in a silence weighted with the desire that had been present all night. Parking the Pathfinder in her driveway, Michael gave her a tender, lingering kiss.

"I'd like to stay with you tonight, Susan."

Her heart was pounding so hard she could feel it.

"I'd like that, too."

"You're sure?" His eyes met hers in the intimate darkness of the Pathfinder.

Reaching across the console, Susan slid her hand along his leg. "Absolutely sure."

Forgive me, my babies, if this is wrong, but I love your daddy so much....

SETH WAS NOT in a good mood when he stopped by Susan's on Sunday. Neither his mood nor his task was improved by the fact that Michael had spent Friday night right there at Susan's house. Or that he *hadn't* spent Saturday night there, as well.

One thing Seth knew. He didn't want to be there now. Didn't really want to be anywhere in particular, if the truth be known, but most especially not there.

Still, he'd promised Michael he'd cover for him. As much as he disagreed with what Michael and Susan were doing, he felt for the guy.

Susan's disappointed look when she opened the door to see him standing there almost made Seth forget that he felt anything for Michael but a very real need to punch his lights out.

"Michael got called away. He sent me instead."

His message grew even more distasteful when his sister calmly accepted Michael's desertion. Nodding, she motioned silently for him to come inside. No questions asked.

"He had to fly to Denver—some business he'd left unfinished that can't wait as long as he'd hoped," he explained anyway. At least that was what Michael had said when his call had awakened Seth from a sound sleep that morning. Seth wanted to believe him.

"The landscapers," Susan said, padding back to the kitchen in her stocking feet. She was wearing sweats again, and a blue flowered T-shirt. "I was just making a coffee cake. You want some?"

"Sure." He wasn't really hungry, but what the hell. "I promised Michael I'd help you with the nursery."

"You don't have to do that, I can han—"

"You can handle it, I know, sis," Seth said, taking her by the shoulders. "But I *want* to help, okay?"

Susan nodded.

"I think I made a big mistake," she confessed later, as they sat in the empty bedroom, looking at the paint swatches and wallpaper books he was holding up.

"I could've told you that."

"No." She shook her head, glanced up at him. "I mean, I really made a mistake."

Seth's heart gave a jolt. "You mean you don't want the babies?"

"No!" She caressed her slight belly possessively. "I want them more than I even knew." She looked away, then said softly, "But I think I also want Michael to be their father."

"Thank God." Seth couldn't help himself. "You've finally come to your senses."

"You don't understand, Seth." Her expression was

guilty as hell. And horrified, too. "I think I *always* wanted him to be a father to my baby—babies. I think I lied to him, Seth. That I lied to me. And I'm scared to death that I tried to trap him with all that talk about no responsibility."

"You don't know if you meant to trap him or not?"

Susan just shook her head again, those damn tears back in her eyes. He'd seen his sister cry more in the past three months than in her entire life.

"Correct me if I'm wrong, but isn't the definition of entrapment to *knowingly* plan to trick someone into doing something he wouldn't ordinarily do?"

He was trying to understand. Trying not to get defensive on Michael's behalf. Trying not to give in to the temptation to lie to his sister and tell her that everything was going to be all right.

"Yes, of course, which I guess means I didn't set out to trap him, but..." She walked into the middle of the room, wrapping her arms around herself.

"Michael asked me the other night what I planned to tell the baby about him, and I didn't have an answer."

Seth was out of his element. Had no idea what to say. Had no idea what you told a kid who was made by *arrangement*.

"I'm so confused, Seth." The pain in her eyes tore at him. "I know that logically, in my mind, I was fully prepared to have this baby on my own, to raise him—her—alone. I'm just afraid I was so busy forging ahead, I didn't stop to listen to my heart."

Seth leaned against the wall behind him, the big

book of wallpaper samples still in his hands. He wished he could help her.

"Or maybe I really did want to raise the baby alone back then. Maybe I've changed over the past few months and I've recently begun to wish Michael could be a father to his babies."

"You didn't tell him about the twins yet, did you?"

"No." She looked helplessly around. "I... couldn't."

"He has a right to know."

Her eyes were filled with fear as her gaze flew to his. "Promise me *you* won't tell him."

Raising both hands, Seth muttered, "Hey, I'm staying out of this. It's between you and him."

Susan's face was anguished, distorted by uncertainty.

He'd never seen her like this. It scared the hell out of him.

"I never meant to hurt him, Seth," she said softly, shaking her head.

"I know that."

"The thing is—" she turned her back to him "—I want it all. I want Michael in my life, however he needs to be there, and I want his babies, too. I guess I should've realized you can't have everything before it was too late to do anything about it."

He couldn't stand to hear her so bitter, so hopeless. "It's never too late, sis." Seth tossed the book to the floor and gave his sister a hug. "It's never too late."

But even as he said the words he was afraid that sometimes it was.

"You asleep?"

"Yeah, but that's okay." Susan rolled onto her back in the dark, the bedside phone at her ear, happy he'd called. "How's your week going?"

Michael was in California meeting with the finance directors of one of Coppel's diversified interests. It had been a little over two weeks since she'd seen him, but he'd been calling. A lot.

"Fine," he said, his voice tired. "Business is good." Another sigh. "You know how old it gets having to walk through a lobby of strangers every night just to go to bed?"

"Yeah, well, there are other options to those fancy high-rises you stay in, Michael," she told him. "You know there are these things called motels where you drive right up to your own front door."

"Don't get smart with me, woman," he said, but she could hear the laughter in his voice. "Point taken. No more whining." It sounded like he'd just torn a sheet of paper off a tablet. Susan could picture him, sitting at the desk in his posh hotel room, drawing pictures.

"The McArthur case starts tomorrow."

"On Tuesday? I thought you were expecting later in the week."

Susan bunched her pillows more comfortably behind her. "Wishful thinking, I guess."

"You ready?"

"Of course."

"You gonna win?"

"Unless a miracle happens between now and then."

"Just remember what I said, Sus, that wouldn't be

the end of the world, nor does it have to be the end of the line for this boy. Something may come up.''

"I hope so.''

"Bobbie Jayne called me today.''

"She knows you're in California?'' Last she knew, he hadn't even told his parents about his promotion.

"She left a message for me in Chicago. I pulled it off my machine.''

"How's she doing?''

"Good…great.'' He paused. "She was in a play this semester in school—a musical, actually, *Oklahoma*—and she had to tell me about every scene.''

Grinning, Susan gazed up at the ceiling, making mental shapes out of the shadows. "That must've been entertaining.''

"Yeah, well, it got even better when she started working me over.''

"What's she want?''

"Drama camp this summer.''

A little uncomfortable, Susan turned onto her side. "She wants you to spring for it?''

"More, she wants me to convince Bob and her mom to let her go.'' He was grumbling, but Susan knew he enjoyed Bobbie Jayne's antics. And Bobbie Jayne's faith in him.

"She talk you into it?''

"What do you think?''

"Good girl—oh!'' She sat straight up in bed.

"What?'' Michael asked, and then, more urgently, "Susan, what's wrong?''

Stunned, she was afraid to move, to speak, afraid

she'd miss a replay. "Nothing. I think I just got kicked," she whispered, staring down at her belly.

"You…what?"

"There!" she said more loudly. "It happened again."

Silence hung on the other end of the line and Susan suddenly remembered who she was talking to—not Michael, she knew that—but the reluctant father of her babies.

"What's it feel like?" His question came softly.

"Um…" She took a deep breath. "Like a bubble popping, I guess."

"Did it hurt?"

"No." Then she added, "Not at all."

"Well, I guess you better get some sleep."

"Yeah." Tears burned the backs of her eyes.

"Good night."

"Good night…"

Susan lay on her side in the dark, holding the receiver in both hands. As if by doing that, she could hold Michael close. But the attempt was futile. He was no longer there.

DRESSED IN a conservative black suit, Susan sat at the defendant's table the next morning, struggling to focus on the arguments she had to present, on the judge. And nothing else. Most especially not on the Tennesee woman, a few years younger than Susan, whose son was facing a tragic life. Identifying with the woman in ways she'd never imagined, she was finding it impossible to be impartial, objective.

How would she feel if they were discussing *her* child?

"Tell the court about your son's mental state, Mrs. McArthur," Joe Burniker said, gesturing toward the room. He was pulling out all the stops, dragging everyone's emotions into play in the hopes of a sympathy call.

Susan sat alone and listened as the boy's mother described the change in her son—from a fun-loving boy who laughed frequently and always had an extra hug to give, to an often sullen, quiet kid who sometimes wouldn't let anyone near him. She tried not to hear the tears in the woman's voice, the unbearable heartache that couldn't be concealed.

Tricia Halliday hadn't even bothered to show up. Not that she was required to come. She paid Susan to represent her. But Ed would've been there, sitting right beside Susan all the way.

"I don't know what you expected me to do with this one, Susan." Joe stopped her on the way back into the courtroom after a break for lunch. "Your case is airtight."

Unable to say a thing, Susan stood her ground and held Joe's gaze head-on.

"You know something I don't?" he asked.

She turned and reentered the courtroom.

"HOW DID IT GO?"

"About like I expected."

Michael's heart sank when he heard the weariness in Susan's voice. He'd barely made it through his business dinner in his haste to get upstairs and call her.

"Is it over?"

"No, we spent the afternoon going over design

specifications. Then there'll be at least another day of medical reports.''

''Remember what I told you,'' he said, feeling helpless. ''There are always options.''

''Yeah. We haven't won yet.''

''So…'' Michael picked up the pen on the desk in front of him. ''Did it happen again?''

''Did what happen?''

''The bubbles.'' He scribbled some lines here. Some there. ''Getting kicked.''

''Oh.'' She paused. ''Yeah, once.''

''Well, I'd better let you get back to what you were doing.'' He had some reports to go over.

''Okay.''

God, he missed her. More than he'd missed her since that first year after their divorce.

''Good night.'' Looking down, he saw a pretty good replica of a toy train.

''Michael?'' She sounded hesitant. Needy. Making Michael hard.

''Yeah?''

''Good night.''

It was another half hour before Michael could concentrate on his reports.

SHE HAD THE WALLPAPER and paint for the nursery on order, and that Saturday Seth dropped by to take her shopping for furniture. She'd spoken to Michael again, twice that week, but was no closer to resolving anything with him. Was beginning to suspect she never would be.

''How you feeling?'' Seth asked as she climbed into the Bronco beside him.

"Great." It wasn't a total lie. She hadn't had any morning sickness for almost two weeks. And the weather outside was beautiful. It was the week before Memorial Day, and the skies were shining on Cincinnati. They'd had sunshine and sixty-degree temperatures all week.

Seth was glancing over at her, grinning, but looking kind of stupid and embarrassed, too.

"What?" she finally asked him. If he thought she was in the mood for teasing, she'd set him straight immediately.

"Nothing." He held up both hands in a gesture of surrender, then started the car. "It's just the first time I've seen you in maternity duds. You look kinda cute."

"Shut up and drive," Susan said, but she was smiling. She'd been clothes shopping the day before and liked the denim jumper she was wearing. Even more, though, she was excited at the changes that proclaimed the lives growing inside her. Every day, the babies she carried seemed more real.

Seth tried to be patient as Susan dragged him all over town in search of the perfect nursery, but by noon, Susan could tell he'd reached his limit. He'd looked at his watch no fewer than ten times. She almost settled for an off-white ensemble with soft roses on the headboards and changing table, just to pacify him, but she couldn't. They weren't quite what she wanted.

She'd go by herself when she could take as much time as she wanted. And send Seth back later to pick up whatever she ended up buying. Or, better yet, have the whole lot delivered.

"How about some lunch?" she asked as they left the last store.

Seth glanced at his watch. "You mind if we take a little drive first?"

"Fine with me." She buckled up. "Where we going?"

"Just driving."

Taciturn all of a sudden, Seth headed out of town, but this was no leisurely drive they were on. The turns Seth took were deliberate, made as surely as if he'd taken the trip a million times before.

"Can I ask you something?" He broke the silence that had fallen between them.

"Sure." She was game for just about anything if it would help improve his mood.

"Why did you decide to divorce Michael rather than give up your job and follow him to Chicago?"

Not the question she'd been expecting. "You want the short version?" she asked, wondering how much to tell him.

"I don't think so, no." He was frowning.

"I'd been with Halliday for several years by then, Seth," she reminded him. "I was well on my way to the top. A move would have meant starting over."

He continued to drive, silent as he watched the road in front of him.

"Halliday Headgear is one of the few successful privately held companies left. My chances of attaining the same level of advancement somewhere else were slim," she went on, choosing her words carefully. "And I loved working for Ed."

"More than you loved Michael?"

That hurt. "No."

"But you loved your career more than you loved Michael."

"No, I didn't," she said slowly. Anyone but Seth would've been told to mind his own business. "My career is part of who I am." She tried to explain what she didn't fully understand herself, anymore. "And I had goals to meet."

"So you could be ready to have your baby when the time arrived," he said. "By the age of forty or the year 2000." He wasn't being judgmental; rather, he sounded as though he were *trying* to understand.

"That," she said, "and other things."

Silent again, Seth drove on. Staring out the window, Susan wondered just where they were going. The houses weren't very attractive here. They'd driven to a part of town Susan had never visited before.

Pulling under a weeping willow that was so huge she could barely see past it, Seth stopped the Bronco. He settled back in his seat and looked out at a field of weeds that was occupied by a bunch of poorly dressed kids kicking a soccer ball around.

"Do you regret the decision you made back then?" Seth asked quietly.

"I didn't regret it then." Not completely. "At least, I didn't regret not leaving Halliday's. I never wanted the divorce. I tried to talk Michael out of it."

"You did?" Seth turned toward her, surprise lighting his dark features.

"Of course I did," she said. How could he have expected anything less? "I loved him. Our marriage was a good one. I saw no reason it couldn't continue.

We could afford to travel back and forth between Chicago and Cincinnati.''

"So Michael was the one who wanted the divorce?"

Susan shook her head, following Seth's gaze out to the field. "I don't think so. He just didn't see any other option. Said long-distance relationships never work. He was afraid of the damage we'd do to each other if we tried to hang on."

"Maybe he was right."

"I guess I thought so at the time."

"You don't now?" Seth's eyes were following the kids around the field as though he knew something about them.

"No. I think we've proven over the past three years that we *could've* made it work."

The kids on the field ran over to a man dressed almost as shabbily as they were, and Seth started up the Bronco.

"Mind telling me why we were here?" she asked him as he pulled around the corner.

He pointed out a dilapidated gray structure with dirt for a front yard. "See that house?" he asked.

"Yeah."

"There's a woman who lives there alone with two kids. Her husband left her a couple of years ago, but not before he'd beaten the life out of her."

"You know her?"

"I did."

"And those kids back there, they're hers?"

"One of them is," Seth told her. "His name's Jeremy."

CHAPTER TEN

SUSAN WATCHED her little brother, the muscle twitching at the corner of his mouth as he tried to act unaffected by what he was telling her. She had a feeling she might have stumbled on the woman Michael thought was responsible for Seth's sudden drinking. Michael just hadn't figured in the kids.

"What happened?" she asked softly.

"I couldn't be a proper father to the kids, being out of town as much as I am," he said, telling her far more than he probably knew. He must really have loved those kids if he'd even considered being a father to them. "They've been deserted enough in their lives. They need someone who can stay around. Someone who comes home at night."

"Oh, Seth," Susan said, her eyes full of empathy.

"I've been thinking about quitting my job, finding something here in town," he shocked her by admitting.

"But..." Susan scrambled for words. "What would you do?" Seth was one of the best structural engineers in the business. He'd not only trained for years to do what he did, he loved his work. And he was in demand all over the country. Not to mention the fact that he made a damn good salary and by the looks of things those kids could use a lot of help in that area.

"Good question," Seth said, sullen again. "Engineering's all I know and I have to travel if I'm going to make enough money to support the four of us."

The four of us. Seth was really serious here.

Making up her mind, Susan whisked up a quick prayer for her mother's forgiveness and decided to tell Seth something nobody but Michael had ever heard.

"You asked me earlier why I chose my career over Michael," she said, hoping this wasn't a mistake.

Seth nodded.

"Well, in the first place, I never saw the divorce as final. I could never quite convince myself that our marriage was over." She grinned nervously. "I guess the past few years have proven that I was right."

At Seth's pointed look, Susan continued. "Mom called me into her room before she died." She took a deep breath.

"I remember." Signaling a turn, Seth headed back toward the more upscale part of town. "Scott, Sean, Stephen and I were all sent to the cafeteria. I think Spencer was still in school."

"Right." Susan squeezed her eyes shut, trying not to remember that day so clearly. "Anyway, she made me promise never to tell you guys what she told me."

"But you're going to tell me." Seth's words were more a demand than a question.

Studying her little brother, Susan wondered if she should. If her secret would help at all. "Mom wasn't always a meek, mothering soul, Seth," she started. "She'd wanted more than just about anything to go school to learn fashion design."

"You're kidding."

Susan had had a hard time believing the news her-self, except when she'd looked into her dying mother's eyes and seen the broken dreams there.

"Anyway." She blinked the memory away. "She married Daddy and he had specific ideas about a woman's place. She was to cook and clean, of course, but she was also the warmth, the nurturing, the moth-ering that every family needs. His role was the pro-vider, the protector."

"Right," Seth broke in impatiently.

"Mom was content to live under Dad's loving care, his protection, happy to have his children, to care for them. For us. Most of the time…"

She stopped abruptly, swallowing back her own tears as she remembered the tears dripping slowly from her mother's eyes that day.

"But growing up, I hated how she always *settled*—how I was supposed to settle, too. It pissed me off that I had to do dishes every night while you guys got to go out and shoot hoops. I had to put away everyone's laundry twice a week while the five of you took turns taking out the trash once in a while. I wanted to play Little League with you and instead I got to watch from the sidelines. Hell—" she laughed without humor "—Dad wouldn't even let me have a turn when he took the five of you to the batting cages. If I got to go at all, I had to be content to watch."

Seth's jaw was working while he stared out the windshield. "I never knew it bothered you so much."

"Mom did."

"Why didn't you ever say anything?"

"I did. All the time. Nobody listened."

"I—maybe you just—we didn't…did we?" Glancing quickly at Susan, Seth muttered, "I guess maybe you're right."

They fell silent, both of them lost in their own thoughts, their own memories. Not all of them bad.

"That day, in Mom's room…" Susan needed to finish what she'd started. "She told me she'd always understood how I felt, that she'd been rooting for me all those years."

"Then why didn't she do anything about it?"

Susan had wondered that herself. Many times. "I guess because then she'd have had to cross Dad and that wasn't something she ever did.

"But that day in the hospital, she spoke up. She told me she wanted more for me than she'd ever had herself, more *from* me than she'd ever given." She looked over at her brother. "She said I was the part of her she'd never had the courage to be."

"That doesn't even sound like Mom."

"I know." Susan remembered her own shock as if she'd only heard the words yesterday. "And that's not all. She told me that only through my courage to be more in life could she finally be complete."

Seth swore. "That's a hell of a burden to place on anyone."

Charging on, Susan had to finish, to get it all out. "She told me to believe in myself, to be strong, to be whatever my heart told me I needed to be." She'd also told Susan, in a breathless whisper, not to forget about the part of herself that was a woman.

"God, sis—" Seth broke off, concentrated on the road in front of him. He was frowning, his knuckles white as he gripped the steering wheel.

"How could she do that to you?" He seemed to be talking more to himself than to her. "To think you've been carrying around that burden all these years...."

"It's okay, Seth." Susan placed her hand on her brother's arm. "I survived." She smiled over at him, showing him that she really was just fine. "If anything, Mom's words set me free."

"Only you would come up with that take on it."

"It's true." She watched the trees whiz by, the fields of wildly growing weeds. "She took away the guilt I'd been feeling my whole life for bucking the system. For needing to make more of myself; for trying to be who I always knew I could be."

"Maybe," Seth grunted. "And maybe she's to blame for your divorce. And for the fact that you're now four months pregnant with fatherless twins."

"Maybe." She didn't want to think about that. "But that's not why I told you all this."

She had a feeling he knew what she was getting at, but he didn't say so.

"The point is, Seth, that if you quit your job—the work you love—you'll never live life to its potential. Regrets will eat at you until you're bitter inside, and sooner or later, they'll explode on someone else."

"Like Mom's did on you."

Parking at a restaurant a couple of blocks from Susan's house, Seth stopped the Bronco, but he didn't get out.

"You know the old saying that if someone gives you lemons you make lemonade?" Susan asked him.

"Yeah," he answered grudgingly.

"Well, the lemons Mom gave me made some really good lemonade."

Giving her one of his "do-we-really-have-to-do-this" looks, Seth waited for her to finish.

"Believe in yourself, Seth," she told him, her gaze pleading with him to take her seriously. "Be strong, not only for you, but for those around you. Don't settle. Ever. Anyway, if this woman really loves you, she won't expect you to give up something that's so important to you." She had his attention. "For God's sake, be whoever it is you need to be, 'cause if you don't, chances are someone else is going to pay for it."

"WE WON."

"I'm sorry." Michael cursed himself for not coming up with anything more useful to say. He paced his hotel room, holding the phone in his hand, hating the confinement. He'd been in Denver far longer than he'd planned.

"When the trial was dragged out that extra week, I really thought Joe was onto something...."

Michael had been concerned about the extra waiting, what it was doing to Susan, physically and emotionally. "You can rest assured that the boy got the best legal care."

"That poor little boy..."

Frowning, he worried about the despondency he heard in her voice. He hadn't seen her in over a month.

"Don't give up on him, Susan," he said, hoping he wasn't offering a bad suggestion. Perhaps it would be best if she just let go, went on, forgot. "You arranged for that funding for his surgery, you found Joe and there might be something else you can do.''

''Yeah. Maybe.''

Michael made a quick decision. "I'm finishing up here in Denver tomorrow or the next day. How would you like to take a day or two off and have some fun?''

''What kind of fun?'' His blood warmed at the sensual promise in her voice.

She was still Susan. Thank God. ''Well, that, too,'' he said, sitting down on the edge of his king-size bed. ''We could make reservations at The Race Book.'' On the Kentucky side of the river, The Race Book was the new hot spot at Turfway Park. ''Or there's a new Trekkie collectible shop in Louisville.''

''The Race Book would be fun.'' She was sounding better already. ''There's no live racing going on this month, but I love the simulcasting. We can bet on a bunch of races at once.''

Yep. Still Susan, all right. One race wasn't enough for her. She had to take on ten at a time. ''Let's plan to go Friday.''

''Michael?''

''Yeah?''

''You can stay here if you like.''

His body sprang to attention. ''I like.''

''Good.''

Something made him push his luck. ''My meetings with the Miller family are set to resume on Monday.''

''You want to stay here for the rest of your time in town?'' He noticed she was just asking, not necessarily inviting.

And yet, he wasn't sure he even wanted the invitation. ''Maybe.''

"Why don't we talk about it on Friday?"

"Fine." He didn't want to talk about it at all. Thing was, he didn't know what he *did* want.

Looking around his hotel room, Michael couldn't find anything he hadn't seen a million times before in the weeks he'd been there. Even opulence dimmed with overexposure.

"How are you feeling?" He had to ask.

"Good." She paused. "Fat."

"Already?" He couldn't picture it.

"Yep."

"Still feeling movement? Kicking?" He hated his curiosity. Hated the constant tension pressing against his temples.

"All the time."

"Well, you need your sleep." Pinching the bridge of his nose didn't help his headache. But he kept trying, anyway.

"I know, Michael. Good night."

She hung up without even waiting for his reply.

TOSSING OUTFIT after outfit on her bed, Susan was frantic by ten o'clock Friday morning. Michael was due anytime, she had clothes all over the room she'd be sharing with him—and she was naked. Which wouldn't have been the problem a few months ago that it was now.

He wasn't going to like her body.

The overalls made her look like a horse. The denim jumper like a cow. And the cotton slacks and knit top like a bright pink pig. Great. He'd think he was in a barn. Dating a farm. He'd probably cancel their reservations at the track and take her to the zoo.

Frustrated tears seeped through eyelids she was squeezing tight in an effort not to cry. She didn't have time to ruin her makeup.

Then again, why not? She'd ruined the rest of her life.

As if in protest, a little body part jabbed Susan in the left side. Another joined in on the right side.

"Great," she mumbled with a weak smile as she opened her eyes to look down at the growing mound of her stomach. "You're in line with my thoughts now. Well, just watch it, you two, some of them are not meant for little minds." She'd just have to trust them to tune out when necessary.

Like when she told Michael about them. Or rather, about there being *two* of them.

Her conversation with Seth two weeks before had backfired. She'd meant the words for him, but the memories had spoken to her, as well. Her mother had told her to be strong. To have courage. She was ashamed of how little courage she'd had where Michael was concerned these past months. But no more.

With that thought, she decided on the cow look and donned the denim jumper. Pulling a brush through the layers of her hair, she was pleased that the natural streaks hadn't lost any of their luster. Maybe if she could keep his attention on her face and her hair, he wouldn't notice that she'd gained fifteen pounds in four months.

She could always hope.

At least until she opened her door to him twenty minutes later. His warm green eyes met hers for a moment. A great moment. But then they started to travel.

"Wow," he said, staring at her belly.

"Yeah."

"That can't be comfortable."

She felt like some kind of freak. "It's not so bad."

For a second, he looked back up to her face, but then, as if drawn by a will of their own, his eyes focused again on her midsection. "You've still got five months to go."

Probably more like four since her doctor expected her to deliver early—but, hey, who was counting. "Women have babies all the time, Michael," she told him, wishing he'd quit staring at her. "It's no big deal."

But it was. And they both knew it.

GRINNING, Michael sat back and watched his ex-wife at work. He'd forgotten how truly amazing a Susan show could be. She'd bet on every race, somewhere between eleven and fifteen of them, had tally sheets spread on the table in front of her, and was somehow watching enough of all the races, on numerous monitors, to keep track of her winnings.

"Damn," she muttered.

Or losses.

He'd given up betting an hour ago, appreciating the sport of Thoroughbred racing a whole lot more than the betting. He was also keeping one eye on the baseball game being broadcast over a nearby monitor.

"Go, baby," Susan said, her eyes riveted to one screen.

Susan, on the other hand, loved the gambling.

Go, baby. Baby. He still felt the shock of Susan's protruding belly every time he thought of her standing in that doorway this morning. He'd known for months that she was pregnant. You'd think he'd have been prepared for the evidence. He hadn't. He wasn't.

"You ready to go?"

He glanced up to find her looking at him. "Only when you are." According to the clock, they'd been there a little more than three hours. And though the racing continued until eleven o'clock at night, he was hoping to have Susan in bed before then.

Placing no new bets, Susan still watched until her cards had dwindled down to nothing.

"How'd you do?" Michael asked, smiling as she frowned over the final tally.

"Up twenty dollars," she announced with satisfaction.

"An afternoon of fun, and money, too."

"Can we walk for a while?" Susan asked as they passed through the elaborate entranceway and back out into the Kentucky sunshine.

Looking around at the parking lot, Michael said, "Here?"

"My leg's cramped." With her hands in the pockets of her jumper Susan glanced up too quickly for him to gauge her expression. Then she perused the hills off in the distance. "Besides," she said, "I need to talk to you and I don't want to do it in the car."

Curious, Michael set off with her, wondering what was suddenly so important that it couldn't wait until they got back to the house.

"What's up?" he asked, when she appeared to be having difficulty getting started.

Another couple of steps, a glance toward the hills again. A deep sigh. "I've known something about this pregnancy for a while now, and I put off telling you, but it occurs to me that, as my friend, you should know.''

He wondered how long she'd rehearsed to get those words just right. ''You know the sex of the child?'' he asked. He'd wondered. He knew they could find things out these days, that most people knew what they were having long before the pregnancy became obvious to the rest of the world.

''No.'' She shook her head. And then looked over at him. ''You think I should?''

''Of course I do,'' Michael walked beside her, hands in the pockets of his jeans. He studied the grass ahead of him.

''Why?''

He probably shouldn't be advising where he didn't belong. ''Seems obvious.'' He looked down at her— shying away from the belly that was so visible from that perspective. ''If you know the sex of your child, you can make smart purchases. Take your nursery, for instance.'' He warmed to the subject. ''You decorate for girl or boy, rather than generic baby, and the room should see the child all the way through toddlerhood.''

''I hadn't thought of that.'' She was frowning. At least he thought she was, based on the tone of her voice.

''You'd make much more practical selections with clothes, as well.'' He kept right on talking. ''And you'd be able to purchase everything before the birth so as to be more completely prepared.''

Hearing himself carry on, Michael shut his mouth,

uncomfortable. Where on earth had all of that come from?

"Okay." Susan wrapped her arms around her middle, brushing his side as she did so. "My next appointment's on the twenty-first. I'll ask about it then."

"Not unless *you* want to, Sus," he was quick to assure her. "Don't do anything on my account."

She nodded, picking up her pace a little as they wandered farther from the raceway. "The appointment's still almost three weeks away. I have plenty of time between now and then to decide."

Good. This was her pregnancy; she should do things her way. "What was it you wanted to tell me?"

Eyes focused straight ahead, Susan said, "There's not just one child to buy for. There are two."

"Two." He wasn't sure he understood. "You're having twins?"

He stopped abruptly, stared at her.

Susan nodded.

"Twins?" He resumed walking, hands clasped tightly behind him now.

"Yes."

Michael glanced down at her, then looked ahead once more. She didn't have much to say, he thought, considering the significance of this news.

"They're sure?" he asked.

"Yes."

"How sure?"

"Completely sure, Michael." She sounded a little exasperated. But oddly sympathetic, too. Seemed to him *she* should be seeking sympathy right about now. Two babies. Hell.

"I've listened to the heartbeats."

Oh. Nodding, Michael walked on. "Maybe they made a mistake." He tried to offer her what hope he could. "Maybe they just caught the same heartbeat twice."

He didn't even know if such a thing was possible, but he had to say *something.* Try to reassure her that things might not be as bad as they seemed.

"I had an amniocentesis. There are two babies."

That was that, then. "God, Sus," he said, putting an arm around her shoulders. "Some luck." What on earth was she going to do?

Two babies. Instead of one child growing inside her there were two. Michael's blood ran cold. Instead of fathering one child, he'd fathered two.

There wasn't a swear word he knew that could express how he felt.

"It *is* luck, Michael," Susan was saying softly, almost dreamily. "At my age, I was probably going to have to settle for an only child, especially since I'm alone."

Aghast, Michael stared at her, his arm falling to his side. "You sound like you're happy about this," he said.

"I am." Her eyes glowed as she met his gaze, glowed with happiness, with awe.

"You're nuts." Brilliant, Kennedy, just brilliant. But he couldn't think of another thing to say.

"I don't think so." She stood up to him unblinkingly. "I get two children but only have to go through one pregnancy."

"You're alone, Susan." Wasn't she getting it?

"Even more reason to go through this only once."

"It'll be two against one." He tried to make this clearer to her. "Two babies to carry, two diapers to change, two pairs of screaming lungs, two hungry mouths."

"Then I guess it's a good thing I have two arms, two hands, two ears and two breasts, huh?" she asked him, completely undaunted.

"You're nuts," he said again and turned back toward the car, leaving her to follow him.

Leave it to Susan to speed blithely ahead, certain she could cope. She had no idea what lay ahead. No idea how busy she was going to be, how exhausted.

He slowed his gait a little, waiting for her to catch up. Of course, it wasn't as though she had any choice in the matter. She couldn't very well send one of them back.

Putting his arm around her shoulder, he pulled her against him, letting her know in the only way he could that he was sorry for what he'd said. His heart gave a lurch as he felt her arm slide around his waist.

He'd fathered not one child, but two.

He was deserting not one child—but two.

CHAPTER ELEVEN

"I'm QUITTING soccer, Mom."

Laura stilled, the pan of spaghetti sauce bubbling wildly beneath her unmoving spoon. When Seth had first left she'd dreaded hearing those words and then cried tears of relief and thanksgiving when they hadn't come. Now, almost ten months later, here they were.

"Why?" Deep breaths. Think.

"It's a dumb game and we have a dumb team."

More deep breaths. She started stirring again, measuring her breathing by the slow steady passes of the spoon. "It's not a dumb game, Jeremy," she told her nine-year-old son. "In Europe, it's as famous as football."

"We have a dumb team."

Where was this coming from all of a sudden? Why?

Most importantly, how did she beat it? Soccer had given Jeremy direction, kept him off the streets and out of the trouble he'd been heading into—fast.

"You guys have had a decent season," she reminded him.

Slouched over the kitchen table, his face twisted by the hands on either side of his cheeks, Jeremy looked miserable. It was Friday night, his sister was at a friend's house for the entire evening, and Laura was making his favorite dinner. By all rights, he should be feeling pretty good.

"We'd've been number one if Seth hadn't quit on us."

Feeling guilty for that, for the fact that the team had suffered, the other boys had suffered, because of decisions Laura had been forced to make, she couldn't deny her son's accusation.

"You've hung in with the team all year, Jeremy," she pointed out instead. "You've practiced hard, improved incredibly." Glancing over, she saw that her son was hanging on her praise. "So why quit now?" she finished softly.

Shocked when tears sprang to Jeremy's eyes, Laura dropped the spoon, turned down the heat on the homemade spaghetti sauce and joined Jeremy at the table. Dinner could wait.

"What is it, honey?" she asked him.

Jeremy looked up at her and his silent anguish broke her heart.

"What is it?" she asked again. Fear was burning her stomach. Something was very, very wrong.

It seemed he was finally going to answer her, but then he shook his head and lowered his eyes.

"Jeremy." With a hand under his chin, Laura gently lifted his head until his gaze met—and held—hers. "We don't shut each other out, you and I." Her voice was as firm as her insides were not. "We promised, remember?"

"I just don't want to go no more," he said sullenly, pulling away from her.

She was getting more frightened by the minute, but

that only made her more determined. "I'm not letting this go, Jeremy," she told him. "We'll sit here all night and all day tomorrow if we have to, but you're going to tell me what this is about."

Chin quivering, he gazed up at her again, his eyes filled with bitterness. With anger. And with a whole load of hurt.

"I saw Seth with another woman."

"What?" Laura's throat closed on her. She didn't know what she'd been expecting, but it certainly hadn't been that. "Where?"

"Across the street from the park."

"Where across the street? When?" Seth had been in the neighborhood? She couldn't even contemplate the rest of her son's bald announcement. Not if she was going to keep her composure.

"Under that big droopy tree, the one that practically covers the road," he said.

"You're sure it was Seth?"

"He was in his Bronco."

"You're sure it was his?" Jeremy had to be mistaken. That was all there was to it.

"It had his work parking sticker on it, Mom," the boy said as though he was questioning his mother's mental capacities. "I could tell by the shape."

"When was this?"

With a shaky sigh, Jeremy slouched back in his chair. His chin was planted firmly on his chest.

"He's been coming practically every week since he quit."

"What?" Laura was so shocked she yelled the word.

As though he'd expected the reaction, Jeremy

calmly nodded. "I don't think he wants us to see him the way he always hides under that tree and doesn't ever get out of the car."

"Why didn't you say anything?" she whispered, her lips frozen. Seth had been around, watching Jeremy, every week all these months?

Not looking at her, the boy shrugged. "I was scared you'd send him away from there, too."

Oh, God. "Jeremy, I told you—"

"I know, Mom. Seth didn't want to marry you. He was going to move on sometime...." He parroted the words she'd said so often those first weeks after Seth had gone.

"But, Mom, I didn't see why you couldn't let him stay around until *he* decided to move on."

She stared at her son silently. Lost. Alone. Afraid.

"I liked having him there," Jeremy said defensively. "Watching us..."

"And that's why you stayed on the team?" she asked, reality dawning.

"A little bit."

Choking back tears, Laura watched the dejected face of her son, completely uncertain what to do next.

"But I'm not going anymore," Jeremy told her, looking up at her with angry eyes.

"Because of the woman." She could barely say the word. Why in hell had Seth done it? Why, if he had another woman in his life—which surely he did by now—had he brought her over here? To watch Laura's son?

She hated Seth the next instant when fat tears welled up in Jeremy's eyes and dripped slowly down his dirt-streaked face. "I don't want to see him with anyone else, Mom. I want him to love you."

Laura pulled the boy into her arms comforting him as she silently wept.

LATE FRIDAY NIGHT, long after he'd made love to Susan, Michael lay awake in the bed he'd once shared with her, in the room that had once been theirs and tried to see a future. The picture was gray, blank. Cold.

"We need to talk, don't we?"

Startled by the soft voice beside him, he turned his head. "I thought you were asleep."

"I was. For a while."

"How long have you been awake?" Why in hell did it matter? Except to distract her from her original question.

"Long enough." Sighing, she raised herself on one elbow, pulling the sheet over her naked breasts.

Michael wished she hadn't done that. Hadn't shown him her beauty and then covered herself. Hidden herself from him. He wanted nothing more than to bury his face between her lush breasts, inhale her sweet scent, love her. Lose himself in her. Again. Forever.

"Even if I couldn't see the misery in your eyes, you're so tense I can practically feel your muscles quivering."

Michael willed his muscles to relax, trying for nonchalance. "Your imagination is working overtime. Go back to sleep, Susan."

"Michael?" She waited for him to look at her.

Which he did. Eventually. "Don't lie to me," she said.

Her beautiful blue eyes, warm with compassion, were too much for him. He couldn't continue the charade.

Leaning over her, he took her lips in a kiss that was meant to distract her and distracted him, instead. Her mouth opened beneath him, soft and welcoming, and he was lost. Nothing else seemed to matter when he was with Susan like this. Only her. Only them. Together.

Until she broke away. "Not now, Michael," she said, shifting toward her side of the bed. "Not like this."

Frowning, frustrated on top of everything else, he sat up—not bothering to cover himself up the way she had. He wanted her. He wasn't embarrassed about that.

"Like what?" he grumbled.

"With secrets between us."

"There are no secrets here."

Laughing without any humor at all, Susan slid out of bed and into a robe so quickly he admired her finesse. But only because he didn't want to focus on anything else.

"I lived with you for ten years, Michael," she told him, "and I've been sleeping with you for the past three."

He knew that but liked the sound of it anyway.

"In all that time, if there's one thing I've learned, it's that it takes you about two seconds to fall asleep after sex." Glancing at the clock, she delivered her closing line in superb prosecuting-attorney form. "It's been exactly one hour and twenty-four minutes and you're still awake. Something's wrong.''

"You timed it?'' he asked sarcastically.

She ignored his remark. "We both know what that something is.''

"We're not in the courtroom, Susan,'' he said, still sitting with his back propped against the headboard. "And I'm not a defendent.''

She wilted before his eyes. But only briefly. Straightening her shoulders, she sat on her side of the bed. "Please talk to me, Michael.''

It was extremely difficult to resist the soft pleading in her eyes, but Michael managed. Barely. "Let's get some sleep, Susan.'' He held up the covers for her to climb back underneath. "If you still want to talk in the morning, we will.''

Susan studied him. And shook her head. "I'm not going to be able to sleep now. And obviously, you're not having much luck at it, either. You might as well tell me whatever you've been thinking for the last hour and a half.''

"Hour and twenty-four minutes.'' He had no idea why he'd said it. Only that he wasn't ready to say anything else. Wasn't even sure what he had to say.

SHE WAS LOSING HIM. Susan knew it as surely as she'd known when to stop fighting him about the divorce. Maybe it was because she was such a good lawyer, maybe because she loved him so much, but she could sense defeat.

"I've been thinking…'' he finally said, and she almost cried. She'd won the battle. He was going to talk to her. But she'd lost the war, and she wasn't ready to deal with that.

"About the babies?" She found the strength to help him when he faltered.

His eyes, when he looked over at her were tired but stony as well. "Yeah."

"And?"

"I don't have any choice in the matter." He sounded like a man who'd just been sentenced to life imprisonment.

"If you mean whether or not I have twins, no, you have no choice," she said. She was having a hard time breathing. And appearing calm at the same time. But she couldn't fall apart. It wasn't fair to him. She'd asked for this. Against his will, she'd coerced him into this. Now she had to let him go.

"That's not what I meant." He actually grinned at her—sort of—as he drawled the words.

Susan grinned back. Sort of. God, she loved the man.

"What matter, then, do you have no choice in?" She couldn't let him distract her. This was too important—for both of them.

Shoving aside the pillow, Michael stood and pulled on his jeans. He zipped them, but left the snap undone.

"I have to take some responsibility for them."

"No, Michael." Susan stood, too, the unmade bed between them. "I did this. I handle it."

"One, maybe," he said, gesturing at her with his hand, then letting it drop to his side. "Not two."

"This isn't your decision to make, Michael, it's mine."

"You're a lawyer, Sus, you know the courts would differ with you."

"This isn't about courts. It's about me and about you. We went into this with promises. And I intend to keep them."

Holding her gaze with his own, Michael asked, "But do you *want* to keep them, Susan?"

He knew she couldn't lie to him.

"Yes," she said, still meeting his eyes. Because the part of her that loved him, that understood him, that couldn't bear to let him down, *did* want to keep her promise to take full responsibility for her children.

Relief flashed across his features, but they quickly shadowed again. "Let me ask that a little differently," he said, and she knew, even before he opened his mouth, what was coming. "Can you honestly tell me that, given the choice, you'd rather do this alone? That you'd rather your children not have a father?"

He'd lived with her for too long. Known her for too long. Heard her prepare arguments for too many cases.

"No."

His shoulders fell. "Like I said, I have no choice in the matter."

"We always have choices."

"I'm a decent man, Susan."

"Of course you are." It hurt her to hear him say that—as if it were something she might not have known otherwise. "But a lot of decent men are divorced, living separate lives from their children."

"They still provide for them."

He had her there. And finally, she understood. Her

plan had one little loophole that had turned into a big one. Michael's conscience.

She felt sick to her stomach for the first time in months.

"So." He sat down on the end of the bed and put on his socks. "The first thing I'm going to do is set up a bank account for their financial needs. I'll get to work on that immediately."

"Michael." Susan sat down beside him and stayed his hand as he reached for his shoes. "It's one o'clock in the morning."

He stopped momentarily, then picked up a shoe. "Well, I can get everything on paper and be ready when the bank opens in the morning."

"I don't need your money." She had to get through to him. To make him understand that he wasn't deserting his children. "I have enough put away to pay for college right now."

"That was when you thought you were having one child."

"I could put three children through college tomorrow if I had to."

Nodding, as though not in the least surprised, he sat there, just holding his shoe.

"I have to do something."

"We don't need you, Michael," she told him, trying with every ounce of strength she had not to cry. If this was what they meant by tough love, she wasn't sure she was going to make a good parent, after all.

Turning, he looked at her, his eyes filled with understanding—and a hint of hopelessness, as well. "I appreciate what you're trying to do, Sus," he said, seeing right through her. Or, probably more accurately, into her. "But even if you don't need me, you can't speak for those babies. One to one, I was trying to justify, but two to one isn't fair odds. Not for you. But also not for them."

"So what are you saying?" Her cheeks felt like ice. Her whole body was freezing. From the inside out.

"I don't know," he told her, gazing straight ahead. "That's as far as I've gotten. Except—" He broke off.

"What?" Her stomach clenched.

He stood, turning to face her, his hands on his hips. "I think that for the next couple of weeks, while I'm in town, I should stay here."

They'd said they'd talk about that. And for a while, she'd been hoping he'd decide to stay. She was used to him coming and going in her life. As untraditional as their relationship might be, it worked for them. Most of the time. But...

"You're always welcome, Michael, you know that, but you don't sound too happy about the idea." She took a deep breath. "And, under the circumstances, I'm not sure I'm happy about it, either."

"It's the circumstances that make it the only feasible idea."

"I don't follow you." She frowned. "You need some space, some time to work this through in your mind, to figure out what to do, what feels right. What'll make you happy."

"My happiness isn't the issue at the moment," he told her, and because she knew he meant every word, her heart started to break. It was too late. She'd done to him the very thing she'd sworn she'd never do.

The thing she was afraid she'd already done. She'd trapped him. Maybe not in her life, maybe not in her home, but in his heart.

"And I've had space," he continued, pacing from the bed to the closet to the door and back again. "Four months' worth with no answers forthcoming."

"But you just found out about the twins today!"

"Maybe." He still paced steadily. "But the issue has been in the forefront of my mind, anyway. It was just a little easier to justify no involvement when there was only one child to consider." Stopping at the window, he stared out into the night. Feeling helpless, she sat on the edge of the bed and watched him.

"Let me stay here, Susan," he said, his voice tinged with a note of begging. It was so unlike Michael, it brought the tears rushing to her eyes before she could stop them. "Let me try for these few weeks, see what I can do, what I can live with."

Let me see how bad it's going to be, this being trapped, she translated for him.

"Of course you can stay," she told him. But there wasn't even a spark of excitement, of anticipation, of happiness, in her acquiescence.

She felt as though she'd just ruined the life of the man she loved.

MICHAEL CAUGHT a flight to Chicago Saturday morning. He'd secured an appointment with the Miller family for a week from the following Monday. He wanted to use the time in between to finalize his market analysis and to check in with team members who were experts in various areas of acquisitions. And he wanted to be settled in his personal life before the new week began. He was going home to catch up on mail, on Mrs. Leets, on his phone messages, to pick up some more clothes—and the Pathfinder. He needed that Pathfinder more than anything, illogically so. As if it represented the only piece of freedom he had left.

While he was home, he called his family, caught up on all the new happenings in Carlisle. They were finally getting a McDonald's. Which was the biggest news Michael had heard from there in a long time.

"How are the twins?" Michael asked when his mother took a turn on the phone.

"Fine. Those babies keep them busy," she said. The same answer he always got, and yet, his little sisters suddenly seemed much more real to him.

"They're a great support for each other, aren't they?" he asked, only just realizing something everyone else had probably known for twenty years.

"Of course," his mother said. "Why wouldn't they be?"

"No reason, Mom." He meant to change the subject then. "Mom?" he asked instead.

"Yeah?"

"How did you feel when you found out you were having twins?"

"Ohhh, I don't know that I remember. Happy, I'm sure."

"Was it hard, you know, that first little bit?"

"Hard?" She paused. "No, I don't think so."

"What about when both of them were crying or needed to be changed, or when you had to go somewhere and lug two babies with you?"

"Well, of course, *that* wasn't easy, but I had you boys and your father—and besides, Michael, you just don't think about those things. You're just too busy loving them.''

Right. There was that. Unfortunately, Michael didn't have any idea how to go about it. *Loving them.*

''Of course, if you asked your father, I'm sure you'd get a different answer,'' Mary Kennedy continued, rattling blissfully on. ''He grumbled a lot when the girls were little. 'Double everything, mostly trouble,' he used to say. But he didn't really mean it. He took such pride in them. In all you kids.''

Because they were the only thing he could take pride in? The only thing he had? But it wasn't a question Michael could ask.

He rang off a few minutes later, not telling his family that he'd be staying at Susan's over the next few weeks. He knew exactly what they'd make of that—adding more pressure that he didn't need. He also didn't want to get their hopes up about something that wasn't happening.

Which was exactly why he also failed to mention the two grandchildren on the way. Until that moment, he'd never even considered the fact that Susan's babies had another entire family who would delight in their existence. Who deserved to have a share of their lives.

With that thought wrapping the chains more tightly around him, Michael phoned his brother Bob. And didn't hang up until he'd secured permission to send Bobbie Jayne to drama camp in August. And then, filled with the need to call his niece back and tell her everything was finalized, he called the director of the camp—reaching her at home—and reserved Bobbie

Jayne one of the last slots. So as the day drew to a close, at least he felt good about something.

He met the new director of finance at Smythe and Westbourne for dinner Saturday evening—as he'd been doing every time he came to town since he'd left the position himself. Melanie Dryson had worked for him for years and was every bit as committed as Michael had been to the continued growth of the investment firm. And while she was very well qualified to do the job, there were still some things she liked to run by him. Sensitive issues relating to employees and to clients.

"I need to give you some new contact numbers," he told her as soon as he'd finished off the steak and baked potato he'd ordered. Pulling out a business card, he scribbled Susan's number under his own. He'd told Melanie when she agreed to take the position that he'd keep her apprised of his whereabouts for as long as she needed him.

"You're through in Denver?" Melanie asked him. She'd had a salad that made him appreciate Susan's more voracious appetite.

"Last Thursday." Melanie was a beautiful woman, a brunette with classical features. Everything about her from her dress to the way she wore her short, layered hair was classy, stylish. She reminded him a lot of Susan—especially the air of confident poise she was never without.

Taking a sip of her tea, she smiled at him. "Have you been to Atlanta yet?"

"Just briefly." He'd made a couple of weekend trips to familiarize himself with the office he was hardly ever going to use. To meet his new secretary whom he used a lot—but only long-distance.

Looking at the card he'd given her, Melanie asked, "So where are you going this time?"

"Cincinnati."

"Doesn't the travel ever get to you?"

"I like seeing different parts of the country, meeting different people." He just wished he could come home at night a little more often. And during his few hours off on weekends, too.

"What about living out of hotels?"

"Not my favorite thing." A bit of an understatement. "As a matter of fact, I won't be in a hotel this trip."

She looked at the card again. At the number. "Staying with Susan?"

"Yeah." He glanced around for the waiter.

"Any chance of you two getting back together?"

"It hasn't even been discussed." He thought of the unrest he'd seen in Susan's eyes when he'd left her that morning, the worry on her brow, remembered the compassion in her kiss. And she was the one going through the real hardship. He was eager to get back to her.

"Maybe it should be." Melanie dipped a tea bag slowly in and out of her cup.

"Melanie..." he began.

"I know." She held up one hand. "We don't ever talk about things like this, and most of the time I'm as opposed to bringing up private matters as you are. But I've been working with you for seven years, Michael. I saw how you were when you first came out here, like someone had just shot your best friend."

He didn't think that was true, but after the night he'd spent, he didn't have the energy to argue with her. So he humored her instead and listened quietly.

"And then when you two started being more than just friends again, you changed. Seemed more at peace. Maybe even happy."

The only reason Melanie had even known he'd been seeing Susan was that he'd had to leave Susan's number when he'd gone to Cincinnati. He wished now that he'd stayed in a hotel.

Michael checked his watch. "I really think—"

"Just a minute, Michael." She reached across to grab his arm, but let go immediately when she had his attention. "You've been good to me," she said. "You gave me a chance in a predominantly male world and offered me fair reward for my accomplishments. I'll never be able to thank you enough for that, but maybe I can help you out for once."

He shouldn't have bought Melanie that glass of wine with dinner. Not that it had ever affected her like this before.

"Help away," he said, bracing himself.

"You and Susan belong together, Michael." He started to protest again, in spite of his recent acquiescence, but she rushed on. "I realize I don't know either of you all that well. Personally, I mean. Hell, I've only met Susan a couple of times, but seeing you together…" She paused and Michael hoped she was done.

"I've heard you talking on the phone to her." Unfortunately, she continued. "The way you build her up, the way you're always willing to listen, even your tone of voice when you talk to her—it's obvious to anyone with eyes and ears that you're soul mates. How else could such an unusual relationship last?''

As Michael sat there, listening to Melanie against his will, a strange thing began to happen. He felt less constricted suddenly, less suffocated. And he felt a sense of…renewed strength. Or purpose, maybe. Or will.

In the long run, it changed nothing. He still didn't have any answers.

But he welcomed the relief just the same.

CHAPTER TWELVE

THERE WERE VERY FEW things in life Susan could control at the moment, which meant she had to put all her energy into controlling what she could. Michael had been living with her for almost a week. Sort of. He'd been sleeping at the condo, even in her bed, but she saw very little of him.

And he hadn't made love to her since he'd returned from Chicago.

Her body wasn't her own; rather, it belonged to two other people she hadn't even met. She had no say over what she did, what she ate, even how much she slept. But there was one thing she *could* do something about. One thing she had to do something about. Ronnie McArthur.

On Friday, a week after her day at the races, she met his plane at the airport, helping his mother wheel the boy out to her car and get him settled in the back seat. Dressed in clean jeans, a short-sleeved knit shirt and tennis shoes, he looked like any other American kid, except for the wheelchair. And the limp left arm.

"Thanks so much for coming," she told them both as she slid behind the wheel of her Infiniti. She hoped to God she wasn't making another major mistake.

"Of course we'd come," Mrs. McArthur said. "We'll do anything that might give Ronnie some hope.'' The woman was tastefully, though inexpensively, dressed in a pair of dark dress slacks and white silk blouse. Her dark hair, cropped short, looked freshly cut.

The boy hadn't said a word since he'd been wheeled off the plane. Susan shot a quick glance at him in her rearview mirror, wondering how to make him smile, and found that he'd fallen asleep.

''He's been excited about the trip since you called on Tuesday,'' his mother said. ''He's exhausted.''

Once she was safely on the freeway, Susan turned her thoughts to the ordeal that lay ahead. ''I have to warn you again,'' she told the younger woman. ''Tricia Halliday doesn't know you're here and I have no idea how she's going to react.''

Susan had spent two sleepless nights worrying about Ronnie McArthur, afraid she might be doing more damage than good by exposing him to the possible heartless rejection of her boss.

''Ronnie knows she's the bad guy,'' his mother assured Susan. ''And he's John Wayne, riding into town to fight the bad guys.''

''An eight-year-old kid's heard of John Wayne?''

Smiling for the first time Susan had ever seen, the other woman said, ''His father's a John Wayne addict. We have videos of every movie that man ever made.''

Susan's worries returned. ''John Wayne always wins.''

''Only at the end,'' Mrs. McArthur said softly. ''And Ronnie will, too. This may not be the end. He knows that.''

"You and your husband sound like pretty remarkable people."

"We just love our son."

"Do you have any other children?" It wasn't a question Susan had allowed herself to investigate earlier. She couldn't get that close.

The other woman shook her head. "We tried, but we only got lucky once." She glanced down at Susan's stomach, the pregnancy fully visible in the new blue maternity suit Susan was wearing. "When are you due?"

"October, but the doctor thinks I'll probably be early."

Frowning, Mrs. McArthur asked, "You're having problems?"

It might just have been politeness, but Susan had a feeling the other woman was sincere in her concern. Even in the midst of her own heartache, she was capable of having compassion for someone else.

"No problem." Susan smiled a little, still feeling a secret thrill when she thought of her babies. "I'm having twins."

"Congratulations!" There was no doubting that Mrs. McArthur's delight was genuine.

"I want you to know," Susan said, biting her lip as she signaled their exit. "If this doesn't turn out well today, I'm not giving up. Not until Ronnie wins."

"Why are you doing this?" Ellen McArthur asked, tears in her eyes.

"Because it's right."

"But you fought against us in court."

And she hadn't slept peacefully since. "That was

right, too," she said, slowing as she hit the exit ramp. "I was under obligation to Tricia Halliday then. But that part's over now, so I'm free to try something else."

"I've never thanked you properly for your help with money for Ronnie's surgery. Or for the lawyer."

"You may not be thanking me shortly," Susan felt compelled to warn again as she pulled into Halliday Headgear, her stomach in knots. After what she'd done to Michael, she'd lost a lot of confidence in her own instincts.

And this was a shot in the dark.

Susan pulled into her reserved parking spot. "I'm curious," Mrs. McArthur said before she turned around to wake her son. "Why do you think a meeting with Mrs. Halliday is going to make any difference?"

"Just a hunch," Susan said. She was going on so little, she should be hanged for putting the McArthurs through this. But Michael had told her to keep looking. She had—and the only thing she'd found was Tricia's aversion to dealing with this entire episode.

Tricia had insisted that she didn't want to know anything about the boy, about his situation. She hadn't gone to court. Hadn't even wanted to discuss the case. Which could all have been put down to the woman's coldheartedness. Except that every other incident Susan had taken to Tricia had been met with professional interest. Tricia always wanted details. And follow-up.

And Susan had discovered on Monday that the woman was on the board of the local chapter of the Children's Heart Association. Not the act of a selfish woman. Nor a woman who was indifferent to sick children.

Her stomach churning, Susan took one deep calming breath before she ushered her guests into Ed's old office a few minutes later. She just kept telling herself that Ed Halliday had loved his wife for a reason.

"Mrs. Halliday, I have someone I want you to meet."

"Oh!" Tricia started to stand, and then, as she saw her guests, fell back into the chair behind her desk.

"Cool room!" The childish voice tumbled into the sudden silence. They were the first words Susan had heard Ronnie say.

"Ronnie!" his mother whispered, leaning over the child's wheelchair.

"It's okay," Susan said, aware of Tricia's striken look, her stunned silence, but more aware of the little boy who desperately needed a chance to live. She knelt down by Ronnie's chair, smiling at the cute little dark-haired boy.

Having heard the child's voice, Annie got up from beneath Tricia's desk and lumbered over.

"A dog!" Ronnie cried, leaning over the side of his chair to pet the old setter.

"Her name's Annie," Susan said, giving the dog a reassuring pat.

"Hi, Annie," Ronnie said, still petting the dog. Annie returned the greeting by licking Ronnie's arm, then sauntered out of the room.

Probably on her way to the stairwell that was always kept open for her.

Ronnie watched her leave, his eyes lingering. "Where's she going?"

"Who knows?" Susan shrugged, smiling. "The cafeteria maybe, or down to the first floor where her doggie door is—it leads to the courtyard. Or maybe she'll go to my office."

"Why would she go there?"

"She likes the carpet."

Ronnie nodded politely, but his attention was straying to the basketball court beside them.

"You ever shoot hoops, Ronnie?" she asked him.

"Used to." His eyes dropped to his lap.

"Well, here." Susan retrieved a basketball from a rack on the wall and handed it to the boy. "It's okay if you miss. I do all the time." She wheeled his chair beneath the basket.

The boy looked from Susan to the hoop and back again. He was ignoring Tricia.

"Go ahead," Susan urged. Another couple of minutes passed in tense silence.

And then, without warning, the boy launched the ball with his one good arm. And actually hit the rim.

"Here, try again," Susan said, placing the ball back in the kid's lap. Ronnie did. And again. And again. He just kept trying, rising out of his chair as much as his limp left leg would let him in his attempts to sink a shot.

And then he succeeded. "Two points!" he hollered, looking back at his mother with a grin.

Ellen McArthur's eyes were brimming with tears.

Tricia Halliday didn't say a word, barely moved, as she watched the boy.

"Cool! What's that?" Ronnie asked, trying to turn his chair to the right. It moved easily enough on the ceramic tile floor, but he still had trouble maneuvering with only one arm.

"It's like an arcade game," Susan replied, wheeling Ronnie over to the big machine.

"It's soccer," Ronnie said, grinning over at his mother.

"That's right, it is," Susan continued, forging on ahead because she simply didn't know what else to do. Tricia still hadn't moved. "You kick the ball into the net like this, see," she said, slipping out of her pumps to demonstrate. "See how it's attached to this rope?"

Ronnie gave a thoughtful nod. "That way the machine can send it right back to you."

"We make headgear for soccer goalies." Tricia's voice fell into the room, freezing all the occupants in midmove.

Straightening slowly, her attention focused completely on her employer, Susan slipped back into her shoes. "They weren't on the production line that day," she said softly.

Still staring at the boy, Tricia flinched. And Susan knew the older woman had understood.

"Come on, Ronnie." With a quick glance from Tricia to Susan, Mrs. McArthur moved to her son's chair, wheeling him toward the door. Susan let them go.

Holding herself regally until they were gone, Tricia faltered the second the door closed behind them. She tried to speak, her eyes bright with anger. But she closed her mouth without saying a word.

She tried a second time, Susan standing mute in front of the soccer game where Ronnie had left her.

And then, slumping back in her chair, Tricia buried her face in her hands.

The sounds of Tricia Halliday's weeping seemed amplified in the silent room, touching Susan in spite of her disdain. She approached the older woman, placing a gentle hand on Tricia's back.

"Tricia?" she asked softly. She wished she felt closer to the woman, wished Ed were there, guiding her.

"I never wanted to do this," the woman cried, her words muffled by her hands.

"Do what?"

Tricia looked up at Susan, her usually immaculate makeup streaked with tears. "Run this company," she said. "I'm a mother, not a businesswoman."

Leaning on the desk beside Tricia, Susan said, "Overall, you've done an impressive job, Tricia. You *are* a businesswoman."

"But I don't want to be." The words were whispered, full of shame, of regret. "I enjoy my volunteer work, I like organizing benefits, but what's most important to me, what makes me the happiest, is taking care of my family."

"And Halliday's is getting in the way of that?" Susan asked. She supposed she could see it, considering that Tricia had three teenagers at home.

Tricia shook her head. "No, it's because of them that I'm even here."

"I don't understand."

"Would you mind terribly if I asked you to sit down?" Tricia's question held not even a hint of the hard woman who'd been her boss these past months. "You're a bit intimidating as it is," she continued, "and it makes me uncomfortable to have you standing over me."

Rounding the desk, Susan sat.

Tricia pulled out a tissue and a compact, drying her tears, repairing some of the damage to her face.

"My oldest son has his heart set on running Halliday Headgear some day." Tricia eventually spoke again, having put her makeup away. She'd regained her composure, but not her coolness. "He's got to finish his last year of high school and then get through college before he can do that."

Susan turned cold. "Are there…money problems?" she asked. She'd had absolutely no indication that Halliday's was in trouble.

"No." Tricia shook her head firmly. "Nothing like that." She gave Susan a sharp look, as if determining how much of her personal business to impart. "Ed has a brother, an older brother, who's never amounted to much. Gambles away every dime he's ever had." She fiddled with the edge of a paper on her desk as she spoke. "But back when they were younger, right at the time Ed was trying to come up with the money to finance this factory, his brother hit a lucky streak playing the stocks. He offered to give Ed the money he needed."

"But this is a privately held company," Susan said, "and you and Ed are the only owners."

"As long as Ed or I—or our kids—are running the company, that's true," Tricia glanced up and then back at the paper. She'd curled the lower right corner and was going to work on the left. "We agreed to pay Ed's brother ten percent of the profits—and agreed that if there ever came a time when one of us was unable to run the company, he'd take over.''

Susan was beginning to understand. "Since that time, the brother's proven that, given the chance, he'd probably run Halliday's out of business," she summed up.

Pushing the paper aside, Tricia looked up. Nodding.

"So *you* have to operate the company until your son is old enough to take over or it won't be here for him when he's ready."

"That's the way it is."

"I had no idea."

"So you see, Susan, I'm here because I'm taking care of my family by making sure that Halliday's is in good shape when my son's ready to come on board here."

"You know I'll help in any way I can."

"I relied on that more than you know. Until recently." Tricia paused, gesturing at Susan's stomach. "But soon you'll have a little one of your own making demands on your time, your priorities."

"Two, actually." Susan felt compelled to be completely honest. "But I still intend to continue working. Especially now that I'll have two children to support."

"The father has denied any responsibility, then?" Tricia asked.

Susan had wondered when people were going to start asking about that. So far everyone had been unfailingly polite. Covering their shock as best they could, offering her congratulations. Susan had made it clear that the choice to have a baby, to be a single parent, had been hers, but she knew people were curious.

She just hadn't come up with an explanation that sounded right. That would satisfy her co-workers' curiosity, yet forestall further questions.

"He hasn't denied anything," Susan told her employer slowly. "He'll play whatever part I ask of him. I'm just not asking."

Tricia nodded, saying no more, and Susan appreciated the older woman's respect for her privacy. She appreciated a lot more about Tricia Halliday now that she understood her better. Except...

"So what about Ronnie McArthur?" She hated to bring up the subject, but she couldn't let it lie. Though only a handful of people knew it, Halliday Headgear was responsible for that boy's injuries.

"I don't know." Tricia's face crumpled again, though she held back any tears. "I'm not bound to come forth with information I'm not asked for," she said.

"Maybe not legally."

"Do you have any idea what it could do to Halliday's to have this all over the papers?" she asked.

"Companies survive bad press."

"Sometimes, but these days most of them have stockholders who own other interests they can fall back on during hard times. Something like this could ruin Halliday's."

"Not necessarily."

"I can't take that chance, not for something we weren't technically responsible for. That face mask wasn't made for soccer...."

Tricia's voice faded away, her eyes turned toward

the soccer game across the room. To the spot where Ronnie's wheelchair had so recently been. And then she looked at the basketball court.

"Ed taught all our kids to play basketball, right there on that court," Tricia said, reminiscing. "By the time they were old enough to hold the ball, he had them down here, trying to teach them to dribble, to shoot toward the hoop. He said basketball formed character."

Susan had heard those words herself. The day Ed hired her. He'd asked her to shoot a few hoops with him. Without hesitation, Susan had kicked off her pumps, shrugged out of her suit jacket, and taken him on. He'd cremated her. But she'd been loyal to the man ever since.

And being loyal to the man meant being loyal to his family. So…what would Ed do in this situation?

"You're right," Susan said, thinking hard. "Halliday's has no reason, no obligation even, to implicate itself. We made a mistake, but so did the people who were told to return the masks. So did the person who made the decision to have Ronnie wear a catcher's mask to play goalie."

She'd drawn Tricia's attention back to her. "But there's nothing to stop us from being philanthropic, is there?" she asked, growing excited as the answer came to her. An answer she felt certain Tricia would support.

"Why not finance Ronnie's recovery?"

"Well…"

"Everyone wins," Susan pressed on. "We give a little boy the chance to get his life back, and Halliday's looks good, too. Think of the media." Susan warmed to her argument now that she finally had one. "Halliday's wins in court, proves itself innocent of wrongdoing, and then turns around and helps, anyway."

"Won't that make it look like we're covering up? Make people wonder if we really *were* at fault?"

"It would have if we'd settled before going to court," Susan said, thankful suddenly that the situation had played itself out as it had. "But not now."

"We can certainly afford to help...." Tricia started.

"Yes!" Susan cried. She jumped up, hurrying around the desk to give the woman a hug. "I think we're going to make a great team, Mrs. Halliday."

"It was Tricia a few minutes ago."

"I know."

"I prefer Tricia."

"Yes, ma'am." Susan grinned. She could hardly wait to go out and find Ronnie and his mother. Could hardly wait to tell Michael.

"You'll take care of all the legalities?" Tricia asked, as professional as ever. With one major difference. She was smiling, too.

MICHAEL BROUGHT home a bottle of sparkling apple juice.

"I'm proud of you, Sus," he said, popping the cork in the kitchen while she dished out the Mexican takeout he'd also brought home with him.

Only Michael could make her feel so complete, so warm and satisfied, with a simple look. A tone of voice.

"I was really worried there for a bit," she admitted

to him. "Afraid I'd made a huge mistake bringing them here."

"You've always been able to trust your hunches."

Until recently, she added silently.

They moved to the table, carrying champagne glasses and plastic plates brimming with rice and cheese enchiladas.

"How are things going with Miller Insulation?" she asked as they ate. This was the most accessible he'd been all week.

"Slower than I expected." He frowned, his fork still. "The family has sent word to everyone in the company that they're to be cooperative, tell our people anything we want to know. But the Millers themselves don't seem eager to sit down and talk."

Did that mean he'd be with her longer than the couple of weeks she'd expected? Could she stand to have him around that long? Or stand to let him go?

HE STAYED with her all evening, watching the news, helping her hang a couple of prints on the newly painted walls of the nursery.

"You're doing a great job in here," he told her, surveying the work she and Seth had done the previous weekend when Michael was in Chicago.

"If only I can find some furniture I like," she said, trying to see the room through his eyes.

"You have something particular in mind?"

"Not really. I just seem to know what I *don't* want."

"What about car seats and stuff like that? Have you started picking up any of those extras?"

"Not yet." She shook her head, afraid to be having

this conversation with him, afraid he'd shut himself off again, as he'd done all week. Afraid to enjoy speaking with him about the babies. Afraid she'd miss what she couldn't have.

"Don't you think you should start looking?"

"I have looked, but there are so many decisions to make and since I'm probably only going to be doing this once, I want to make the right choices." She slid down to the empty nursery floor, leaning against the wall, and gazed up at him.

Michael joined her, leaning against the opposite wall. "What kinds of choices?"

Telling herself not to hope that he was going to change, Susan still couldn't suppress her delight as she told him about changing tables and diaper bags, car seats that also did duty as carriers. "And then there's a stroller," she said. He was listening carefully.

"You'll need a double stroller, of course," he said.

"Right, but they have these ones where the babies ride side by side, and then other ones where they ride in front of each other."

Michael frowned. "What are the benefits of each?"

"Side by side, they see each other, can play with each other, and I can tend to both at once." He looked so good to her, sitting there in a pair of cutoff sweat shorts and white tank T-shirt. So natural. Even surrounded by the colorful wallpaper and clowns on the walls.

"The problem with that stroller is that it's so wide, which makes it difficult to get in and out of places. Plus," she added, thinking as she went, "they might fight with each other, pull each other's hair."

"So what about the other kind?"

"When I'm pushing, I won't be able to see the one in front. And they won't be company for each other."

"But if one's crying, the other won't see and immediately join in."

She hadn't thought of that.

"Of course," he added, "there's always a chance that the one in back will toss something and hit the other on the head—especially if the one in back is a boy."

Susan's heart leapt when she saw the grin on his face. Maybe there was hope, after all.

Just maybe.

CHAPTER THIRTEEN

SETH MISSED his sojourn across town that Saturday.

"C'mon, Mr. Carmichael, I'm sorry already. Now throw the damn ball."

Silently, Seth waited, raising one eyebrow at the rough-looking kid. One of the toughest of his friend Brady's underprivileged kids.

"Shit." And then, "I meant to say darn, okay?"

It took everything Seth had not to grin. He gave his best effort at looking stern, instead.

"Ah, hell, I didn't mean shit, neither." Realizing that he'd just sworn again, the boy hung his head, his arm dropping to his side and the baseball mitt he'd been holding out for Seth's pass dropping along with it.

Seth relented. "It's okay, Paul, you're trying so we'll let that be enough for now."

Paul glanced up, his face alight with a real grin— probably the first Seth had seen in the three weeks since he'd first started spending a couple of Saturday hours with the boy. "That's bitchin' of you, man..." Paul stopped, grinned again, and said, "I mean, that's *swell,* Mr. Carmichael." He enunciated very carefully.

"Call me Seth."

The twelve-year-old looked as though Seth had just

given him an in with the Cincinnati Reds. "Sure, man," he said, trying to seem tough. "I mean Seth."

Seth threw the ball to Paul before the kid embarrassed himself any further. And for the next couple of hours he forgot his own troubles as he tried to make the life of a hardened young man more palatable. Paul had been picked up for shoplifting, but he had a history of expulsions from schools across the state. Other than the shoplifting, he'd never really done anything horrible; he was just disruptive and refused to follow rules.

It had taken Seth maybe five minutes to figure out that the toughest thing about the kid was his mouth. And another five to find something that mattered to the boy. Baseball.

From there, getting him to follow rules was a cakewalk. No rules, no baseball.

But great as it felt to be working with a kid again, to be contributing something useful to society, nothing seemed to ease the ache Seth felt every time he thought of another boy who'd needed him. A boy he'd made promises to. A boy he'd deserted.

He tried not to think of the boy's mother at all.

MICHAEL HAD completely taken over the third bedroom of the condo. Previously Susan's study, the room had become his hub. When he wasn't out at the Miller Insulation plant or in meetings, he was in that room working.

"Michael, we have to talk." Susan was standing in the doorway.

He didn't want to talk. He thought he'd made that quite clear to her over the past week. Until he knew what to think, until he understood things himself, he had nothing to say to her.

"You've been here for more than two weeks and I don't see how this is accomplishing anything," she said. "Unless it's hurt the good things we had going for us."

"Such as?" He looked up from the papers he'd been trying to study.

"We haven't made love since you moved in here."

Yeah, well, that was one of the things he couldn't explain. "I'm not here to make love."

"Why are you here?"

He wished to hell he knew. "Because I'm the father of the two children you're carrying."

"So?"

"So, that's why I'm here."

"What is this supposed to accomplish?" she asked, leaning against the door frame. God she was lovely. Almost five months pregnant with his children. He couldn't remember ever seeing her so beautiful.

Which was just another of the things he couldn't explain.

Sighing, Michael put down the papers. They hadn't been holding his interest, anyway. "I don't know what's supposed to happen, Susan," he admitted. Maybe he was just seeing how long he could stand to be there, how long before he started to suffocate. Or capitulate as his father had.

"I don't know, either." She wandered into the room, dropped down to the couch. "We talked more when you were across the country."

Yeah. And he missed those easy conversations. Frowning, he tried to find a way to express what he wasn't sure of himself. "I need, somehow, to separate you from the children, separate my relationship with you from the children."

He needed to make love to her. So badly he'd woken up with a hard-on every morning for the past week. Gone to sleep with one, too, for that matter.

"Why?" The question was soft, understanding, making it difficult for him not to reach further.

"Because I already know how I feel about you."

"How's that?"

Picking up a pencil, Michael pulled the message pad away from the phone and drew aimlessly. "You're my best friend. The person I always think of first when I have something to share."

"I was starting to wonder if that had changed."

He looked up when he heard the tremor in her voice.

"The question has never been about you, Sus." He met her gaze openly, intent on reassuring her on that score, at least. "We've always been able to give each other the space we needed to do what we had to do, yet at the same time provide each other with understanding and encouragement."

"And why do think that was?" He knew she wasn't testing him for answers she already had. Rather, she sounded as though she were trying to understand it herself.

"Because we were two of a kind." Finally—an answer *he* had. "You were hell-bent on not becoming your mother and I was just as determined not to become my dad."

"Yeah, I guess." The oak-grain layers of her hair glowed in the evening light.

"Both of them were forced by family responsibilities into roles that weren't satisfying to them, your mom by giving up herself, her own dreams, my dad by being trapped in a job he hates."

"But family responsibilities bring joy, too." Her arms rested atop her protruding belly.

"And sometimes—like with your mother, my dad—they weren't a joy because of the cost."

"I'm not so sure of that," Susan surprised him by saying. "The cost was great, granted, but perhaps some of the joy was, too."

Feeling strangely deserted, Michael said, "Sounds like you've changed a bit."

"Not really." Susan continued to hold his gaze. "Doing my job, being my own person, is still important to me." He was immensely relieved to hear that. "I just want *more* now. I'm adding another, new dimension to who I am."

It seemed so logical when she said it. But what was going to happen when she was forced to choose? When Susan the lawyer was at odds with Susan the mother? She'd have to choose Susan the mother, of course; she'd left herself no other choice. And that was where he strangled every time. Being left with no choice scared him to death.

"The thing is," she said after a pause, "I don't know how much longer I can stand having you here, knowing you don't want to be here."

Michael cursed himself to hell for putting that look in her eyes. "I want to be here," he told her, surprised at the truth.

"Out of duty?"

He didn't know. Probably, at least to some extent. But...

"I've always wanted to be with you whenever I could."

She sat watching him, her legs curled beneath her, her sleeveless cotton dress billowing around her. He'd never wished more that he was different, that he was the kind of man she deserved, the kind of man who wanted it all—home, work and family. The first two he wanted. He'd just never wanted the third.

"Can you give me a little more time?" he asked her now, praying he'd experience some kind of revelation soon, some sign that would show him the way. Lord knew, he wasn't finding it by himself.

"If you'll promise me something."

"What?"

"That the minute you *don't* want to be here, you'll leave."

"Susan..."

"That's it, Michael." Her eyes were filled with conviction. "I don't want you here out of duty or any other misguided sense of moral expectation."

He didn't want to make the promise. Wasn't sure he could keep it. But he was giving her so little as it was. Far, far less than she deserved or had the right to expect from him. He owed her this.

"I give you my word."

He only hoped it wouldn't come back to haunt him.

HE STAYED PUT all day on Monday the twenty-first of June. He'd rescheduled a couple of meetings with department heads at Miller Insulation so he could remain in the temporary office he'd set up in Susan's study. He'd been trying to make sense of the report his market analyst had faxed over that morning. They were researching sites for a couple more factories in other parts of the country so they'd be ready to begin production as soon as the Miller deal went through.

Michael was also working on profit margins—comparing the projected cost of production and distribution against the estimated consumer price.

And he was reaching for the phone every time it rang. He hadn't asked Susan what time her appointment with the doctor was, so had no way of knowing when he could expect a call from her.

Although he'd tried, he couldn't quite forget that she was finding out whether they were having sons or daughters. Or one of each. The fact that he might care enough to want to know scared the hell out of him.

As it turned out, the time of her appointment didn't matter. Susan didn't phone at all. When five o'clock rolled around, and he realized she wasn't going to, he'd convinced himself that he was glad. It was probably for the best if she didn't include him every step of the way.

TOO BURSTING with news to go home and pretend she wasn't, too excited to keep her newfound knowledge to herself, Susan returned to the office after her late-afternoon doctor's appointment and called her father.

"It's a boy *and* a girl!" she said as soon as he picked up the phone.

"One of each, eh, girl?"

Beaming, Susan glanced at her desktop calendar. "Yep."

"I wish your mother were here. She'd be beside herself."

"I know, Pop. Me, too."

Silence fell with their shared loneliness. "You sure you know what you're doing, girl?" Simon Carmichael asked a little self-consciously. "Sure you aren't just bucking convention for the sake of bucking it?"

She wasn't *sure* about anything anymore. Except that she loved her babies with all her heart and couldn't imagine not having them. "I know you all think I'm crazy, Pop, but I'm a big girl now, almost forty. Certainly old enough to make my own decisions."

"If you say so." She heard the doubt in his voice. The resignation, too. "You know you can call if you need anything, anything at all."

"I know, Pop, thanks."

"You hear any more from that ex-husband of yours?"

Susan hadn't told anyone who'd fathered her children, hadn't told anyone except Seth that she hadn't done this clinically, but she knew they all assumed—maybe even hoped—that Michael was responsible.

"Actually, he's been staying at the condo for the past couple of weeks. He's in town on business." She had no idea what had made her say that. Susan had learned long ago to keep her private life private. Not many people understood her untraditional choices. And she'd grown tired of defending them.

"Good."

"Good?"

"I'm glad he's there. A woman needs a man around to take care of her at a time like this...."

Susan tuned out.

Some things just never changed.

SUSAN CALLED her brothers next, reaching everyone but Seth who was in town but not anywhere Susan could find him. The brothers' reactions were all similar to her father's. With the exception of Stephen, who'd been in the middle of some important nuclear-scientist thought when she'd called and probably wouldn't even remember that they'd spoken. None of them—including Seth—really understood her. They all thought she was off her rocker. And they all told her to call if she needed anything.

If she did, they'd come running. En masse. She knew that as surely as she knew they'd never include her in their annual golf outing. As surely as she knew they loved her unconditionally.

She could hardly ask for anything more.

Except maybe a lover who'd make love to her.

Pulling onto her street around seven o'clock that evening, Susan frowned. There was an old and completely unfamiliar car parked in her drive. She wasn't expecting anyone. The visitor had to be Michael's.

What a night for him to have company.

"Okay, you two, we'll just have to keep our news to ourselves. Probably for the best, anyway," she said aloud, parking out in the street in front of the condo. Michael couldn't even come to terms with generic babies, let alone the pair who'd just taken on form and personality. "Just see that you play nice, tonight, kids."

Someone kicked in response as she got out of the car, and Susan laughed.

One of each. She couldn't believe how lucky she was. A son *and* a daughter. Boy clothes and girl clothes. Brownies and Cub Scouts. Makeup and fast cars. She'd have it all.

Or so she told herself.

"I'll just be going then," a construction worker, minus his hard hat and tool belt, was leaving as Susan approached the front door.

"Thanks for bringing him by," she heard Michael say from the shadows of the foyer.

"No problem," he called. And then, "Ma'am," as he strode past Susan.

"What's—"

With a finger to his lips, Michael nodded toward the living room just as they both heard a resounding crash.

And a very loud curse.

"Seth?" Running into the living room, she saw her brother picking himself up from the floor, clutching pieces of a broken lamp.

"Sorry, sis," he slurred. "It moved."

"Seth Carmichael, sit down before you break anything else," she commanded, worried sick about her brother. If he kept this drinking up, he was going to find himself in jail.

"I've got coffee started," Michael said, helping Seth onto the couch. "I'll go get him a cup."

"Pud a liddle whiskey in it, would ya." Seth's attempt to point landed in his lap with a thud.

"Forget it, buddy." Susan wasn't even a little bit sympathetic.

"Ah, Sus, lighten up."

"Not till you sober up, Seth, and then we're going to talk."

Two cups of coffee later, Seth was a little more manageable, but not much. It was all she and Michael could do to keep him in her living room—he was hell-bent on leaving for someplace that served liquor—while trying to preserve Susan's belongings in the process. There'd been another casualty after the lamp. A ceramic vase she'd bought in Mexico.

"C'mon, Seth, old man," Michael said after he'd vacuumed up the shattered pieces of the vase. "It's cold-shower time."

"I 'on't need a shower."

"Yes." Michael was gritting his teeth as he heaved Seth off the couch, shouldering the majority of the younger man's weight. "You do."

Pulling clumsily out of Michael's grasp, Seth sniffed in the general vicinity of his underarms. "I stink?"

"You're drunk, man."

"I know." Seth smiled happily. "Ain't it great?"

Frightened by the implications of Seth's emotional state, Susan got out a clean towel and collected a pair of Michael's pants. Keeping her eyes averted, she delivered them to the guest bathroom.

"I'll make a fresh pot of coffee," she said and left the two men to their task.

She owed Michael big-time for this one.

"I got no undies on," Seth announced, entering the kitchen twenty minutes later. His speech was still slurred, but at least he was walking on his own. More or less.

"Sorry, brother, I don't share Skivvies." Michael

came up behind him. He was still wearing the twill shorts and polo shirt he'd had on earlier. They were drenched.

Guiding Seth to a chair, he turned to Susan. "I'm going to change." And then to Seth. "Your sister's in no state to be chasing after you," he said sternly. "You stay put until I get back, got it?"

"Yessir." Seth grinned. "Got it."

It had been so long since she'd seen that grin on her usually fun-loving, easygoing brother. She hadn't realized how much she'd missed it. She wondered if she'd ever see it again without its being alcohol-induced.

The more Seth sobered up, the more depressed he became. By ten o'clock that night, the three of them were seated around the kitchen table, not a smiling face in the bunch.

"I've looked everywhere I can think of, and there's nothing," Seth was saying, staring into yet another cup of coffee. "No decent jobs around here at all."

In spite of her confidences the day he'd taken her out to the ghettolike home of his ex-girlfriend, Seth was still talking about finding a new job, one that didn't require as much travel. Sharing a silent communication with Michael, Susan remained silent.

"Sure," he continued, not looking up. "I can get work, had lots of offers, but nothing that pays enough to support myself properly, let alone anyone else."

Susan wanted to help him. To tell him that no woman was worth doing this to himself. That there was nothing wrong with his job, with him. That other engineers got married.

Michael reached for her hand under the table, giving it a squeeze. Holding on.

"Funny thing is," Seth said with a humorless laugh, "I'm not like you, Michael." He stared up at Michael. "My job isn't my identification. It's not everything to me."

Jaw tight, Michael nodded—and let go of her hand. Susan's gaze darted from one to the other. Seth saw Michael's job as his *identification?* Like he had some kind of emotional—not logical—dependence on it? Was that true? And if it was, why hadn't she seen it?

"I like what I do," Seth went on. "Hell, I love what I do. I'm damn good at it."

"The best." Susan finally had to say something.

"I don't know about that." Seth sent her a slanted glance. "But the bottom line is, it's all I'm trained for. It's all I *can* do if I'm to make a decent living."

Relieved that Seth was finally coming to his senses, Susan relaxed in her chair. "There's nothing wrong with that."

"Yeah," he said bitterly. "There is."

Michael was frowning. "Why?" he challenged.

"Because unlike you, old buddy, I want a family."

"Uncle Bill, on *Family Affair,* was an engineer," Susan quickly pointed out. "And he raised three kids."

"He had Mr. French," Seth argued.

"But he didn't have a wife—or mother—for the kids," Michael said, joining in.

"And those kids couldn't have asked for a better life," Susan said. "Buffy and Jody were happy, well-adjusted children. And why? Because they always knew they were loved."

As if realizing as much himself, Michael nodded. "Cissy, too," he added. "Sure, there were times when they missed Bill, but they did fine."

"Just think how excited they got whenever Uncle Bill was home. Think of the quality time he spent with them."

Seth listened, his face lighting with a trace of hope. But only briefly. Shoulders slumped, he finished his coffee and stood up. "You two are really sick, you know that?" he said. "You're talking about a thirty-year-old television show like it really happened. This is real life. Now will one of you please take me home?"

"Not yet," Susan said firmly as both men started to stand.

Staring at her, they both settled back in their chairs. "Yes, this *is* real life Seth, and in real life, there are a lot of kids who have no father at all. And there are thousands of kids right here in this city whose fathers live in the same house with them, are home every night, and are still strangers to them."

"So?" Seth's question wasn't quite belligerent, but Susan had a feeling he'd wanted it to be.

"I guess what she's saying, man, is that a good weekend dad is a hell of a lot better than no dad at all."

"What I'm saying," Susan said, taking in both men with her lawyer stare, "is that any kid who has a good dad—even one he sees only once or twice a year—is a damn lucky kid. Just knowing the man's out there to lean on, to call, to go to for help, even if that help comes over thousands of miles of phone wire, gives the kid an edge."

Susan's heart sank when she saw the indulgent look shared by two of the most infuriating men in her life. "Of course, this comes from the woman who thinks that caring for two children will be just as easy as caring for one," Michael said.

"The same woman who's planning to continue her career as always, in spite of midnight feedings, colicky babies and mornings with messy crib sheets, diapers and babies."

Tuning out Seth *and* Michael, she felt sorry for both of them. They were just too stubborn to realize they really could have it all.

SUSAN WAS already in bed by the time Michael returned from Seth's. Strangely depressed himself after the evening with his ex-brother-in-law, he undressed quickly and slid in beside her. Instantly hard, just from her warmth, he moved a little closer. She was asleep. She'd never know if he stole a little comfort.

Slipping his arm carefully around her belly, he settled himself on his side behind her and closed his eyes. There were many forms of torture. And many forms of heaven. He figured he'd found one of each.

The first time it happened, he was drifting in a state of semiconsciousness, floating in and out of a dream.

By the second kick, he was fully awake, waiting.

Heart beating rapidly, he lay completely still, resisting the urge to cup his hand around that movement. To claim it.

There was a baby in there. Alive. Real.

Another kick came, but this blow landed on his forearm. Either the sucker was a fast mover or...

There were two babies in there. Two lives he'd

helped create. Amazingly, he didn't feel any immediate sense of foreboding, any of the familiar chains
closing around his throat. They'd follow. He knew
that. But for now…

Exhausted beyond the ability to analyze, Michael
moved a little closer. Flattening his hand softly
against Susan's stomach, careful not to disturb her,
he gave in to the need to connect with his children.

And then, oddly comforted, he slept.

MICHAEL WAS GONE when Susan awoke the next
morning. If not for the indentation of his head on the
pillow beside hers, the rumpled covers, she'd never
have known he was there.

She'd dreamed of him all night long.

To the point of frustration. She was horny as hell.

Based on the way things were going, she was almost relieved when he called her at work later that
morning to tell her he'd be gone for a couple of days.
He had to make a quick trip to Atlanta.

She needed a break from the tension. A little time
to herself to distinguish between her needs and her
wants. To be honest with herself.

A little time to determine whether or not she could
let Michael come back.

CHAPTER FOURTEEN

AS IT TURNED OUT, she didn't have a chance to make that decision. Michael was in her study, deeply involved in a telephone conversation when she arrived home from work on Thursday. She'd been playing phone tag with him all week and, as a result, hadn't spoken to him since he left.

She wasn't sure if that was deliberate or not. Her fault or his.

She just knew she'd never been happier to see him there.

Embarrassed by the relieved tears that sprang to her eyes, she gave him a quick wave and hurried in to change her clothes. Or rather, to get herself under control. Changing her clothes was an afterthought.

"New dress?" Michael asked, following her into the bedroom a few minutes later.

"Uh-huh, bought it yesterday." She turned and modeled it for him. "You like it?"

A light cotton, tank-style sundress, Susan had found it so comfortable she'd actually picked out seven of them. In varying shades. Tonight she'd chosen the dark-gold one because of the way it brought out the highlights in her hair. "I do like it," he said, pulling her into his arms. "I like you, too."

She saw his lips descending, her heart quickening

so fast it stole her breath. Too needy to think, she welcomed him, kissing him back as desperately as he was kissing her.

He was touching her again.

He felt so good, she trembled.

"It's been one hell of a long three weeks," he grumbled against her lips. And then he consumed them again. Consumed all her senses. The light musky scent of his aftershave, the salty taste of his lips, his voice deep and low moaning his desire, the coarse touch of his thick dark hair sliding through her fingers, the sight of him, there, with her.

The long fast had ended. And her celebration was too intense to deny him anything he asked of her.

His hands worked their familiar magic as he quickly stripped her of the dress she'd just donned. A moment later, he'd added her bra and underwear to the pile on the floor.

"You've blossomed," he said, splaying his hands across her breasts, cupping them.

"Mmm-hmm," Susan murmured, inanely proud of herself.

"I've missed you." Lowering his head, he took her lips again, holding the contact as he urged her back on the bed.

His suit and other things soon landed on the floor with hers and then he was inside her, his hands everywhere, his body her only reality as he brought her to one of the fastest climaxes of her life.

"Guess being pregnant has its side effects," she gasped, out of breath and slightly embarrassed by her unusual haste.

Stilling inside her for a moment while her tremors

subsided, Michael grinned. "Care to do research on that theory?"

"Anytime." She was promising him everything. Anything he wanted. As much as he wanted. Knowing that, in the end, he might want nothing at all.

And then she was floating again, caught up in the power of his loving as he accompanied her toward an incredible climax, her name on his lips.

HE LAY BESIDE HER afterward, belly to belly, just as he'd loved her, until one of the babies gave a kick so mighty it made her grunt.

"Whoa, there, little fella," she murmured without thinking. She'd been having complete conversations with the kids ever since she'd found out their sexes.

"So you know they're boys?" He hadn't moved an inch, but Susan could feel Michael's distance as physically as though he'd gotten up and left the room.

Shivering, she pulled the bedspread up.

"One of them is," she said softly, tucking the spread around her belly.

Michael's gaze flew to hers, serious, searching. "There's one of each?"

Susan nodded, biting her lip.

He turned over, lying flat on his back, eyes wide-open as he stared at the ceiling.

In spite of herself, Susan was a little distracted by the gorgeous perfection of his body. And his unselfconsciousness where his own nakedness was concerned.

At least with him to concentrate on, she didn't have to focus on what might really be happening.

"I suppose one of each is best." He broke into her thoughts, his chin firm as he made the assertion.

Stunned at his calmness, she rose on one elbow and stared at him.

"I would imagine raising a girl is vastly different from raising a boy. So even if this is your only pregnancy, you still get a chance to do both." He turned and looked at her.

Afraid to move, to disrupt the tender mood between them, Susan tried to read him. Tried not to be disappointed when she couldn't.

"That's what I thought," she said instead.

"Might make things a little more difficult as far as some of the practicalities are concerned." He was staring at the ceiling again.

"How so?"

"Well, they won't be able to share clothes for one thing."

"But I get to buy both now, little dresses *and* little suits."

Michael was off the bed so fast, Susan's head was spinning. He grabbed a pair of denim shorts out of the drawer she'd emptied for him when he'd first come to stay, then pulled them on.

"I'm hungry," he announced abruptly as he chose a shirt from the closet. "Italian sound okay to you?"

"Sure." These days, any food sounded okay to her. She got up more slowly, untangled her clothes from the pile on the floor.

"I'll run and get some take-out," he said, tying his tennis shoes with a flourish. "Be right back."

And he was gone. She'd barely stepped into her underwear.

MICHAEL WORKED most of Saturday, partially because he wasn't getting a good feeling about the Miller deal. There was no indication of anything going sour. Exactly the opposite. But *something* bothered him....

He'd also kept himself busy because he'd known Susan would be home. And spending the day together, like any normal couple, didn't seem wise.

Yet, when he finished late in the afternoon, he was inordinately disappointed to go looking for her and find her gone. And then relieved when he saw the note on the kitchen table.

She was at the complex pool. He was welcome to join her there if he wanted to.

He didn't know if he wanted to or not, but ten minutes later, dressed in black boxer trunks and carrying glasses of iced peppermint tea, he joined her.

"I thought you might be thirsty," he said, settling down on the lounge chair next to her. She was wearing a black, flowing maternity suit that looked sexier than the bikini he'd seen her in the year before.

"Thanks." She smiled at him as she took a glass of the tea and sipped greedily. He wished her eyes weren't hidden by the dark lenses of her sunglasses.

"You been in?" he asked, pointing toward the pool.

"A couple of times. The water's nice."

If he got any hotter, he was going to have to go in, too. Or give himself away. He'd loved Susan again the night before, but frequency didn't seem to have any more quelling effect on his libido than abstinence did. He watched a couple of kids playing water tag at the other end of the pool.

"How'd the work go?"

"Hmm?" He glanced over at her again. "Oh. Fine."

"This deal's certainly taking longer than you originally figured. Is the family hesitant?"

"Not really." Michael took a sip of his tea. The combination of icy liquid and hot sun was pleasant. "They've made the decision to sign whenever I tell them to."

"So what's holding you up?"

"Nothing particularly valid, I'm afraid."

Sipping her tea, Susan frowned. "That doesn't sound like you."

He looked away. "Miller Insulation isn't just a way for this family to support themselves. I'm paying them millions, and the money isn't that important to them."

"Surely they were excited by making that kind of money so quickly."

"At first, of course." He met her gaze, searching for understanding, for confirmation of something he was only beginning to understand himself. "But it doesn't seem to hold much allure anymore. The company seems to represent some kind of bond for them, probably because they all sacrificed together to start it. Now it's something that holds them together."

"Kind of like Halliday Headgear, a family venture. Or like Halliday's will be when Tricia's sons are grown."

"Maybe." Probably. "Could you ever have pictured Ed Halliday being happy doing anything other than running Halliday's?"

"Of course not," Susan said without hesitation.

"He loved every minute he spent there. Leaving would have killed him before the heart attack did."

Michael nodded, his chest heavy. "Miller Insulation gives that family reason to get up in the morning. Running the company fulfills them. When I buy them out, I take away one of their major reasons for living."

He hated sounding melodramatic, but he was afraid there was complete truth in what he was saying.

"Have they given you any indication that they want to back out of the deal?"

"None." Michael shook his head. "That's the damnedest part. They're going to go through with this as soon as I give the word."

"How does that make you feel?"

No one but Susan could get away with asking him a question like that. No one but Susan would get an answer.

"Like a damn criminal."

He glanced over at her, not at all surprised to see her nodding. "So what are you going to do about that?" she asked.

"I don't know, smarty-pants," he mocked her. Then, just in case, he asked, "Do you?"

Shaking her head, she shrugged, sent him an impudent grin. "I'm sure you'll figure it out, whatever it is."

Michael set down his glass. "Thanks for the vote of confidence," he said, rising. "I think." With that, he dove headfirst into the pool.

HE MADE LOVE to her every night that next week. Driven by something he didn't understand, or maybe something he *did* understand and wasn't ready to acknowledge, he loved her with an urgency he'd never known before. Not even when their divorce had become inevitable, the final court date imminent, had he been filled with such a sense of energized desperation.

One way or another, his time at Miller Insulation was coming to a close. His time in Cincinnati was coming to an end. And, as that day drew near, he found he didn't have any plans not to go. He wanted to tell Susan that he'd stay, that he'd be the perfect father to her children. But he couldn't. He just didn't have any confidence in his ability to do so. He was afraid he'd suffocate within a week of the declaration. And he couldn't lie to her.

One of the babies moved again on Wednesday night, just after Michael and Susan had made love. It wasn't a kick this time, but a heel or something sliding across her entire belly, sticking out as it went. They both watched its progress.

"Can you feel that?" Michael whispered, as though he'd disturb the children if he spoke any louder.

"Of course," she laughed. "You try being rubbed from the inside out."

Michael couldn't imagine the feeling, but he knew what it felt like to carry a lead weight around in his chest. A weight that was getting heavier by the hour.

He'd never experienced a stronger need to get up and go, to run as far and as fast as he could. Or to stay.

"Have you decided what to name them?" he asked instead, studying the mound of her stomach.

Susan frowned. "I change my mind at least twice a day. There are so many names I like."

That sounded like Susan. If she could get away with it, she'd pin a minimum of six names on each kid.

"Remember to pay attention to initials," he told her, rolling over to lie on his back, staring at the shadows on the ceiling. "Kids can be awfully cruel when they tease, and names and initials always seem to be a target."

"So I can't name her Katy Kathleen 'cause she'd be KKK, huh?"

Katy Kathleen *Kennedy*. *His* name. That he'd given to Susan and she'd kept after the divorce.

"Right," he said, jumping up as if self-propelled, shrugging into his robe. "Want a snack?"

"I'm not hungry," Susan surprised him by saying. She was always hungry these days.

He shouldn't have been surprised, though. He wasn't hungry, either.

But he escaped to the kitchen anyway. Dished himself a bowl of ice cream he didn't want. And then, while it melted beside him, took up paper and pencil and doodled.

What was the matter with him? What in *hell* was the matter with him that he checked out anytime she got too close, anytime those babies got too close? Michael wished to God he knew. Wished he could control the claustrophobic dizziness that assailed him anytime he tried to force himself into a decision about the children.

One thing was for certain. He couldn't keep on like this much longer. Couldn't keep hurting Susan. There didn't seem to be much point in moving forward when there were some fundamental things that couldn't be changed.

Zack Kennedy. He looked down at what he'd written. A good name for a boy. Short. Strong. Solid.

If the boy were his, he'd name him Zack.

LAURA WAS getting desperate. In the four weeks since Jeremy had announced he was quitting soccer, the boy had been late for school six times, he'd been held for detention twice, and failed an exam. Looking around to make sure no one was paying attention to her, she stole over to the computer cubicle in one corner of Jenny's classroom and logged on to the Internet. She was at the school to volunteer, but the class was having reading time. That gave her fifteen minutes.

Moving around the Internet much more slowly than her kids would have done, she managed to find a search engine, and then a button to click on to find people. A prompt asked her to type in the name of the person.

She did that. And waited nervously, glancing over her shoulder every couple of seconds. It wasn't that anyone cared whether she played around on the computer; she just didn't want to have to explain what she was doing. Not even to herself if truth be known.

Had she no pride?

And then, just that easily, up popped a listing— name, address, phone number. And even a place she could click on to see a map.

She clicked. And printed. Snatching up the page as

soon as the printer let go of it, she folded it and slipped it inside her purse.

She was armed.

MICHAEL WAS making her walk on a treadmill. He'd brought one home the day before without even discussing it first and set it up in her study. "To make the birth's easier," he'd said.

And because Susan was so crazy in love with him, so thrilled that he'd cared enough to buy the stupid thing, she was treading quite sweatily Saturday morning.

She just wished Michael looked as pleased to have her on it as he'd looked bringing it home the night before.

"You sure you feel okay?" she asked for the second time.

He glanced up from the papers he'd been studying. "Fine, why?"

"I don't know." Susan held her side as she trod, wondering why something that was so good for you had to feel so bad. "You've been awfully quiet."

"We've only been up for half an hour." Head bent, he returned to the business in front of him.

She tried to catch his eye the next time he glanced up. He managed not to notice.

"My folks invited us to their place tomorrow." His words came out of nowhere.

Susan's heart gave a little jolt—even more than it was already jolting. She'd always adored Michael's parents. But she hadn't known he'd told them—

"There's a family reunion planned, a picnic."

A Fourth of July picnic. And she'd been planning

to stay home and get caught up on laundry, reading, lying by the pool—anything that would keep her close in case Michael had some time to spend with her.

"Are you asking me to go?" she finally murmured when he said nothing else.

Arms crossed at his chest, he sat back in his chair. "They don't know about you."

There was no reason to feel disappointed. After all, she'd assumed as much. "About the babies, you mean."

"About any pregnancy at all."

Susan nodded. She understood. "So you're going alone." And she was on her own for the holiday. No big deal. She had that laundry and reading and...

Coming around to the front of the desk, Michael leaned back against it, close enough for her to touch. "I don't know what to tell them, Sus."

"You don't have to tell them anything," she panted. "I'm not pinning these babies on you."

"They know we still see each other...."

"What if I'd had artificial insemination?" One foot in front of the other. Nothing more than that required. Just one foot at a time. Easy. "Insemination was always one way to meet my goal." Not that she'd have done it. She'd need to know far more about the father of her child than the reports prepared by a clinic.

"Those babies..." He swallowed, looked down at her bulging stomach covered by the cotton T-shirt and shorts she was sweating in. "They're my parents' grandchildren, Susan. My parents are their grandparents. They have a right to know each other."

She hadn't dared hope that could ever be. At least, she'd tried not to.

"They have as much right as your father has to know them," he said, his chin jutting almost defensively.

"Is that what you want?" she asked him. Didn't he know that all he had to do was say so?

Michael stood up, strode to the window, lifted it to let in a fresh Cincinnati breeze. "I don't think it matters what I want or don't want in this situation," he said. He'd moved to the far wall, straightening a picture. Susan was getting dizzy—keeping up with him, treading and breathing, all at once.

They were right back to square one. And she wasn't sure how much more energy she had. "Of course what you want matters," she told him. She couldn't seem to come up with another way to tell him that she wasn't going to be responsible for ruining his life. That he was under no obligation, that there was no reason for him to give up what he was to become something he was not.

"Not in this case." He sat back down beside her. "The children are people, Susan, with rights and freedoms of their own. My parents, too. What right do you or I have to keep them apart?"

She frowned. She hadn't thought of it like that. Hadn't thought her choice to become a mother would have such far-reaching effects on so many people. "I just—"

"Sure," he interrupted, his brow furrowed. "We can keep them apart easily enough in the beginning. But what about later?" He turned and locked gazes with her. "What happens when the children find out about me and look up my family? I'll tell you what. They'll all have lost years of a relationship that they'll never be able to regain. Can you do that to them? To any of them?''

She couldn't even think about doing it. But she couldn't *not* do it, either, if that was what Michael needed. ''You've given this a lot of thought.''

''Haven't you?'' He looked surprised.

''I really believed that my decision to have a baby was a very personal one,'' she said, studying a spot on her off-white carpet. She'd never felt less intelligent in her life. ''And that as long as I was willing, ready and able to bear the total responsibility on my own, I was doing no one any harm.'' She turned off the treadmill and came to a stop.

''I wish it was that easy.''

''Yeah,'' she said, sharing a sad smile with him. ''Me, too.'' And then, softly, ''I'm sorry, Michael. I never meant…''

''Shhh.'' He placed a finger on her lips. ''I know.''

She cradled her stomach, loving the babies too much to feel that having them was wrong. And yet…

''So what are we going to tell my parents?''

As much as she wanted to go home with Michael, to be welcomed into that fold, she knew she couldn't. ''We don't have to tell them anything yet, do we?'' she asked. ''At least until the babies are born.''

She had to give Michael all the time she could, all the freedom she could, to determine for himself what part he'd play in their lives.

''My mother and sisters would have a shower for you.''

She would have loved every minute of it, too. ''I'll

have just as much fun picking everything out on my own," she said instead.

"But they'd love to do that, and more. To share in the anticipation of the coming babies. My mom would start sewing immediately. And bragging."

"Michael." She stepped closer to him, running her fingers through his hair. "You aren't responsible for everyone's happiness, you know," she said. "Yes, they'd probably like knowing right now, but it's not going to kill them if they don't. You need to think of yourself."

"Seems to me that's all I've been doing since this whole thing began. Probably before that, too."

"No more than anyone else," she told him adamantly, "and less than most."

He said nothing, just walked with her as she headed toward a shower. "You've spent your entire career listening to your customers, making sure you give them only what they need, not what it would most benefit you to sell them. They come away from transactions with you feeling cared for, not used."

"That's just—"

"And what about Bobbie Jayne?" she interrupted. "Every time that child needs a bandage, you're there, not only paying for it, but making sure it's properly applied."

He propped his shoulder against the door of the bathroom. "She doesn't ask for much."

"That's not the point." She pushed off her tennis shoes and socks. "The point is, you care, and you help, every single time she calls. And what about Melanie Dryson?"

"What about her?" A sexy half grin lingered on

his face as he watched her strip down, piece by sweaty piece.

"You stuck your nose out more than once to see that she got the promotions and the credit she deserved."

Completely naked, Susan stepped into the shower, pulling the curtain behind her.

The water, once it warmed, felt wonderful on her skin, soothing muscles that were already tired so early in the day.

"How 'bout I give you something *you* deserve, stripping like that so delicately right in front of me?"

Opening her eyes, Susan saw Michael standing in the shower with her, utterly gorgeous in his masculine perfection. Utterly naked. And wanting her.

"How 'bout it?" she asked him.

He proceeded to do that very well. And if there was a hint of desperation in their lovemaking these days, she tried very hard not to notice.

CHAPTER FIFTEEN

"Can I ask you something?" Susan asked later, watching as he brushed his wet hair into some semblance of order.

"Of course."

"These past three years, before I got pregnant, were you happy?"

He waited so long to answer her stomach tensed.

"I was content, sure."

Content. Not happy. Why wasn't she surprised?

As she toasted bagels and Michael mixed up some orange juice, Susan wondered if he'd ever been happy. If he even knew what the word meant. If, maybe, the problem wasn't about goals and dreams and being who you were, but about never reaching quite far enough. Never asking for it all. And never relaxing enough to even know if he had it.

Needing to put some distance between her and Michael, Susan went shopping right after breakfast. Baby clothes and toys, bottles and diapers were all happy things. And she got really, really happy. So happy that there was barely room for her in the Infiniti when she finally called it quits midafternoon. She had enough stuff for three baby showers. And she even had mints and chips and probably some peanuts to go with the loot. She'd have herself a party.

Another strange, and very old, car was blocking her drive when she arrived home. Heart plunging, she groaned. "Ah, Seth." If he was blasted this early in the day, she was taking him straight to detox.

"Close your ears, little ones," she instructed firmly as she headed empty-handed up the walk. The baby shower was going to have to wait.

On the alert, she let herself in, listening carefully to gauge how bad things were.

Shock held her immobile two steps inside the door. That wasn't Seth's voice.

"You're such a nice man." The voice was definitely feminine. And the woman just a tad too fond of Michael, in Susan's opinion.

And since the house was Susan's, hers was the opinion that counted. Set on charging the living room like a pit bull, she stopped suddenly, struck by a thought that left her weak and shaking.

Michael mattered that much to her. The idea of him with another woman was enough to make her insane.

She was acting as if he still belonged to her. As if he were her husband—and the father of her children. She could no longer hide from the truth. She was not only hopelessly, illogically, passionately in love with him, she truly didn't think she could live without him. For real. Until that moment, she'd never actually faced the fact that she might have to try.

Which meant she *had* tried to trap him.

As her thoughts fell over themselves, they became increasingly dangerous. If she felt these things, wasn't it possible, probable even, that Michael felt them, too? From her? That all the while her mouth had been telling him he was free to go, her eyes and heart were telling him something completely different?

Oh, God. Her fingers to her lips, she searched for a way to escape.

"Susan? Is that you?" Michael was calling her.

She made a dash for the hall, but ran into Michael as he came out of the living room. "There's someone here to see you," he said. With one glance at her face he stopped.

"You okay?"

Nodding her head jerkily, Susan tried to think, to behave normally. "Just have to go to the bathroom." She blurted the only thing that came to mind. "You know how it is with pregnant women."

Babbling like an idiot, she made a dash for their bedroom, ran into the adjoining bath and locked the door.

For want of something better to do, she splashed water on her face—and then repaired her makeup.

"I can think about this later," she told her children who were protesting the butterflies that were sharing their space. "I'll get rid of whoever's come to see me, if she really did come to see me, and then claim I need a nap."

With a plan, she felt a little better, but stopped again, just as she was about to open the bathroom door.

"I really do need a nap," she said to her stomach. "I wouldn't lie to Michael, not ever."

Except she had. She'd been lying all along.

MICHAEL WATCHED Susan closely as she joined them in the living room. Relieved to see that her color was back, he smiled at her. She'd been sickly white when she'd first come in from shopping.

Their guest jumped up from the couch as Susan approached. "Hi," she said, holding out her hand. "I'm Laura Sinclair."

Michael almost felt sorry for the woman, standing up to Susan's intimidating once-over—followed by her clear lack of recognition.

"What can I do for you, Ms. Sinclair?"

"You've never heard of me." Michael's sympathy for their pretty blond guest grew. Her glance darted toward the door.

"Laura's the woman Seth told you about," he said quickly, before the other woman decided to run.

"*You're* Seth's woman?" Susan asked, her eyes wide as they took in Laura's long blond hair, faded blue jeans, the old but neatly ironed blouse that accented her tiny waist. "He's got better taste than I realized." Susan grinned and Michael, standing with his hands in the pockets of his shorts, relaxed just a little.

Laura's brow was still furrowed, her eyes worried. "So you have heard of me?"

"I actually know more about you from what Seth hasn't said than what he has," Susan said frankly. "Have a seat." She led the woman over to the couch. "Can I get you something to drink?"

Classic Susan, handling everything, Michael thought with admiration. Almost six months pregnant with twins, she'd been shopping all day, and with a quick trip to freshen up, was now playing the perfect hostess.

Laura declined the drink, but she sat. After Susan had joined her, Michael sat, too, in a chair opposite them.

"You're probably both wondering why I'm here," Laura said, twisting her fingers in her lap as she gazed earnestly from one to the other.

Susan sent Michael a worried look. And because he knew her well enough to read her mind, he quickly reassured her.

"I explained to Laura that I was an old friend staying with you while I'm in town on business."

"I'm sorry," Laura said, still fidgeting with her hands. "I didn't catch your name."

"Michael," he and Susan answered in unison. Both forgoing the surname that would surely bring more questions than either of them was prepared to answer.

"Then you're—" Laura broke off, bright color creeping up her cheeks. "I'm sorry," she said. "It's just that Seth told me a lot more about you two than he apparently told you about me."

"Oh," they both answered again.

Damn. Restless, Michael stood. "I'm going to the kitchen for some tea. You ladies sure you don't want anything?" he asked.

He barely heard their requests for tea because he was already down the hall. Escaping from the watchful eyes of a stranger who knew what he'd done. Fathered a child with the full intent of abandoning all responsibility for it.

Escaping, too, from the pressure that had been slowly building all these months. The pressure to just give in. He'd had to leave before he made promises he wasn't sure he could keep. He'd almost told Laura that it wasn't the way she thought, that Seth didn't know everything. He'd almost told her he was in town because he had every intention of marrying Susan again. And of being a proper father to his children.

He poured three glasses of iced tea, the peppermint tea he'd begun to favor since her pregnancy.

And had himself more firmly under control as he carried them to the living room. He'd done nothing but grant his ex-wife a favor, given her something that apparently mattered more to her than life itself, saved her from throwing herself at the mercy of some unknown man who might have done far worse than leave her with his child growing in her womb.

So why, since that fateful Super Bowl weekend, had he felt no higher than a slug in the mud? Unfortunately, he was pretty sure it had nothing to do with Atlanta losing.

SURPRISING HERSELF, Laura liked Susan. A lot. She was intimidated by Seth's older sister. Sure. Who wouldn't be? The woman was a hotshot lawyer, and gorgeous to boot. Six months pregnant and her hair was styled and beautiful, her makeup impeccable. And the only place she'd gained any weight was her stomach. Laura had had fat arms. She'd hated that.

But she wasn't there on a social call. She waited until Michael returned with their tea, and then dove in before she could change her mind again and bolt.

"I'm sorry to bother you both," she heard herself say and followed the words with a silent reprimand. She'd decided to think more positively. Which meant presenting herself in a positive light. She tried again. "Thanks for seeing me."

"You're welcome," Susan said, grinning at Michael, who remained silent. Laura was so envious of them it hurt. It was obvious just being with them during this short period of time how attuned they were to each other.

Laura had once believed she and Seth were that connected, too.

"I just had to do something," she blurted as the pain rose once again to swamp her.

"About what?" Susan's voice was warm, her eyes soft and concerned.

"I've made a mess of things." As usual. "And now I'm not sure how to go about fixing them."

"And you thought I could help?"

Laura had a feeling the woman could do anything she put her mind to. "You know Seth so well," She tried to explain what had sounded so good in the middle of one of her many sleepless nights. "I thought maybe you could give me some direction."

With another quick glance at Michael, Susan included Laura in her smile this time and said, "I'll certainly try."

"I have a son." Laura decided to get it all out there. Licking her dry lips, she yearned for the tea she'd yet to touch.

"I know. Jeremy. I've seen him."

"You have?" Laura was incredulous—and confused.

"Mmm-hmm." Susan nodded encouragingly. "The same day I found out about you."

"Where? When?"

"Seth drove me by a ballpark where Jeremy was practicing soccer. And then around the corner to point out your house."

"That was you?" Laura wanted to laugh, her relief was so great. And to cry.

"What do you mean?"

"Was that maybe six weeks ago?"

"Seems about right."

Hope sprang even in hopeless hearts, it seemed. And then Laura recalled what else Susan had said. "You've seen my house?" She hadn't meant to say the words aloud. Trying to make herself as small as she could, she hoped Susan wasn't worried that Laura was getting her couch dirty.

"Yeah," Susan said. "Seth was staring at your door—and I've never seen such longing in his eyes."

"You must have been mistaken," Laura whispered. Seth had walked out that door of his own accord. Mostly.

"Uh-uh." Susan shook her head so vigorously, the layers of her beautiful hair slapped her face. "I've known Seth his whole life. I could feel his misery as clearly as if it were my own."

Afraid to hope, for fear of her inability to survive another letdown, Laura looked for other possible explanations. And finding none, she changed the subject. Reminded herself what mattered.

"Jeremy saw the two of you," she said.

"Oh."

"He told you this?" Michael asked, speaking for the first time since he'd brought in the tea. His glass was empty.

Laura nodded. "And he hasn't been back to soccer since."

Susan gasped. "Nooo." The one word was so sincere, so full of honest empathy, Laura almost wept. She should've known Susan would be a wonderful person. She'd practically raised Seth, and he was the most honorable man she'd ever met.

"It seems Seth has been watching practices and games from a distance since we, uh, broke up." The explanations came a little easier. "And because of that, Jeremy kept playing. He figured Seth's being there meant Seth still loved us."

"He does."

"Susan…" Michael said in a warning voice.

"He does, Michael," Susan said, meeting her ex-husband's gaze head-on. Laura wished she had half of Susan's gumption. "He does," she said again to Laura. "I don't know what happened between the two of you, but there's no doubt how much my brother loves you."

"Just not enough to marry me." Laura forced herself to acknowledge the truth.

Susan frowned. "How do you know that?"

Sighing, Laura remembered back to that last awful night. She'd handled things so badly, coming at Seth without a hint of finesse. She tried to tell his sister what she'd done—and couldn't. She started to cry instead.

"What happened?" Susan asked, sliding closer to take Laura's hand in her own.

"The kids were getting too attached," Laura said, not bothering to fight the tears. She only had so much strength.

Michael shifted in his seat, drawing Laura's attention, but he didn't say anything, just sat there and frowned. She turned back to Susan.

"My kids have been through a lot."

"I know." Susan's eyes were full of understanding. "Seth told me."

Grateful that she'd been spared that particular explanation, Laura said, "So you can understand that I couldn't risk putting them through another rejection." Laura tried to tell the story without thinking about that last night with Seth. Wiping a tear as it slid down her cheek, she took another deep breath.

"It was getting to the point where they couldn't wait for Seth to come so they could tell him whatever good news they might have. They hung on his opinion, even asked his permission for things."

"And that bothered you?" Susan asked. "Threatened your place as their mother?"

"Good heavens, no!" Laura almost laughed. "I thought it was heaven."

Susan looked a little confused. "So what happened?"

Staring down at her hands, she confessed the rest. "I gave Seth an ultimatum. Told him we either had to have a firm commitment between us or I had to end things right then. Because the kids were already telling their friends he was going to be their new father."

"They couldn't just be happy having him around as a friend of the family?" Michael asked. His hands were clasped, fingers against his lips, as though he were intensely interested in Laura's plight.

She'd wished so many times that things could've

been different for her and Seth. But now she had yet another reason. Her life would have been so blessed if Susan and Michael could have been part of it.

Embarrassed, she was glad her thoughts were her own. What audacious liberties she was taking, even imagining Susan as family.

"It wasn't the time he spent with them or whether or not he lived there so much as the impermanence that bothered me," she finally said. "If Seth didn't love me enough to give me some kind of commitment, then chances were he'd be gone without warning some day." She spoke to both of them. "Whenever someone else came along, or he just plain got tired of me and my kids. I couldn't take that chance. Not with Jeremy and Jenny being so vulnerable."

"Did you explain all of this to Seth?" Susan asked.

"I tried to." Laura was remembering again. Seth had looked so betrayed. She was no longer sure what she'd said.

"The thing is..." Susan spoke slowly, not glancing toward Michael this time. "I think Seth is under the opinion that he'd have to quit his job to be with you."

"What?" Laura squeaked. "I've never heard anything more ludicrous in my life. Seth would never think that!"

"Then why is he drinking himself to death in between scouting all over town for a job that will pay him a decent enough wage to support a family of four?"

Heart pumping hard, Laura froze. "He's doing that?"

"Susan..." Michael warned again.

"I'm sorry, Michael." She cut him off before he

could say anything more. "But I won't see my brother kill himself over something it might be possible to fix. Anyway, I certainly can't hurt him any more than he's already hurting himself."

"Laura." Susan turned back, her gaze intent, full of purpose. "Do you have a problem with Seth being out of town for much of the week?"

She shook her head. "That's the way it's always been."

"Right. So why does he think it has to stop?"

"I have no idea."

"I don't know, either," Susan said, frowning. Like a helpless child Laura simply waited for Susan to come up with an explanation.

"Because he can't be a proper father to those children if he's gone all the time." Michael's words fell quietly into the room.

"Who says?" Susan asked defensively.

"Why not?" Laura challenged simultaneously. "Seth's been more of a father to my kids than their own father ever was. He was over every weekend, coaching ball, playing with them, making them feel important."

Michael's face was resolute. "Our marriage couldn't survive with one of us working out of town, and I hardly think parenting takes less time and commitment than marriage."

"How do you know our marriage couldn't work?" Susan said, staring at Michael. "You never gave it a chance."

"You knew as well I did that it wouldn't have

survived, Susan, or you would never have agreed to divorce in the first place.''

''That's beside the point, anyway,'' Susan told him, leaving Laura to wonder if Susan had ever really given up on her marriage or just given in to Michael. ''We were dealing with you living in another state, working full-time in another state. Seth lives here. He's home every weekend. He just happens to travel, too.''

''All I can tell you is the man believes he can't be a proper father and do what he does, too.''

Laura's heart was beating fast again, though not with fear. With an emotion she was afraid to name. ''He's told you that?'' she asked. Michael sounded awfully sure.

Glancing at Susan, Michael bowed his head once, slowly, and raised it again.

Laura took that for a yes.

''And that's why he left us?'' She looked from one to other, hope an unfamiliar flower blossoming inside her. Taking her breath away.

''I think so,'' Michael said.

''Me, too.'' The tears in Susan's eyes won Laura's heart forever. ''If he's been contemplating quitting his job to be a father, I'd say there's little chance it's anything else.''

''Do you know where he is today?'' Laura whispered, tears flooding her own eyes.

''At home.''

Laura minded her manners enough to down her tea in one long gulp, and then, with embarrassing haste, grabbed her purse and ran. She had a very stupid man to set straight.

And then she was going to spend the rest of her life loving him to distraction.

CHAPTER SIXTEEN

"An Sooz! An Sooz!" Susan's stomach roiled as two-year-old Joey barreled into her.

How'd she ever get herself into this?

Grabbing him up, she pretended her back didn't hurt as she settled him atop the mound of her stomach. "You're supposed to be sound asleep, little man," she said, heading back toward his nursery.

She'd been looking forward to this evening ever since Scott and Julie had asked her the previous week to baby-sit for them. She'd been eager to get a taste of the joys she'd been anticipating all these months.

She hadn't figured on Joey having his own plans.

"I wet," Joey announced, right about the time Susan started to feel an uncomfortable warmth seeping through her maternity blouse.

"You sure are wet," she said, hugging the little body against her. After all, it wasn't his fault she'd let him have three glasses of water that first hour after she'd put him to bed. He'd looked so darn cute, holding that cup by its handles.

"I wet," Joey said again, nodding his head.

Ignoring the tug on her back muscles, Susan hauled the toddler up to his changing table and set about repairing the damage. Getting the clothes off him was the easy part. But then, instead of lying there quietly the way she thought he was supposed to, Joey started squirming around. He almost got away from her as he tried to chase a butterfly that was pasted to the wall above the changing table. Susan grabbed his ankle just in time and returned him to his back.

He made it all the way to his knees when Susan reached for a new sleeper. He'd been after the laughing Pooh bear that time.

"The wallpaper comes down off my nursery walls tonight," Susan muttered, thinking of all the colorful things dancing across the twins' walls at home.

Joey started to cry when she forced him back down to the table. "Shhh," she said, drawing imaginary lines on his belly to distract him. After several tiring minutes of coaxing and fighting surprisingly strong little limbs, Susan finally had him lying still.

Prepared now, she placed her body half on the active child as she slid the dry diaper beneath him.

Joey giggled. And peed.

Susan swore. She was going to cry, too. Until she saw the big blue eyes gazing up at her, watching. She smiled instead.

"Okay, Joe, me boy, no more of that," she said in a funny low voice. The little boy laughed.

Stripping off her wet blouse, Susan stood in her bra and maternity shorts trying to be cheerful as she grabbed a fresh diaper.

Five minutes later, the task was done; he was clean diapered, dressed. Suddenly sleepy, Joey cuddled against her as she finally lifted him from the changing table. He smelled of baby powder and little boy, and Susan gave in to the temptation to hold him for a while, rocking him back and forth. He seemed to grow heavier as he lay against her. In less than five minutes, he was sound asleep—from imp to angel-face.

Susan walked softly, slowly, to Joey's crib, trying to figure out how to get down the side bar with the child sleeping in her arms. She discovered, that it was the least of her problems. Because first, she was going to have to change the soaking wet crib sheet with the child asleep in her arms.

She knew from her experience earlier in the evening—and from Julie's warning, which she'd so stupidly ignored—that the second she put Joey down anywhere but in his crib, he'd be awake again.

And Susan was pretty sure she didn't have the energy to survive that.

SUSAN WAS HOT. Sweat rolled down her back and pooled at the waistband of her ugly maternity underwear beneath her green tent of a dress. All this discomfort, just because she'd walked from her car to her office building. July was quickly moving toward August, and Cincinnati's weather wasn't being nice to her.

Tricia met her at the door, on her way out someplace, and taking one glance at Susan, swung back.

"Come on," she said, linking her arm with Susan's. "Let's get something cold to drink."

Tempted to give in to self-pity and allow herself to be led, Susan held strong instead. "Weren't you going someplace?" she asked, trying to remember where Tricia was headed. "A meeting with the insurance people, maybe?"

"I'm their best customer. They'll wait," the other woman said.

Fifteen minutes later, Susan was ensconced in a quiet booth at Tricia's club, sipping a decaffeinated frozen latte and marveling how friends could be found in the most unexpected places.

Over the past six weeks, she and Tricia had formed an unusually frank relationship built, at first, on mutual respect, but more recently, on mutual affection, as well.

"Michael's still gone?" Tricia asked as the waitress left them.

Susan nodded. He'd been gone almost constantly since the Saturday they'd seen Laura. And though she knew the Miller deal had been put on hold for at least a month, she couldn't help worrying that Laura's visit had something to do with his extended absence.

"He's still calling?"

"Almost every day."

Chin puckered, Tricia nodded as though pleased. Susan was pleased, too. So pleased she scared herself. The frequency of Michael's calls could simply be the result of a misguided sense of duty.

"So what have you decided to do once the babies are born?" Tricia asked. Though her boss was impeccable as always in her violet suit, not a black hair out of place, Susan now knew the woman beneath the facade.

"Hire a nanny for in-home care."

"Good, that's what I'd do, too. I can get you some names if you'd like."

"That'd be great." With all the charity and church work Tricia had done over the years, she knew everyone in town. "I'd feel a whole lot better working with referrals than with a service."

As they sipped their coffee, they talked about Tricia's earlier days with young children at home. And then about her current days with teenagers ruling the roost. Susan couldn't wait for either. They both sounded like heaven to her.

"How was Amy's dance?" Susan asked. She'd yet to meet the fifteen-year-old, but she'd already grown very fond of her through her mother.

"She went with one guy and came home with another, but she had a wonderful time."

Susan smiled, her glass completely empty. "Wouldn't it be wonderful to be fifteen again?"

"Yeah." Tricia's eyes were downcast, and teary when she glanced up again. "I met Ed when I was fourteen," she said. "He was the only man I ever dated."

"I never knew that," Susan said, amazed. "You seem so worldly."

Tricia grinned through her tears. "I am worldly, just a one-man woman."

Susan sipped a bit. "So have you thought any more about having Eddie come into the office after school?"

"Yeah. I think I'll do it."

"Good." It was Susan's turn to grin. "No more worrying about what he's doing with his time. Plus, he'll get a taste of the business he's so eager to join, and it'll relieve a little of the weight on your shoulders."

"He won't be ready for any decision-making."

"No, but just having someone to bounce things off will help."

Reaching over the table, Tricia covered Susan's hand with her own. "I already have that, Susan. I wish I knew how to thank you."

"Believe me, Tricia," Susan said, "you've done far more for me than I'll ever be able to do for you."

And she had. Tricia had become the rope Susan was hanging on to as she faced life without Michael. Before, she hadn't believed it mattered so much, and she'd coped just fine. But now that she had the inside scoop on her stupid heart, she couldn't seem to get through a night without crying herself to sleep.

THAT SATURDAY, while walking the treadmill, Susan entertained herself with possible plans for the day. She still had so much to do, and only a couple of months in which to do it. She'd been in for her sixth-month checkup the week before, and the doctor had told her again to expect an early delivery. And *not* to expect to accomplish much during her last month. She warned that Susan would be too big to move around comfortably.

Susan figured she was already at that point. But who was she to know?

"Okay, Zack, you still need overalls and tops, a dress outfit, and little-boy shoes." Someone threw a hard blow to just beneath Susan's ribs, and she chose to believe it was her son responding.

"And no more of that while I'm walking," she panted. "It's hard enough to breathe." She paused then forced herself to tread some more.

"Now, back to business." A few more heavy

breaths. "Baby girl, you have all your clothes, but I'd like to get a couple more girlish receiving blankets. You two are probably going to throw up a lot and I don't know how much time I'll have for laundry."

Thinking about that, Susan continued to walk and to stare at the desk Michael had used during his stay with her.

"I'll call a laundry service as soon as I finish showering this morning."

Someone moved again, not so much a kick as a drag. "Zack, don't tease your sister about her lack of a name," Susan said. "If I hadn't found your daddy's note under the toaster, you wouldn't have one, either."

Her timer went off, signaling the end of a murderous half hour, but Susan walked a bit longer. Her feet could still move one in front of the other, and she hadn't finished her list yet.

"We have to stop by the office, and I don't want any argument from either of you," she said as sternly as she could with no breath. "No acting up today, guys. That's how I make the money to give you everything you want."

All quiet.

Good.

"And then I promised to make three dozen cookies for the battered women's center fund-raiser. They have to be delivered by ten o'clock tonight." She stared at the desk some more. *Step. Step. Step.* "Yeah, I suppose I could do another few dozen. Those ladies need a lot of things, and now I know how much it costs just to keep newborns in diapers."

Sweat was dribbling down the backs of her knees

by the time she finished walking. But Susan was smiling as she headed into the shower.

"With all this walking, you two are practically going to slide out in my sleep," she told her stomach.

Right before she passed out.

"SETH?"

"Yeah?" Seth rose up in bed, glancing at the clock. Only seven-thirty on Saturday morning. He still had a couple of hours before he picked up Paul from Brady's house. And then he was driving out to Laura's....

"Could you come over?"

"Of course." He was out of bed instantly, pulling on yesterday's jeans. "Is there a problem?" he asked, forcing his voice to remain calm. If Susan was having some kind of emergency, he needed his wits about him.

"I'm just a little scared."

Shrugging into a T-shirt, he grabbed his keys and wallet off the dresser, taking the mobile phone with him as he made his way to the front door. "Is someone bothering you? You hearing noises?" he asked quickly. "Hang up and call the police."

"No, nothing like that." She didn't sound any stronger.

And then it hit him. Oh, God. No. "Is it the babies?"

"I don't think so," she said, but she'd started to cry. "I just fainted, okay? Can you come?"

"Hang tight, sis. I'm on my way."

He dialed Michael's hotel room in Atlanta from his cell phone. And breathed a bit easier once he knew

Michael was on the first flight out. He called Brady next and talked to Paul, explaining why he'd have to miss their date at the batting cages. And then he called Laura, just needing to hear her voice.

These babies meant everything to Susan. He was afraid to even think about what would happen if she lost them now.

"I HAVE TO MAKE six dozen cookies before tonight." Michael heard Susan's voice as he let himself into the condo with his key.

"Like hell you do," he said, striding into the living room. She'd fainted less than four hours ago.

Susan's head swirled so fast, she should have been dizzy as she strained to see Michael. He couldn't have mistaken the welcoming light in her eyes, or the wide smile on her lips. But in the next instant, he might have been forgiven for thinking so. She turned on Seth who'd been lounging in an armchair.

"You called Michael." That obviously didn't please her.

Seth shrugged, apparently not at all fazed by Susan's anger. "Of course I did."

"I'm glad he did," Michael said, sitting gently beside her. She lay on the couch, propped up by pillows. She was wearing one of the summer shifts she'd bought when he'd still been living there, but she filled it out a hell of a lot more now than she had then.

"There was no reason," Susan said, her eyes imploring him not to overreact. "I'm just fine."

"You've been to the doctor?" he asked, certain she had, but needing that reassurance anyway. He wanted to run his fingers through the layers of her hair, too—and to kiss the pout off those lips.

Susan nodded. "She says I'm fine. I just overheated walking on *your* treadmill."

Understanding dawned. "You went for longer than half an hour, didn't you?"

"Um, a bit." She looked down, picking some imaginary lint off her dress.

"And you were probably walking on an incline at a faster speed than you should have been."

"Just trying to make the delivery as easy as possible," she said. "Dr. Goodman told me to do as much as my body would allow."

He couldn't believe she'd just said that, as if the doctor's words were a strong defense on her behalf. "Then, why didn't you?"

"Because there's no meter that tells you what it will allow," she said crankily, sitting up beside him. "Your body only tells you when it doesn't allow something."

"Laura's on her way over." Seth jumped into the conversation. He sat relaxed in his chair, with a huge grin on his face. "She had to drop the kids off at a swim party, and then she's going to help Susan bake cookies."

Michael looked at Susan, his expression serious. "You aren't baking today."

"It's no big deal, Michael," she said, brushing him off with a wave of her hand. "I can sit at the table the whole time. Besides, there's nothing wrong with me that a good dose of air-conditioning can't fix."

Alarm returned, cramping his stomach. "What exactly did Dr. Goodman say?"

"Just that I overheated. Nothing more."

"She also said Susan shouldn't try to do quite as much now as she did before she was pregnant."

"Believe me, baking a few cookies isn't nearly what I had on the agenda for today," Susan quipped dryly.

Standing, Michael went for the phone. "Would you mind if I called her myself?" he asked Susan, waiting for the number.

"Yes, I'd mind!" Susan stood, too—but very slowly, Michael noticed. "I'm not a child who needs looking after," she muttered.

"She really did say there's nothing to worry about," Seth added, resting his head against the back of the chair. "The babies are fine. Susan's fine."

Still uncomfortable, Michael turned to Seth. "Did you ask if there's any reason Susan shouldn't stay here alone?"

"I asked," Susan snapped. Fainting certainly did nothing for her disposition.

"And?"

"None."

"She said there's no reason at all," Seth elaborated.

Michael wished his friend's words had reassured him. But they hadn't. The pressure in his chest grew until he knew his time was up. Susan could have been in serious trouble that morning, and she'd been there all alone. He couldn't take a chance that something like this would happen again.

Which meant that whether he chose to or not, he was going to have to come to terms with living a life he'd never wanted. Being a man he'd never needed to be.

He just didn't know how in hell he was going to pull it off.

"YOU AND LAURA set a date yet?" Michael asked later that afternoon. He and Seth were in the nursery, assembling the furniture Susan had purchased sometime since Michael's last visit.

"She wants to wait until after Susan has the babies," Seth said easily. "She wants Susan to stand up with us."

Michael froze, crib directions in hand. "You've actually asked her to marry you?" He'd been ribbing Seth, not expecting a serious answer.

"Yep." Seth pushed his way under the crib, clutching a screwdriver.

Grabbing a wrench, Michael held the bolt Seth was twisting a screw into. "I'm happy for you, man," he finally said. And shocked. He knew Seth and Laura were seeing each other again, but the last he'd heard, Seth was still holding out on tying her kids to an absentee dad.

Seth looked up, wearing the stupidest grin Michael had ever seen. "Yeah, me, too," he said sheepishly.

The bolts on the first crib finished, Michael went back and double-checked every one of them. A tiny life was at stake here.

"My work satisfactory?" Seth asked, laughing at him. He was standing across the room, the pieces of the other crib spread at his feet.

"Smart-ass," Michael said, wishing he felt a little more like laughing himself.

Without directions this time, they silently set to work on the second crib.

"So, what made you change your mind?" Michael asked about halfway through.

"The kids," Seth grunted, twisting a bolt so tight Michael was surprised the screw didn't break right off. Seth was making damn sure Michael didn't have to check his work a second time.

"I thought the kids were the reason you *weren't* asking her to marry you."

"They were until a couple weeks ago, when Jeremy broke down one day on the soccer field. He thought I wasn't marrying his mom because I didn't love him and Jenny, didn't want to be their dad. He thought they were keeping her from being happy. It suddenly became clear to me that while having a man at home every night might be good for them, having a father who loved them was more important."

Michael wished he could believe it was that easy.

"Besides," Seth said from beneath the second crib. "I'm home every weekend. I can still coach, help them with their homework, take them to the zoo, keep tabs on their friends."

Michael wasn't home on weekends. He was lucky if he made it home long enough to turn on some lights.

"And if they act up during the week, I can yell real good by telephone."

"Sounds like you've got it all worked out." Michael removed plastic wrap from the second mattress and dropped it in the crib.

"You know," Seth said conversationally as he laid

out the pieces for the changing table. "You might give marriage some thought yourself."

"Lay off."

"I see you're as open-minded as usual."

Studying the directions in his hand, Michael concentrated on leaving Seth with his head intact. "You have no room to talk, little brother," he reminded the other man.

Seth got the hint. Setting to work on the changing table, neither of them spoke for quite some time.

"Tell me why you work every hour of every day," Seth finally said.

"Because I love what I do."

"More than you love being with Susan?"

"Of course not," Michael snapped. And then wished he hadn't. Seth's eyes took on an I-told-you-so-light, even if he didn't say the words. But he had it all wrong.

"Look, man, I know how you grew up." Seth had started in again, and Michael wondered what it would take to shut him up. "Susan says you were working odd jobs by the time you were ten just to help out. That you were buying all your own clothes by the time you were in junior high. And all through high school you held down a full-time job at the local grocery."

Michael tried to tune Seth out. Everything he was saying was old news. Irrelevant news.

"You put yourself through college on loans and two part-time jobs, and then had to pay off the debt as soon as you graduated."

"You can stop anytime," Michael said. Silence

was less boring. "This bar goes across there." He handed Seth the piece he'd been looking for.

"I understand why the career choices you made seven years ago were necessary. Why supporting yourself while getting far enough ahead to send money to your family was utterly important."

Though he still wished Seth would simply be quiet, Michael was a tiny bit gratified to know that he had his friend's endorsement on what had—until today— been the most difficult decision of his life.

"But why now?" Seth went on. "You've got to be loaded."

"I do okay," Michael acknowledged. It was one of the few things he had to feel proud about.

Seth studied the diagram for assembling the drawers that were supposedly going to line up on one side of the table. "It seems to me—" he dropped the page and took the pieces Michael had assembled and was already handing to him "—that your life has changed drastically in the past three or four years, but you've never reassessed your goals accordingly."

"I am what I am," Michael said. He wouldn't kid himself, or try to pretend that things were better than they were. If he was going to commit himself to a life of regret, he was at least going to do so with his eyes wide-open.

He could just hear Coppel's voice when he handed in his resignation. They'd probably be able to hear him from Atlanta to Ohio. And Michael could hardly blame him. Only an immature idiot took a job like Michael's and quit a few months later.

Seth stopped what he was doing and stood, hands on his hips, while he looked straight at Michael. "All

I'm saying is that maybe you should give some honest, open-minded thought to your life," he said, his eyes unusually serious. "You've been pushing yourself at a frantic pace your entire life—since childhood, for God's sake. Isn't it just possible that this need to give everything you are to your career comes more from a lifetime of pushing, of habit?"

"You don't understand," Michael said automatically. No one ever had.

"Maybe not." Seth went back to putting the gliders on one drawer while Michael worked on another.

"My career isn't work to me." Michael needed to explain it for himself, if not for Seth. "It's who I am. I'm very good at what I do." Michael felt bound to make Seth understand.

"I know you are," Seth said, sliding his drawer successfully home. "But with nothing else in your life, what's the point?"

WITH LAURA'S HELP, Susan turned out eight-dozen chocolate chip cookies. Seven dozen of them were packed and ready to go by the time Michael and Seth finished the nursery. They were allowed to consume the remaining twelve, along with a couple of glasses of milk.

And then Laura and Seth had to head out. It was getting dark, and Laura's kids would need to be picked up soon.

"Don't they look great together?" Susan asked Michael as they stood together in the doorway watching Seth walk Laura to her car. He was carrying the boxes of cookies, which he was going to deliver for Susan before meeting Laura at her house.

It made Michael uncomfortable to watch them. They weren't really even touching, unless you counted the number of times they rubbed elbows as they walked, but he could feel their closeness.

"Laura was telling me they're looking for a house not far from here," Susan said.

"They are?" Seth hadn't mentioned anything about a house.

"Yeah." She waved as the other two pulled away and then shut the front door. "Then whenever Seth's out of town, Laura and I will be nearby."

And that would make it easier for Seth to play surrogate father to Susan's children as well, Michael surmised. But he needn't have worried. Michael intended to do his duty.

"We need to talk." Grabbing Susan's arm, he pulled her to a halt.

"Here?" They were still in the hallway.

"The kitchen's fine, I guess," Michael said, leading the way.

When she got to the kitchen, Susan immediately busied herself drying the dishes and utensils she'd left in the drainer. Suspecting it wasn't good for her to be on her feet for long, considering the day she'd had, Michael found a towel and helped her.

"What's up?" she asked after they'd worked silently for several minutes. She knew something was wrong. She could tell by the way he wouldn't meet her eyes.

"I'm going to quit my job and move back home."

The bowl in Susan's hands slid to the floor, shattering into tiny pieces.

CHAPTER SEVENTEEN

BLOOD RAN down her leg. Susan saw it there. But she didn't feel a cut. Didn't feel anything at all except disbelief. And a crazy sense of unreality, as if she'd stepped out of her life and was watching from the sidelines.

"Watch where you walk." She heard Michael behind her as she bent to pick up the bigger pieces. She had to get a paper towel before her blood dripped on the floor, too.

Michael appeared in front of her, trash can in hand as he reached for a piece of glass. "You're hurt!" he cried when he caught sight of her leg.

Hauling her up—all 160 pounds of her—he set her on the counter and examined her laceration more closely.

"It's nothing," she heard herself say. Glancing down as Michael cleared away the worst of the blood, she wasn't so sure. The soiled washcloth looked kind of scary.

"You were lucky," he said, probing around the cut.

Susan winced, but was almost glad of the pain. Glad to feel something more than cold.

"It's just a small cut and there's no glass embedded. Are the bandages and antiseptic still in the same place?''

Nodding, Susan sat dutifully still while he collected supplies, patched her up and then cleaned up the rest of the glass. All the while, she was thinking that if Michael was really coming home for good, she should be ecstatically happy. So why wasn't she?

And then it hit her. *Michael* was why she wasn't happy. He wasn't happy. There'd been no joy in his resolute statement. Come to think of it, she hadn't seen him smile since he'd arrived.

''Were you planning to ask first or just move right in?'' She blurted the thought aloud when he was down to the last slivers of glass.

He stopped sweeping and looked up at her. ''You'd tell me no?'' It had obviously never occurred to him.

''I might.''

''I don't believe that.''

''Believe it, Michael,'' she said, her heart splintering into as many shreds as the glass in the trash can.

Finishing with the broom, he put it away, then came to stand in front of her, arms across his chest. ''You can honestly tell me you don't want me living here with you?''

No. She couldn't tell him that.

''I won't have you here out of a sense of duty,'' she said instead. ''And I know that's what this is about.''

''You can't know that,'' he argued, strengthening her belief. ''Only I can know what's going on inside me.''

She noticed he hadn't denied her accusation. ''I know *you*, Michael.'' She made to slide down from the cupboard and he was there, assisting her to a kitchen chair as though she were some kind of invalid.

His courtesy, coming as it did out of a sense of duty, not shared love, hurt her more than she'd have thought possible.

"I can do it myself," she said, shaking him off.

"Fine." He sat, as well.

"So you're suggesting this because it's what *you* want above all else."

"I know that it's right for me to be here where I'm needed."

"I don't need you here," she told him truthfully. Not in the way he thought. Not for practical or financial maintenance. She could take care of herself—and her babies—just fine. She was beginning to suspect he didn't even understand *how* she needed him, and if that was the case, he'd never be able to provide for that need. She needed him emotionally, elementally, more deeply than anything physical. She needed him in a way that was stronger than any other connection in her life. She needed him to need her, too. Needed to be a priority to him, not a pasttime.

He watched her silently for several minutes, his jaw twitching slightly from tension.

"I can't believe you said that." He broke the silence that had fallen, speaking stiffly. "We both know it isn't true."

"I know no such thing." She adopted his tone. "Dr. Goodman said just this afternoon that I'm fine here alone—"

"But after the babies come—"

"I can afford a nanny," she finished before he had

a chance to. She couldn't allow him to convince her, even a little bit, that his being there was necessary. Because his being there wasn't right.

"A nanny doesn't take the place of a father."

"And neither does a man whose heart isn't in it."

He sighed heavily, leaning his forearms on the table. "I'm trying here, Sus."

"I know." She put every ounce of love she had for him into those two words.

"I want you to marry me again, soon."

She'd heard that in her dreams a million times. And in her dreams, the answer was always yes.

"Before the babies are born, you mean?" she asked now.

"Of course."

"So they're legitimate."

"Exactly," he said, obviously breathing a little easier with what he saw as her capitulation.

"No." Never had a word hurt so much. Never had she been more sure of anything in her life.

"No?"

"No." He'd better get it soon. She didn't know how much longer she could hold out.

She'd created this mess and it was up to her to fix it. She'd made his life hell, and now she had to put things right for him.

His face a study in disbelief, he said, "You won't marry me."

"No, I won't marry you."

Falling back hard in his chair, Michael stared at her. "You're doing this for my benefit, aren't you?"

"Not really." Cradling her belly with her arms, she shook her head, surprised to find that the words were completely true. "I'm thinking of all of us, and maybe me most of all."

"How's that?"

"I had a proposal of passion once, Michael. I know how that feels, to want something with such intensity. To be wanted that much. I can't settle for less."

She was getting through to him. His eyes were no longer disbelieving. Questioning.

"You're still the only woman for me," he said. She knew he was remembering back, as she was, to that first proposal so many years ago.

"But we're different now, smarter," she whispered. "And I can't make the same mistake twice."

Michael bowed his head, but not before she'd seen the relief flash across his features. That look cut her to the quick, hurting her so badly she couldn't even breathe at first. And when she could breathe again, she couldn't stop the burning behind her eyelids. She bowed her head, too—until she could swallow the telltale tears, sweep them away. Pretend none of this mattered.

For the sake of her babies, she had to be strong.

"And you're okay with this?" Michael asked. "Honestly?"

If she had any hope of convincing him, she was going to have to look him in the face. And not cry.

And try to lie.

"I'm completely certain it's for the best."

Which was about as much of an answer as he'd given her earlier when she'd asked him what he wanted above all else. They'd be better off if they'd learned to lie to each other somewhere along the way, she told herself wearily.

Leaning forward, his elbows on his knees, Michael reached for her hand, holding it securely between both of his. "And you're okay with my coming and going as I have been?"

No! Susan froze before she voiced the thought. After all, what was her alternative? Never to see him again.

"As you have been lately, where you stayed for a while at a time, or as you have been over the past three years, stopping in for a day or two whenever you could?"

What did it matter? Either one would break her heart.

"In my current position, the most I'd be able to spare is a day or two now and then. Unless I find another company in Cincinnati that I'm interested in buying out."

Pulling her hand from his, Susan retreated further into herself, talking silently to her babies. *We'll be just fine, guys, we'll be just fine.* She repeated the litany over and over.

"No, Michael, I'm not okay with that." The words came straight from her heart. She'd had no intention of saying them. "Every time you leave—" she looked down at her belly "—I miss you more."

She had to stop. To take a deep breath. "I think I've used up my strength fighting that loneliness, Michael. I'm tired of missing you." Meeting his eyes, she begged him to understand. To forgive her for not being able to be everything he needed her to be. "If I can't have you here full-time, I think I'd rather not have you here at all." She took another deep breath, and then, like a runaway train, just kept on talking. "I think it would be best for the babies, too."

Frowning, Michael folded his arms over his chest. "So we're right back where we started," he said with frustration. "I need to quit my job and come home."

With the pain so intense, Susan couldn't help considering, just for a moment, if maybe that wouldn't be better. To have part of Michael instead of none.

She couldn't fight the tears any longer as she saw the haunted look in his eyes. "Did you feel completely trapped the whole time you were staying with me this spring and summer?"

"No." His answer shocked her. Gave her hope. Until he smashed it again. "But I always knew I could leave, that I hadn't committed myself to anything. I always had the safety net of knowing I only had to stay as long as the job kept me here."

"Get out, Michael." Susan was through. Couldn't take any more of his honesty. "Just get out."

"I can't leave you like this, Susan."

"I want you to," she said unemotionally. "Really." And she did. She just couldn't hurt anymore.

"Maybe you and the kids could come on the road with me."

Her foolish heart jumped at this last hope for happily-ever-after. Only to fall flat once more.

"What and enroll them in a different school every three weeks when we had to move on?"

"They wouldn't be in school for years."

"What about a pediatrician? We'd just have floating medical records? Three-month check in Denver, ear infection in Albuquerque, croup in Atlanta and six-month check in Washington State?"

"I've never been to Washington State."

"Not yet, anyway," she said, ashamed of the bitterness rolling from her tongue.

"It was only a suggestion, Susan."

"An impossible suggestion."

"Maybe I'm not the only one with a problem here."

"What's *that* supposed to mean?"

"Your entire life, you've been fighting for your own freedom, your right to have complete say over your own life."

Eyes burning, she met his gaze. "You know why."

"Yes," he acknowledged. "I even understand." Leaning forward, Michael continued to hold her gaze. "But did you ever stop to think that maybe part of our problem, from the very beginning, has been your need to go it alone? You're so afraid of being like your mother was, of *becoming* your mother, that you take your ability to handle everything to extremes."

"That's not a very nice thing to say."

"But it may be the truth." She didn't like the compassion she saw in his eyes. Not when it was directed at her. "Look at how you reacted the minute I suggested you quit your job here to follow me. You didn't give the idea a second's consideration before you were shooting it down."

"You can't raise children on the road, Michael."

"Maybe not, but did you even consider it? Try to picture it for a second? See if the idea had any merit at all?"

He knew she hadn't.

"Maybe this control thing is why you gave in to the divorce with so little fight." He paused, as if waiting for her to reply. Susan didn't have anything more to say.

"It could explain why you've been contented with our arrangement all these years," he said, speaking more quickly now. "In a sense, you had it all—a lover who adored you, and your freedom, too."

"Thank you, Dr. Kennedy." She didn't want to hear what he was saying.

"Right to getting pregnant, this could apply," he went on, ignoring her sarcasm. "You didn't *ask* me what I thought about our having a baby. You'd already made all the decisions on your own and only came to me for stud service."

He didn't quite hide the pain he'd felt at her callous treatment, leaving Susan ashamed. She'd had no idea he'd seen her request like that.

"When you found out you were having twins, you handled the initial impact on your own, waiting until you'd come to terms with it before telling me. Same thing when you found out we were having a son and a daughter." He just kept rattling things off, making her feel about as likable as cow dung. "I might not have been thrilled about this pregnancy at first, but we were talking about it regularly by then. I'm even the one who suggested you find out, yet when you did, I didn't hear about it. You know—" he looked down at his hands "—I waited by the phone that entire day, waiting to hear from you."

"I didn't know..." Tears flooded her eyes as she pictured him sitting there. Waiting.

"How could I have known?" she whispered.

"You couldn't. And I'm not saying you weren't perfectly within your rights to do all these things, Susan. Hell, I'm sure my actions prompted many of them. But maybe if you weren't so eager to go off and handle things, I'd feel differently...."

"Do you think so?" Susan slid down on her knees, laying her arms in his lap as she looked up at him. "Do you really think you'd get over feeling trapped if I...changed?"

"I..."

She could see the truth in his eyes.

"No, because part of the problem is yours, too, huh?" she asked, still leaning on him as tears rolled slowly down her cheeks.

He didn't say anything for a long time. Susan savored his warmth, soaking it in while she could. Garnering her strength for the days and years ahead.

She kneeled there until her back started to cramp, the cut on her leg to throb. And then, painfully, she stood. "You need to go," she said.

His eyes locked with hers, filled with pain—and regret—but resolution as well. Slowly, so slowly she thought she'd die, he nodded his acquiescence.

"You'll call—"

Cutting him off, she shook her head. "Not for a while, anyway." Not until she was strong enough.

His hand on the doorknob, he stopped and turned, meeting her gaze where she stood, hugging herself, at the end of the hall.

"I do love you, Sus, more than anyone else on earth."

She knew he did. And that probably hurt most of all. She opened her mouth to speak, but her throat was so clogged with tears, no sound came out. She nodded.

He stood there a few minutes longer, his throat working as he watched her.

Then, silently, he turned his back and walked out of her life.

Sobs shook her body as she watched him drive away. But somewhere she found the courage to say what she'd tried to say while he was still in her house.

"I love you, too, Michael. I love you, too."

CHAPTER EIGHTEEN

THE LITTLE BOY could hardly walk, but man, could he run. So fast his father was having a hard time keeping up with him. Stopped at a streetlight in Chicago a couple of miles from home, Michael watched the father finally catch up before the child ran head-long into the street. The man scooped the boy into his arms so high so fast, Michael had to wonder if the kid would be sick. The man was angry, scolding the little boy as he held the toddler in front of him. Then he wrapped his arms around that little body, holding the boy close, burying his face in the child's neck....

The drivers behind Michael started to lay on their horns. The light was green and he was sitting through it.

Michael gunned his engine.

He'd left Susan more than a month ago, and he still couldn't get on with his life, couldn't get her off his mind. Couldn't get his mind on anything else. He finally had his freedom—what he'd been craving for months—and the crazy thing was, he still wasn't happy.

He called his closest friend as soon as he was inside his door.

"Seth, I'm losing it, man," he blurted. He couldn't

believe he'd said the words. Wanted to snatch them back.

"I wondered how long it'd take you to call."

"Just tell me how she is," he said. If he knew she was all right, he'd be able to get on with things. Quit worrying about her and worry about the Miller deal that had been hanging on the edge far too long.

"She's fine," Seth said. And then, as if taking pity on Michael, added, "She's huge. Can't reach her feet at all."

"How's she put on her shoes?"

"She and Laura went out and bought a bunch of slip-on things, a pair in every color known to man."

Pacing his living room, Michael nodded. She'd handled that problem in typical Susan fashion. That should make him feel a little better.

"She's only working part-time at the office right now. Tricia brings most of the stuff to the house."

"It's that hard for her to get around?" Michael asked. See, he *was* needed there.

"Not once she's standing." Seth chuckled. "It's just a bit of a chore for her to get up."

He knew it. She needed help.

"So how's she managing to take care of herself?"

"She's found a way to get up, of course," Seth said with admiration. "But it involves some rolling and sliding, and she refuses to do that at the office any more than she has to."

Oh.

"So, how you doing, brother?" Seth asked quietly, seriously.

"Fine. Great." He lied.

"Doesn't sound that way."

Running his fingers through his hair, Michael glanced down at his impeccable suit, his shiny designer shoes, and didn't find a single thing he liked. "I should be feeling fine," he said. "She threw my offer to marry her right back at me, which certainly relieves any feelings of guilt I'd been harboring."

"She told me."

"You think she meant it?" Maybe that was the problem. Maybe he didn't believe Susan's claim that she didn't want him around. Maybe that was why he still didn't feel free.

"Yep. I know she did."

Michael swallowed. Seth's words should be liberating. They shouldn't hurt.

"I guess I just need a little more time to realize I did the best I could and my best wasn't good enough. That I'm truly free."

"You wanna know what I think?" Seth asked. But he didn't wait for an answer. "Of course you do or you wouldn't have called."

"Smart-ass."

"Yeah, well, you got the smart part right. Here's the thing." Seth's voice lowered, filled with respect. "I think maybe you had to be free from any sense of obligation to be able to determine how you really felt. And maybe, just maybe, what you're feeling now is the true problem."

"I'm not following you."

"You've been feeling trapped, right?"

Michael stood by the window, looking out into the gathering dusk. "Right." That was an understatement.

"And you blame the feeling on your impending fatherhood."

"Of course." He'd only started feeling claustrophobic after Susan had brought up the whole pregnancy thing.

"What if it was something else, instead?"

"Like?" He rubbed his forehead, as though he could actually make the throbbing go away.

"Maybe what's been trapping you is your job. Maybe it's your career keeping you from what you really want, not the other way around."

No way. "I love what I do."

"Yeah, man." Seth's voice sounded almost sad. "I know."

"Don't tell Susan I called."

"Don't worry, I won't."

"You'll call if she needs anything?" That understanding had been in place forever.

"No," Seth said. "I don't think I will."

Michael was struck dumb—and left with a dead phone at his ear. Seth had hung up.

SHE HAD TO CALL HIM. After five weeks of running their last conversation over and over in her mind, Susan knew she couldn't leave things as she had.

Through a series of phone calls, she caught up with him in a hotel room in Nebraska.

"Susan?" At least he didn't sound mad. "What's wrong?" No, not mad, only worried sick.

Smiling in spite of her admonitions not to do anything stupid, like get her hopes up, she said, "Nothing, at least nothing immediate."

"You're okay?"

"Fine." She looked down at the beach ball that had taken over her stomach and propped another pillow under her head. She had pillows everywhere these days. Here on the couch, on a chair in the kitchen, in her car. She'd bought an even dozen just to make sure she had enough.

"And the children?"

"Huge." *Don't listen,* she mouthed to the beach ball. "How's work?"

"Good. Busy."

And then the pleasantries were out of the way and a heavy silence fell on the line.

"Nothing's changed. I know that—it's just...I wanted to clear something up."

"What's that?" He still didn't sound annoyed. As a matter of fact, he sounded as though he didn't mind her calling him at all.

But then, she'd been the one who'd insisted on no contact.

"You said something that night, a few things actually, that weren't accurate, and I need to set the record straight."

"Yes?"

"You weren't just a stud service, Michael." She couldn't believe she hadn't had a little more finesse than that. "When I asked you to be the father of my child, it was because I didn't want a child at all if it couldn't be yours."

"You never told me that."

"I know. I didn't want to put that much pressure on you."

He chuckled. "Lady, if you think you didn't put pressure—"

"I know," she interrupted. Damn, he sounded good. It was wonderful just hearing his voice. Her two-ton body felt better than it had in weeks. "I'm sorry, Michael. And one other thing." She rushed on before she could chicken out. "Being in control of my life doesn't mean more to me than you do." She'd given the matter a lot of thought, continuous thought, over the past weeks. "Maybe at one time it did, maybe even when we got divorced, but I've changed, Michael."

She didn't know why it was so important to her that he understand this. But it was. Michael knew her better than anyone, and she needed his view of her to be accurate. Almost as though she couldn't be who she was unless he saw her that way.

"Michael, I don't have to fight anyone else's preconceived notions anymore. Not my father's ideas. Not my brothers'. Not anyone's. I have confidence in my strength to be true to myself, in my ability to handle whatever comes my way." Confidence gained, in some part, during the past five weeks. She'd managed to live without Michael. To survive. "And so—" She broke off, swallowed back tears. "It's no longer a threat to share who I am."

Michael was silent so long she was afraid he'd fallen asleep. "You there?' she finally whispered.

"I am." He fell silent again, but only for a second. "I'm proud of you, Sus. You've grown up."

"Yeah."

"Your children are very lucky to have a mom like you."

The warmth, the sincerity in his voice was her undoing.

"Well, I gotta go—"

"Take care."

"I will. Bye." She didn't wait to hear him echo the word. Her heart just couldn't take it. With her finger on the disconnect button, she cradled the phone to her chest and bawled like a baby.

SITTING IN AN AIRPORT almost a week after his conversation with Susan, Michael was still thinking about the things she'd said. He knew there was a message in there for him. He just hadn't figured it out yet. But he would. He wasn't going to rest until he found for himself the peace he'd heard in Susan's voice.

A woman with a double-wide stroller was trying to maneuver between the rows of seats at the gate where he was waiting to catch his flight to Atlanta. Michael moved his briefcase and carry-on to make room for her.

"Thanks," she panted, falling into the seat next to him.

Now that she was closer, he could get a peak at the cargo in her stroller. She had a couple of sleeping babies wrapped in pink blankets.

"How old are they?" he asked quietly.

As she glanced down at her daughters, the exhaustion completely left the woman's face, to be replaced by a very proud smile. "Three months."

Michael nodded politely and picked up a newspaper he'd been trying to read earlier.

"You find that stroller preferable to the front-and-back kind?" he asked, peering over the top of his paper. Just in case he talked to Susan again, he'd let her know.

"Yeah." She really was pretty, Michael thought, taking in her clear skin and unmade-up face, her straight brown hair. Her generic slacks and top. There was just something about her expression, her air of— what? Happiness? "—I just want to be able to see them both at all times," she was saying and it took him a minute to realize she was still talking about the stroller. "Besides, I want them to be company for each other."

Sound reasoning. Michael nodded. And returned to his paper.

Until one of the babies whimpered. Everyone knew a baby crying was hard to ignore, so he didn't even try. He watched, instead, as the woman bent to her child, gently patting her back and cooing her to sleep again.

"You do that well," he felt compelled to say.

"Thank you." She grinned at him. "I've had practice."

"They wear you out then, two at once?"

"Only when they get up every other hour during the night, and don't synchronize their schedules."

"They get up every other hour at opposite hours?" he asked, appalled.

"Not often," she laughed, "but sometimes."

"Doesn't that get old fast?"

"No." She glanced down at her babies, that glow lighting her face. "They're only this little for such a short time, what's a few hours less sleep in return for more hours with them?"

Sound reasoning, he thought again. Michael told himself to return to his paper. Held it up in front of his eyes. But focused, instead, on the bundles in the stroller beside him.

"You have kids?" the woman asked, noticing his interest.

"I'm expecting twins."

Michael had no idea where the words came from. He'd had no thought of uttering any such thing. But suddenly, with a stranger babbling excitedly beside him, his way became clear.

Seth had been absolutely right. He'd been searching in all the wrong places.

His ex-brother-in-law had been right about something else, as well. Michael's entire identity had been wrapped up in his career. He was what he worked. Until this moment.

Suddenly, with one sentence, he'd become something else. A father.

He couldn't get up fast enough, get out to the Pathfinder, then home to his condo to make some calls.

"Wait!" the woman beside him called as he hurried away. "Aren't you on this flight?"

He turned halfway just long enough to call back, "Not anymore." And hurried out into the rainy September day.

BY TEN O'CLOCK the next morning, Michael was stepping into his mentor's penthouse office in Atlanta, a firmly sealed envelope in his hand.

"You needed to see me immediately?" Coppel asked, taking off his glasses as Michael approached his desk. "Ready to demand a partnership already?"

The man was smiling, a picture of confidence.

"No, sir." Michael paused. "I—"

"You want a raise, then," Coppel nodded toward the seat in front of his desk. "Fine, sit, we'll discuss it," he said.

Michael remained standing and that was when Coppel noticed the envelope clasped between his fingers. Coppel froze, his gaze moving slowly from the envelope in Michael's hand to his face and back again.

For the first time in Michael's acquaintance with Coppel, the older man looked unsure, giving Michael pause.

"That better not be what it looks like," he finally said.

"It's a letter of resignation, sir." He'd thought the words would be harder to say, had expected them to stick in his throat.

They didn't.

"No, it isn't," Coppel said, snatching his hands off the desk as Michael reached over to pass him the envelope.

"Yes, sir, it is."

"I'm not accepting it."

For a moment, as his life sped before his eyes, Michael turned cold. Was he making a horrible mistake? Acting rashly? Irrationally?

"Whatever the problem is, we'll fix it," Coppel said, as though he could sense Michael's split-second waver.

In that instant, Michael felt a peace he'd never known before. He was already fixing the problem.

"I'm going to be a father," he told the billionaire—the man he'd always aspired to be. "Of twins."

Coppel paled. Sinking back in his chair, he stared

at Michael, his shoulders falling with disappointment. He suddenly had nothing to say. To Michael, he looked, for the first time, like what he was—an old man. A lonely old man.

"I'm sorry," Michael said. And he was. But not for himself. He was sorry for a man he still admired the hell out of, but one he now knew he never wanted to be. Because life held far more riches than the billions James Coppel possessed.

Laying the envelope on the older man's desk, he walked silently out.

THE NEXT two and a half weeks flew by. Michael spent about eighteen of the twenty-four hours in each day on the telephone in his condo, leaving only long enough to get more coffee and toilet paper.

He spent hours on conference calls with the Miller family. After he'd resigned, they'd finally turned down the offer of a buy-out. He didn't feel morally correct in assisting them with the financing to accomplish on their own, on a smaller scale, what Coppel would have done with the company. But he felt great about turning them over to Melanie at Smythe and Westbourne. Coppel Industries still got a piece of the pie. And the Miller family had their lives back.

The rest of the time he spent calling every contact he had in the finance industry, setting himself up, laying the groundwork for the rest of his life.

But as his plans fell into place, he found he wasn't nearly as anxious as he would have expected, no matter how things fell out. He loved finance. But he no longer *had to be* in finance. He had enough money already; if he invested it properly, he could actually retire now. Or he could go into the cartoon business...

One person he didn't call was Susan. Not until his plans were solid. Until he had a complete package to sell her. He wasn't going to take a chance on another rejection.

Finally, when all he had left to do was wait for return calls, he phoned his father. At the gas station. He'd done that purposely, so he'd have his father to himself. Sam Kennedy deserved to be able to express the disappointment that would be coming—something he never did in front of Mary.

"I've left Coppel, Dad," he said, getting the job done right off.

"Oh?"

"Yeah." He'd expected more, but maybe his dad thought he had to protect Michael, too, from his own dissatisfactions. Didn't Sam realize that Michael had known for years about his dad's regrets, how he'd lived vicariously through Michael's career moves?

"You had a better offer?" So Sam's hopes hadn't been dashed yet.

"Nope."

"You've finally decided to slow down then? Live some?"

What?

"I'm going into business for myself," he said, too confused to do anything but report the facts. "Financial consulting."

"Isn't that a bit risky?"

Here it came. "Yes, frankly, it is, but with my contacts, I've already got enough business lined up to keep me busy."

"Not too busy, I hope."

"I don't get it, Dad. I thought you'd be disappointed in me."

"Hell, no!"

Michael sat straight down, only half aware that the couch was there to catch him. He'd never heard his dad swear in his life. "I don't worry much about Bob," Sam said, shocking Michael further. "His job's steady, he's got a good wife. And the twins, they both married fine, hardworking men, and they've got your mother. But you—" Stunned, Michael just sat there listening.

"All you've got is money and that can't warm a fella's heart much."

"But—"

"Don't get me wrong, son, I'm mighty proud of everything you do, brag around town about you every chance I get, but I'd trade it all for you to have even half the time, the love, I've had with your mother all these years."

"But—"

"I thought when you married, Susan, well, maybe… But I guess the time wasn't right."

"You could have been an engineer or a scientist or something," Michael blurted, beyond caring that he sounded more like his brother than the educated man he was.

"And then I wouldn't have had you."

"Didn't you ever wish you hadn't?" Michael wished he could take the words back the instant he heard them. Those thoughts belonged to no one but himself.

"Is that what you thought?"

"Who could blame you, Dad?" he said. Now that he'd brought it up, they might as well get it all out.

"Never, not for one instant, have I regretted having you," Sam said. Michael had never heard his dad so angry at him. At Bob, maybe. But not at him.

"How could you not?" He'd known since he was just a kid that he'd been responsible for ruining his father's life.

"Son, that's something I can't explain to you. Only a parent understands how it feels to hold your first-born in your arms, to actually know the joy that surpasses all understanding, to feel the awe. To know that, God willing, this being will be a part of you for the rest of your life—and beyond. No scientist could ever invent something as great as that."

For a man who couldn't remember ever being choked up, Michael was having a hard time finding his voice.

"I, uh, have something else to tell you, Pop," he finally said.

"What's that, son?"

"You're going to have a bit more of that joy coming up really soon."

"What?" He'd confused Sam now.

Grinning from ear to ear, completely free for the first time in memory, Michael said, "I've got a son and a daughter due to be born in less than a month."

"Susan's pregnant?" Sam yelled so loudly Michael had to take the phone away from his ear. "With twins?"

"Yep," he said.

Nothing in his life had ever made Michael feel quite so good.

THE PHONE RANG some time after Michael had fallen asleep that night. Rolling over drowsily, he made up his mind to tell his family that further discussions would have to wait until tomorrow—or at least until he got some sleep. He'd heard from all of them, his mother and sisters, at least half a dozen times that evening, as they made plans for their new babies.

"Michael? It's Seth."

Instantly wide awake, Michael sat up. "What's wrong?" The other man sounded panicked.

"Susan's in labor. The pains are really far apart, but the doctor says this is it." Seth spoke so fast, he was out of breath when he'd finished.

"I'm on my way—"

"Thank God. I can't do this one for you."

SHE WAS ALREADY in her birthing room by the time Michael made it to the hospital. Seth met him at the hospital door and hurried him up to the maternity floor, where a nurse was standing by with sterilized paper clothes for him to pull on over his jeans and sweatshirt.

"How is she?"

"Still has a little way to go," Seth said. "The doctor was just with her, but she's in there alone right now." And Seth obviously didn't like that fact one bit.

"Does she know I'm coming?" he asked Laura over a frenzied Seth's head.

Laura shook her head. "He didn't want her fretting in case your plane was delayed or the babies came early." *Or she didn't want me here,* Michael finished.

He wasn't going to worry about that. He'd win her over. Even if the package wasn't gift-wrapped yet.

He'd been so frantic to get there, but when the moment came to enter Susan's room, he hung back.

"Where are your kids?" he asked Laura.

"At Seth's house. His dad, Sean and Stephen are with them."

And Spencer and Scott—the only two with kids, and hence, not as mobile—were at their own homes pacing, he was sure.

"Get in there, man," Seth said between gritted teeth, pushing Michael through the door.

Prepared for the worst, preparing himself to see Susan gripped with searing pain, he went in.

She turned when the door opened, still laughing at something she'd been watching on television, and Michael just shook his head. She even underestimated the trauma of giving birth.

THE LAUGHTER DIED on Susan's lips when she saw who'd come in the door.

"Thank God," she whispered and then, to her horror, burst into tears.

"Susan?" Panic lining his face, Michael was beside her in an instant. "What can I do, love? Are you okay?"

"I'm fine, Michael," she sobbed, grabbing at him desperately, pulling him down until he was half lying on top of her.

"You don't sound fine—"

"Just hold me, Michael," she said, still crying. "I thought I could do this without you, but when it came right down to it I was so scared and I didn't know what to do and there was no way to stop it from happening, but I just couldn't do it...." The words tumbled over themselves, but Michael caught every blessed one of them. "Ohhh..." she cried out as a contraction began.

"Shhh, Sus, save your strength," he said. "I'm here now, for good."

Riding out the pain, she clutched him tightly, and then as it subsided, she pushed him away. "For good?" She just couldn't afford to hope. She needed all her strength to get her babies born. And Michael, after all, was Michael.

Grinning, he spread his arms wide. "Meet Michael Kennedy, Finance Consultant," he said.

"Michael?" She studied every inch of his face, hardly recognizing the light in his eyes, the easy smile on his lips.

"I quit Coppel's three weeks ago, Sus," he said, all playfulness gone. "I only hope you can forgive me for taking so much longer than you to grow up."

"You're sure?" she whispered.

"I'll tell you all about it later, but rest assured, I've never felt better in my life."

He'd grown up? Hadn't she just said that about herself the last time they'd— Of course she had. But how was it possible that Michael had done such an abrupt about-face?

Susan didn't know how this miracle had happened, but she knew suddenly, with complete surety, that it had.

"Oh, Michael. Ohhh!" The love and happiness in Susan's voice changed instantly, first to surprise, and then agony as, without further warning, their children decided the time had come to make their appearance.

COMPLETELY UNPREPARED for the speed with which things happened after that, Michael just went with the flow, his only job to give Susan whatever strength he could, however he could. Barely aware of the people moving in and out of the room, the instructions and orders, he stayed at the head of her bed, telling her over and over again how much he loved her.

And when, less than half an hour later, he heard the first cry of his newborn child, he was afraid to turn around, to claim for his own the joy that awaited him. How on earth did he deserve to be there? What right did he have to accept the bounty he'd fought so hard?

"Aha," the doctor said, sounding pleased. Michael saw Susan pulling forward, her chin to her chest, as she strained to see. "Your daughter's the oldest," Dr. Goodman told them.

"She doesn't have a name!" Susan said, and burst into tears.

"Shhh. We'll name her, Sus, just as soon as you finish here. We can do it together," Michael said, glad to have something to do, to distract him from the miracle taking place around him.

"Here, daddy, why don't you hold your daughter while Susan and I work on getting that little guy out here."

The worry in Susan's eyes as she watched him gave Michael the strength to turn around, to reach out his arms to that tiny, messy bundle, and bring her close to his heart. The oddest sensation came over him, filling his entire being, until the pressure built behind his eyes. He had no idea he was crying until the first drop slid out onto his face. Hadn't, until that moment, known he was capable.

Less than ten minutes later, Susan held their son against her, exactly as Michael still cradled their daughter. Her gaze moving from little Zack—she was going to have to explain that one—to his precious little no-name, her eyes finally came to rest on Michael. And with that look she made silent promises of love and a future filled with greatness. A future he knew would be grander, fuller, than any he could imagine.

"You see, Michael?" she whispered. "Life offers so much more than mere contentment. If you live right, and you're very, very lucky, you get happiness, too."

She always was the smartest woman he'd ever known.

EPILOGUE

"DAEY SHIT, daey shit!"

With one hand plastered over his daughter's mouth, Michael sat. And found himself on the floor in the front of the biggest Christmas tree he'd ever seen. Using him as a stepstool, which Michael was sure was the intention, Rosemary climbed onto his lap and reached up to get the lighted Santa ornament she'd been after since they'd arrived at his parents' home that morning, the morning of Christmas Eve.

"What did she say?" Mary came running in from the kitchen, her apron smeared with flour and pumpkin-pie filling and Michael had no idea what else.

"She told me to sit down, Mom," he said, bobbing the child up and down on his knee, hoping to keep her quiet, at least until there were no witnesses. And keep her grabby fingers away from the lighted tree at the same time.

Mary laughed, a full-bellied, honestly happy laugh. "I knew Susan would teach her right."

Laughter erupted from the kitchen. Susan and Laura eavesdropping, he was sure.

The Kennedy household was filled with smart-mouthed women, the mouthiest one of all being his year-old-daughter, Rosemary, named after both her grandmothers. Zack toddled over, grabbing a fistful of Michael's sleeve with a hand smeared with drool and the rest of an oatmeal cookie his grandmother had given him.

He grunted. And then grunted again, eyeing his sister with purpose. He wanted his share of his daddy's lap. But, as always, Rosemary had beat him to it. The poor guy never got a word in edgewise. Which explained why Rosemary's vocabulary was approaching more than a hundred words. And Zack could grunt.

Laughter erupted from the kitchen again just as Rosemary connected with a cross-stitched ornament and yanked. Needles sprayed across the huge piles of presents beneath the tree. Branches rocked. Michael held his breath.

Rosemary held up the ornament with a proud grin.

"Uncle Michael! Uncle Michael!" Jenny, bundled up in her winter coat and snow pants, cheeks red from the cold, came tearing into the room.

Michael turned just in time to catch the child with his semifree hand as she hurtled herself against his back. "We're home!" the child cried. "I get to watch Zack and Rosemary now."

"They're all yours." He handed his daughter carefully to the eager girl.

"How was the sledding?" he asked Seth and Jeremy as they followed Jenny into the room.

"Here, let me get him," Jeremy said, hurrying over to take Zack from his sister. "You hold her."

She gave in, but only because she couldn't possibly carry both of them, Michael suspected. Carefully, Jenny handed over one of her cherished cargo.

"Sledding was great." Pulling off his gloves, Seth

stopped beside the tree that dwarfed the Kennedys' living room.

"Yeah," Jeremy said, aiming the words over one shoulder. "Uncle Brady came over and brought Paul, and Paul showed me the coolest trick. We made it all the way down the hill on our shoulders, both of us on one sled."

Raising his brows he looked to Seth for confirmation—and for verification that his brother-in-law hadn't lost his mind allowing the boys to take such a risk.

"I tried it first," Seth defended himself, shrugging his shoulders. "Once you've got your balance, there's nothing to it."

"Except breaking your neck," Michael muttered. He'd been remarried to Susan for more than a year—remarried to her and divorced from his work—and he still wasn't used to the Carmichael physical prowess. He'd known they were highly athletic. He just hadn't realized there was no sport they couldn't conquer. It was only one of the things he'd missed learning the first time around. He'd found many more over the past year. Things he'd been too busy working to notice before. Like the fact that his wife liked to wallow in bubble baths for hours. She read something nonfiction every day, too.

And her father was addicted to chocolate.

"How's Paul doing?" Michael asked softly as Jenny and Jeremy led the babbling Rosemary and grunting Zack down the hall to the playroom.

"Good." Seth looked satisfied as he shrugged out of his coat. The boy had left Brady's group home for disadvantaged kids a few months before. "He's living with his grandparents, taking to his new school, even made the junior varsity basketball team.''

''Jeremy still following him around like a lost puppy?''

Seth grinned. ''Every chance he gets.''

Silently watching the fire flickering in the fireplace across the room, Michael couldn't help but admire his brother-in-law. Seth had done it all. Married Laura, become a great father to her kids, kept his job, and he still found the time to see the kid he'd volunteered with the previous year, when he'd been estranged from Laura and her kids.

''So you really shut down the office for the week?'' Seth asked, joining Michael on the floor. He lay on his side, head propped on one hand.

''Yep.''

Seth stared at Michael, lifted Michael's hand. ''Hold it there,'' he said, letting go in midair.

Holding his hand out in front of him as instructed, Michael stared at his brother-in-law. ''Why?''

''You're not shaking,'' Seth said, as though he were a doctor searching for a diagnosis. ''You been drinking?''

''No!'' Michael laughed and dropped his hand.

''You're sitting still, doing nothing, no bobbing knees or jittery joints. I'd say that means you're re-laxed!'' Seth crowed, and then, just as quickly he grew serious. ''I'm glad.''

''Yeah, me too.'' All in all, the year 2000 had been one of the best yet.

Getting up to put another log on the fire, Seth asked, ''So how's business?''

''Great. Better than I projected.''

"You might think about hiring some help."

Stretching, Michael moved onto his back looking up at the tree. "I'm way ahead of you," he said. "I have a new writer starting the first of the year."

"Can I get you boys anything to eat? It'll be another couple of hours before Christmas Eve dinner." Mary bustled into the room.

"I'm fine, Mom," Michael said, wondering if he'd be able to slip in a little nap while the women finished up in the kitchen. His dad wasn't due back from the station for another hour.

"Susan just talked to her dad. He's home from Florida and he'll be coming with Spencer and Scott and their families for dinner tomorrow," Mary reported happily. With his sisters and brother and their families, that would make twenty-five for Christmas dinner. Mary was so ecstatic, Michael wondered what was keeping her feet on the ground.

"Dad's back?" Seth asked. "How'd he do in the tournament?" The elder Carmichael had joined a senior PGA tour the previous spring.

"Placed eleventh," Susan called from the kitchen.

"Did you remember to bring his present, Seth?" Laura asked, joining them in the living room. She lowered herself gingerly into an armchair and settled back as though she'd like never to get up again.

"I did," Seth said. He crawled over and laid his head against his wife's very extended belly. "How's daddy's little girl?" he asked in baby talk.

"She's daddy's girl, all right," Laura grumbled good-naturedly. "She's been kicking field goals most of the afternoon. It's just too bad daddy isn't the one to field them."

Everyone laughed, including Michael. This was what he'd cashed in his old identity for. The true riches. He thanked God every day that he'd found out in time what they were.

MUCH LATER that night, Michael pulled Susan close as she snuggled beside him in his old bedroom in the attic.

"You think they're down for the night?" he whispered.

"Sure of it. They're exhausted."

They weren't the only ones, but exhaustion had never felt so good.

"Michael?"

"Hmm?"

"We can tell each other anything, can't we?"

Michael stiffened. Was there trouble in paradise? Had he missed something? She wasn't finding life as perfect as he was? Maybe working from home wasn't enough for her anymore.

"I've always thought so," he answered slowly.

"Good."

Was that it, then? She'd just needed reassurance? A confirmation of what they'd become to each other over the past year?

"I'm going to have another baby."

Michael flew out of the bed. Was actually standing naked beside it before déjà vu set in.

"Are we talking about a baby that already exists or is this one of those in-the-future things?"

Leaning on one elbow, she peered at him through the darkness. "In the future."

Relief washed over him, and Michael sank back

down to the bed. As much as he hated to tell her no, ever, he knew what he had to do. "I don't think it's a good idea, Sus." He'd ease into it; maybe she wouldn't take the news as hard.

"Of course it's a good idea." She sat up. "Look how blessed we've been with Rosemary and Zack. How could we possibly not want more of that?"

"Our house is a mess most of the time, we've gone for days and days without having sex, we're both tired a lot, and neither one of us is as well-dressed as we used to be. Hell, I went to work with bananas smeared on my sleeve the other morning."

"My house was never clean, sex is all the more incredible for the wait, we were tired when we worked fourteen hours a day, and who cares if my eyeliner's a little crooked now and then?" She paused. He could see her brow furrow even in the darkness. "Oh, and the bananas." She paused again, thinking. "A built-in morning snack!"

"I'm serious, Susan," Michael said, afraid to see her risk another pregnancy. She'd made it through the last one; why did they have to take any more chances? "You'd be forty-two by the time it was born."

"Yeah?" she challenged. "So?"

"I'm worried about you. Another pregnancy could wear you out. Not to mention midnight feedings all over again."

Susan leaned down until she was lying against him, her generous breasts pushing against his chest. "It'll be a piece of cake," she said, kissing him lingeringly. "After those two, I can handle feedings in my sleep."

She kissed him again, and Michael forgot why her words were nonsense. He forgot everything except how very much he loved her. How thankful he was that she'd waited for him to come to his senses and bind himself to her completely and forever.

And as they slowly, naughtily, brought in the joyous holiday, he made his first installment on another blessed event. He didn't know why he'd even bothered arguing.

Surely he'd learned by now that when Susan put her mind to something, she always got her way.

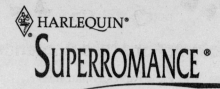

HARLEQUIN®
SUPERROMANCE®

By the Year 2000: BABY!

What have *you* resolved to do by the year 2000?
These three women are having babies!

Susan Kennedy's plan is to have a baby by the time she's forty—in the year 2000. But the only man she can imagine as the father of her child is her ex-husband, Michael!
MY BABIES AND ME by **Tara Taylor Quinn**
Available in October 1999

Nora Holloway is determined to adopt the baby who suddenly appears in her life! And then the baby's uncle shows up....
DREAM BABY by **Ann Evans**
Available in November 1999

By the year 2000, the Irving Trust will end, unless Miranda has a baby. She doesn't think there's much likelihood of that—until she meets Joseph Wallace.
THE BABY TRUST by **Bobby Hutchinson**
Available in December 1999

Available at your favorite retail outlet.

HARLEQUIN®
Makes any time special ™